CW00746773

https://www.brindlebooks.co.uk

WELLINGTON'S DRAGOON 5:

THE ROAD TO MADRID

BY

DAVID J. BLACKMORE

Brindle Books Ltd

Copyright © 2024 by David J Blackmore

This edition published by
Brindle Books Ltd
Wakefield
United Kingdom

Copyright © Brindle Books Ltd 2024

The right of David J Blackmore to be identified as author of this
work has been asserted by him in accordance with the
Copyright, Designs and Patents Act 1988.
ISBN 978-1-915631-22-0

All rights reserved. No part of this publication may be
reproduced, stored in a retrieval system or transmitted, in any
form or by any means, electronic, mechanical, photocopying,
recording or otherwise without the prior permission of
the Copyright holder.

Acknowledgements

In the first instance, I must thank all my readers, particularly those who tell me how much they have enjoyed the books. They make the effort worthwhile. Amongst them I must mention Cameron Brown and Gill Cameron-Waller who got in touch to tell me about their ancestors who served in the Sixteenth in the Peninsular, respectively Troop Sergeant Major John Whitmore and Private James Thornton. These two now make brief appearances, and might do so again.

The usual suspects continue to support my efforts, Gillian Caldicott and Neil Hinchliffe, who read the draft and tell me where I've gone wrong, and Janet McKay, who helps and advises in many ways. The members of the local writing group who continue to encourage me, the writing challenges we set ourselves are a good break from this series. Mark Atkinson keeps me in the saddle, regularly, and makes possible the photography for the cover.

I must, of course, thank Emma Garbett for the cover photography and design and Richard Hinchliffe of Brindle Books who makes it all happen.

Introduction

'The Road To Madrid' takes newly promoted Captain Michael Roberts back to the Peninsular and sees him joining the army on the staff of Sir Stapleton Cotton. There are reunions, old partnerships renewed, new friends made and old enmities continued. As is the nature of war, and particularly the dirty war, there are losses. True to form there is romance, but not too much. Michael seems to be getting a little older and wiser.

As you might guess from the title, this book takes the story into Spain and covers the period of the horrors of the siege of Badajoz and Wellington's great victory at Salamanca. Our hero is faced with new challenges, and Wellington expects results.

In order to avoid possible confusion, I have to explain that in Wellington's army there were two Colonels Lord Somerset, who both appear in this book. They were two of the sons of the 5th Duke of Beaufort. The elder, Edward, a brevet full Colonel, commanded the 4th Dragoons, part of Le Marchant's brigade that charged so successfully at Salamanca. His younger brother Fitzroy, a Lieutenant Colonel, was Wellington's military secretary and is perhaps better known as Lord Raglan, the British commander in the Crimean War. As is the tradition in the British Army, Lieutenant Colonels are always addressed and referred to as Colonel. Fortunately, Edward only appears with his regiment while Fitzroy is only found at Wellington's headquarters.

There are, of course, horses, but the Peninsular was a graveyard for them, you have been warned.

The Road to Madrid

Chapter 1

The man's age could have been anything between thirty and sixty. His face was grimy, weatherbeaten, deeply tanned. He squatted, wrapped in a grubby blanket, by the entrance to the British Army's headquarters in the Royal Palace of Belem, just outside Lisbon. The sentries ignored him. He was universally known as 'Mercurio', after Mercury, not because he was either quick or shiny, but because he was a reliable messenger for any small errand an officer might require run. No one knew his real name, or was bothered by that. He was reliable because of his prodigious memory, he never failed in any errand, and made a sufficient living from the tips he received.

This living he supplemented by keeping a mental record of all the comings and goings at the Palace. These he shared every few days with his friend at a run down coffee shop in one of the poorer, more disreputable parts of Lisbon. His friend, Senhor Loiro, had informed him that he was a keen follower of the progress of the war against the tyrant Napoleon, and would be grateful for any information on the comings and goings of the British army, from regiments and battalions to individual officers. He paid well for what Mercurio told him.

At the moment Mercurio was watching a small party of four men and six horses near the main entrance to the Palace. Behind them was one of the local carters, he knew him by sight, and from the amount of baggage loaded in the cart he put them down as new arrivals. They were leading the horses, and one, an officer by his uniform, handed the reins of his horse to the only other man in uniform and walked towards the Palace, leaving the others by the gates.

Occasionally his friend would ask him to look out for something in particular. It was just such a request that came back to him now. The young officer, in the dark blue uniform with silver braid of a light dragoon, approached the entrance. He was unremarkable save for a vivid scar that ran down his left cheek.

The sentries saluted and the officer addressed the orderly Sergeant standing just inside the entrance way. "Captain Roberts, Sixteenth, reporting to General Peacocke. I know the way." The officer spoke clearly, confidently, and passed through into the Palace.

Mercurio grinned to himself. His friend had asked him to look out for a light dragoon officer called Roberts some months ago. He would have something extra to pass on today.

A few minutes later Captain Michael Roberts of the Sixteenth Light Dragoons was saluting General Peacocke, in charge of the army depot in Belem. Peacocke returned the salute and held out a hand for Michael's orders. "Thank you, Roberts." He glanced at the orders with a slight feeling of uneasiness. There was something about Roberts that did that to him. "Yes, well, there have been some changes in your orders, Captain."

Michael frowned, "Sir?"

"Yes, yes, now, where are they?" He searched through a mass of papers, scattering them in his nervousness and desire to see Roberts on his way. He muttered under his breath as he scrabbled about his desk before holding up a sheet of paper with a triumphant "Yes! Here we are. Now, let me see. Yes, you are to report to Viscount Wellington before you join Sir Stapleton, and before that you are to see Mister Stuart." He glanced at Michael. "Why the Ambassador should want to see you, I can't imagine. Don't want to know, none of my affair. Still, there we are, those are your orders." He handed the sheet to Michael. "You will have heard that Ciudad Rodrigo has fallen to us?"

"Yes, sir, as soon as we landed."

"And Crauford? Mortally wounded during the assault, apparently." He was referring to General Robert Crauford, commander of the Light Division.

"Yes, sir, a damn shame. I met him a few times up around Gallegos."

"Did you indeed? Yes, well, I expect Wellington will be on the move somewhere soon enough. No doubt you will be wanting to join him as soon as possible?"

"Yes, sir."

"Splendid, let us hope Mister Stuart does not detain you too long. Now, off you go. Oh, and, err, congratulations on your promotion."

Michael saluted again and left Peacocke's office and a General who felt nothing less than relieved.

Out in the ante room to the General's office, Michael paused to read his new orders. His heart sank. He wanted nothing less than to get back to the army and fight against Napoleon. These orders told him to offer Mr Stuart every possible assistance for as long as was required. Then, instead of joining the staff of Sir Stapleton Cotton, Wellington's cavalry commander, he was to report to Viscount Wellington. He had expected the usual two weeks to prepare, which would have allowed him plenty of time to see to things at his house in Lisbon. He was looking forward to seeing his home again, and his childhood nurse, his babá, Senhora Santiago, to seeing what progress Bernardo had made to restoring the garden to the glory his late mother had achieved, but he had a feeling that he knew exactly why Stuart wanted his help.

He had worked for Stuart before, successfully hunting down French spies in Lisbon. The last time Michael had exercised his skills in counterintelligence, before being sent to England, the result had been more deaths at his hands than he cared to think about. Well, it couldn't be helped, and if that was what the visit to Stuart was about, he was ready, even, he would have to admit, eager. The dirty war, as he thought of it, was necessary, he was good at it, and it excited him. It also had a very personal dimension for him.

He strode away and passed out of the Palace, barely registering the orderly Sergeant and the sentries, returning their salutes automatically. He took no notice of the figure huddled against the wall. Outside, the day was mild, the sky cloudy, the wind a gentle breeze. It would get hotter, a lot hotter as the seasons progressed, but he was glad his party were getting a gentle introduction to the weather. They were waiting for him beyond the gates, Hall, his batman, White, his valet cum general servant, and Bradley, his groom. They held the horses, waiting patiently. He had decided that, after almost two weeks cooped up in stalls on the transport ship, they would walk the horses to his home. He took the lead rein of his favourite, a black called Johnny, from Hall and gave them all a quick glance. Bradley was leading his own horse, Jasper, and another of Michael's, Robbie, a dark bay. Hall had his troop horse, another black called Billy, and Michael's other black, Thor. White, still not entirely at ease around horses, was leading his horse, Beau. Behind them came the local carter, his cart piled high with baggage and drawn by a single, sad looking mule.

Michael called to the carter in Portuguese, "Senhor, are you ready?" A wave and a nod told him he was. "Right" said Michael, addressing his little party in English, "it's not a long walk, about four miles. Just watch where you're putting your feet, they're not fussy where they empty their chamber pots. Walk, march."

Mercurio had stayed at his post and watched as the officer returned and rejoined his party, which set off towards Lisbon. As soon as dusk fell he would make his way into Lisbon and find his friend. He hugged himself in anticipation of a little more money than usual.

As Michael led the way into the familiar streets of Lisbon, he could hear his party exchanging surprised and wondering comments at what they were seeing. The numerous coffee shops, taverns and the Portuguese in their traditional dress. It reminded him of his arrival with Lloyd, his former batman, now

Corporal Lloyd. He wondered how marriage to the former and most redoubtable Maggie Taylor was finding him. He smiled to himself. Sergeant Taylor had always been well turned out, perhaps Lloyd was now. Thoughts of marriage brought Roberta to mind. He wondered if she was now married to da Rocha and felt a little wistful. They had been the best of friends, lovers and she had taught him a lot. He wanted to see her, and ask her about Catarina Cardoso. He had not parted from Catarina on the best of terms, and he admitted to himself that he had used her shamelessly, something Roberta had angrily pointed out. However, Catarina was an attractive woman, she had admitted to an attraction to him, and you never knew. He expected to be in Portugal and Spain until the war's end, whenever that might be. There was plenty of time to find out where he stood with her.

Behind him he heard Hall swear. "Bloody Hell, look what I've trodden in, you'd never see anything like that in Dorset!"

Bradley laughed. "Nay, nor in Yorkshire, lad, but we're a long way from home."

They walked on and Michael's thoughts turned to home, to England, to Cornwall at least. He was happy to have made his peace with his uncle and wondered, sadly, if he would see his grandfather, the Reverend Isles, again. He had been well enough when they parted, but he was well into his seventies. He decided that he was unlikely to see Elizabeth Trelawney again. Their parting had been fond, but, he suspected, due more to their shared experience than anything else, he was under no illusions about the view she must have of him after all he had told her. Probably considered him to be some sort of dishonourable denizen of the under belly of society, a spy, a killer. No better than Renard, sitting in his Paris office and despatching assassins after him, killing at a distance, but responsible all the same. No, she now belonged in the past. His thoughts turned back to Catarina Cardoso, She, however, was another matter, and there was his quinta that she wanted to buy. He saw possibilities.

.   .   .

In Paris, Matthieu Renard sat in the grand office that befitted the head of intelligence for Portugal and Spain. He had got over his anger at discovering Roberts had escaped the assassin sent after him in England, and it didn't take him long to decide a course of action. He called in his chief clerk. "I want instructions sent immediately to Lisbon, as quickly as possible. That bloody English officer, Captain Roberts, is on his way there, and I want him killed." The clerk hesitated and Renard snapped at him. "Well, what is it, man?"

"Err, I beg your pardon, Monsieur, but that order has already gone, months ago."

"What? What do you mean?"

"Um, when you sent the same order to Rochambeau, Monsieur, there was some confusion, as we knew the man Roberts' regiment was in Portugal. The same order was sent to Lisbon, Monsieur. I'm sorry."

Renard began to laugh, almost hysterically. "You mean to say that when this man arrives in Lisbon, our agents..., always supposing we have any left? Is Loiro still active?"

"Oh, yes, Monsieur, you may recall that we received a report from him last month that was itself only a month old."

"Ah, yes, of course, good, then our agents should know what to do when he arrives. Loiro does well, getting information of new arrivals."

"Oh, yes, Monsieur."

"Yes, indeed, it couldn't be better. But send the instruction again anyway, just to make sure."

"Yes, Monsieur."

"Now get out!" As the clerk stole away Renard hugged himself for warmth and went to warm himself by the poor excuse for a fire that failed to warm his large office.

.   .   .

Michael led his party to the back entrance to his house, where the stables and small paddock stood below the garden. As they clattered over the cobbles a head and shoulders suddenly appeared over the wall that stood at the edge of the garden, at the top of the drop to the paddock. A voice called out "Senhor Miguel" and an arm appeared and waved frantically.

"Hello, Bernardo!" Michael called back in Portuguese. "Run and tell them in the house that we are here, then come and help with the baggage." The head promptly disappeared.

Michael turned to his party. "Tie the horses up here for the moment, White, Hall, get the baggage off the cart, Bradley let's have a look in the stables."

Michael pulled open the wide door and went in followed by Bradley, who took a long slow look around.

"What do you think?" asked Michael.

"Ah reckon they's reyt 'ansome, Captain Roberts, reyt 'ansome. Dry, plenty of ventilation, looks like good drainage too. Very snug, sir,"

"Good. That door leads to the tack room, the hayloft is above, and beyond there's a room for you, but you'll take all your meals in the house while we're here."

"Now that's reyt grand, sir."

Michael left Bradley to look around, paid off the carter and set off towards the house. As he got close, a door opened and an elderly Senhora came hurrying towards him. It was Senhora Santiago, his childhood nurse and now housekeeper.

"Senhor Miguel, oh, Senhor Miguel" she cried out. They met and he stooped to give her a hug.

"Hello, babá, how are you?"

"Oh, getting old, Miguel, but feeling younger for having you home again."

He looked over her head to where an elderly man had appeared from the house. "Hello, Senhor Santiago, it's good to see you."

"And you, Senhor, and you." He beamed at Michael.

An hour later it was beginning to get dark, but the baggage was in, the horses settled in their stalls, introductions had been made and there was quite a crowd in the kitchen. In addition to the new arrivals, there were the Santiagos, Bernardo Garro, his boyhood friend and now his gardener, and Senhora Pinheiro and her son Frederico. The two Senhoras were bustling about preparing dinner for all while the men stood looking at each other awkwardly, as strangers will on first meeting. Michael decided it was time to leave them to get acquainted.

"Senhor Santiago, is there a fire in the dining room?"

"Yes, Senhor, I lit it half an hour ago."

"Then I will dine there. Can you find me a bottle of something suitable to celebrate my home coming? And open a few for your dinner as well." Santiago nodded and Michael switched to English to address his men. "I will leave you here for dinner, there will be wine, be careful of it, it's not ale," he grinned at them, "but no doubt you will discover that for yourselves! And while you are at it, start to learn some Portuguese."

The dining room was as he remembered it, high windows, with long, heavy curtains keeping out the damp evening air. A fire burned cheerfully, and Michael turned a chair from the table to sit facing it. A moment later Frederico appeared with a bottle and a glass.

"Thank you. Just put them on the table where I can reach them"

Frederico did as he was bid, but seemed to hesitate to leave. Michael glanced away from the fire to ask him "What is it?"

"Senhor, I..., err, I am sorry to bother you."

"Yes, well come on, I won't bite!" He smiled encouragingly.

"Yes, Senhor. Err, you have come with many men, Senhor. Will you still want me to go with you to the army, like Francisco did?"

"Ah." Michael turned to look at Frederico properly. "Do you want to?"

"I don't know, Senhor. You hired me to do that, and I don't want to lose my place, but I like it here, and my mother worries about what might become of me. She also worries that if I stay here I might be conscripted into the army, Senhor."

Michael poured himself a glass of dark, ruby red wine and took a sip while he watched Frederico who was practically hopping from leg to another in embarrassment. "Well, it is too soon for me to say. I expect to be in Lisbon for a while, at least two weeks, I suspect longer. So, there is plenty of time to think about it. For both of us."

"Yes, Senhor."

"Good, now off you go."

Frederico almost bolted from the room, but returned moments later, leading White and Hall who were bringing Michael's dinner. Michael spoke to him, "Frederico, light the candles for me, please." Then, while he did so, he asked White and Hall, "Is everything well in the kitchen?"

"Oh, aye, sir" answered Hall, "there's some right good smells coming from the cooking, sir, but I've no idea what it is."

Michael laughed. "Senhora Santiago is an excellent cook, so I am sure it will be good, even if it's nothing you have ever had before. So, go, enjoy."

Senhora Santiago had put together a fine dinner of grilled chicken and a plate of grilled sardines. With the wine as well, Michael felt well and truly back at home. The meal was quickly finished, then he sat back in his chair, sipping the wine, and enjoying the feel of the fire on his back. It was, he realised, the first time he had been on his own since the transport had sailed from Falmouth. Then the realisation came that he was very much on his own, he had no lover in his life. One way or another that happiness was fleeting and elusive.

.   .   .

In a dark and dirty coffee house down a squalid alley in the poorest part of Lisbon, Mercurio sat opposite Senhor Loiro in a booth well to the back and deep in shadow. Loiro was well wrapped up against the cold, damp night air, his collar pulled up high and his wide brimmed hat pulled low. From under the hat his blond hair hung down limply and the light of the single, guttering, tallow candle revealed his startlingly bright, blue eyes. He was listening patiently to Mercurio's gossip.

"But that's not all." Mercurio paused, dramatically and glanced around the almost empty coffee shop. Loiro rolled his eyes. "Do you remember asking me, some months ago, to keep an eye open for an English cavalry officer? By the name of Roberts." He paused for effect, and took a sip of the weak coffee in front of him.

Loiro didn't remember, but he knew Mercurio's memory and if he said he had, then he most probably had. "What of it?," he asked, while he ransacked his memory for the name.

"Well, he arrived today. Captain Roberts of the 16th, he said, Light Dragoons from the uniform. He's got a great, white scar down his cheek, looks a real nasty piece of work."

As he spoke it came to Loiro. There had been an instruction from Paris that this man was to be killed. He hadn't taken much notice because it had appeared to be a duplicate of an instruction sent to London. He had to admit, to himself, that he had completely forgotten. The instruction, however, had come from no less than Renard himself, as such it had to be considered important, a priority.

"Do you know where he is?" Loiro asked.

"No, but I am sure I can find out. Why do you want to know?"

Loiro ignored the question and asked, "How?"

"I'll ask the carter who took the baggage."

"Good. Let me know as soon as you can." He placed a small pile of coins on the table. "Here, there's a little extra as well."

While Mercurio was gathering up his payment, grinning at the bonus, Loiro slipped out the booth and disappeared into the night. He was in a hurry. There was a man he needed to find, and it was unlikely this Roberts would be in Lisbon for more than two weeks. That was what was usually allowed to an officer to finish preparing to join the army. He also needed to get a message off to Paris. If he succeeded, he hoped for reward, possibly even a recall to Paris, away from this squalid way of life.

Chapter 2

The following morning Michael set off, alone, to see Mister Stuart, the British Ambassador in Lisbon and the man responsible for intelligence matters in Portugal and Spain. He had dressed in his civilian clothes, not wishing to draw any attention to himself. He was quickly admitted to the Embassy and shown into Stuart's office where the Ambassador was pouring out coffee. He walked to meet Michael, his hand outstretched.

"Captain Roberts, it is a pleasure to see you again," adding as they shook hands, "and let me congratulate you on your well deserved promotion. Coffee?"

They were soon settled in a couple of comfortable chairs with a low table and the coffee things between them. Stuart began.

"First, let me apologise for securing your services again. I am sure that you would prefer to be joining your comrades and the army, but when I read of your appointment in the Gazette, I wrote to Viscount Wellington asking him if he could spare your services for a little while. As the matter bears on military matters, he was happy to accommodate my request." He smiled at Michael who nodded his understanding. Stuart went on. "I don't expect you will be surprised to hear that we have a little problem that I am hoping you might be able to resolve for us. It is not widely known, nor should it be, that we have agents in Bayonne, the last garrison town in France before the Spanish border. The bridge there, across the Adour, is effectively the gateway to Spain. Our agents count every man, horse and cannon passing in either direction and send that information to me. You can, I am sure, appreciate how useful that is to Viscount Wellington?" He paused for a mouthful of coffee.

"Yes, sir, I can see that."

"Yes, indeed. Well, the problem is, you see, I suspect that the French have a similar arrangement here in Lisbon."

"Ah!"

"Yes, ah! But the difficulty is that I have no concrete evidence to prove it, and certainly no idea who is involved. I have had General de Silva's assistance, and he has investigated without success. He, frankly, thinks I am mistaken. However, I have had intelligence from Madrid that strongly suggests the French are getting some information, if not complete, on the arrivals and departures through Belem and Lisbon. It is possible this information is reaching Paris, although God knows how."

"I see, sir."

Stuart smiled. "Good. So, what I would like you to do, as you have probably already guessed, is to look into the matter for me." He paused to sip his coffee. "And, should you discover such an arrangement, I should like you to put an end to it." He gave Michael a small, disingenuous smile. "It is, of course, a pressing matter, particularly now that Ciudad Rodrigo has fallen. You have heard that, I suppose?"

"Yes, sir."

"Yes, of course. Well, if information can get out of Lisbon it might give the French a hint as to what Wellington intends next. Though, God knows, I certainly don't know, and I rather suspect that Wellington is the only man who does. However, a fair guess would be an attempt on Badajoz. Supplies for that would come from Lisbon, and if that happens, it must not be discovered by the French."

"I see, sir."

"Good. Now, I think it would be advisable if you speak to General de Silva. I have already written to him, but I don't want him throwing a sulk because we are running our own investigation. He's a good fellow and his police are very effective. You might like to tell him that we have absolute confidence in him and will, of course, ask him to act if you discover anything. I, err, also took the liberty of saying that it is only because you are available that we are doing this. I believe he likes you, so that should help to settle any ruffled feathers." Stuart smiled again. "I fear that such is the lot of the diplomat. Or soldiers on loan to the diplomats."

"Yes, sir." Michael was silent for a moment as he thought about the challenges of the task. "I might well need some assistance, sir."

"Ah, yes, of course, what had you in mind?"

"There are some Portuguese who have been of assistance to me before, sir. I should need to pay them for their help, sir."

"How many?"

"No more than four, I think, sir, probably only two or three."

"How much?"

"I don't know, sir, that would depend on what help I need and what I can negotiate with them."

"Very well." Stuart stared at the ceiling for a moment, and then continued, looking Michael straight in the eye. "I shall leave that to your discretion, and trust you to be economic with your country's money."

"Yes sir."

"Very good. Well, I shall not detain you any longer." He smiled. "And do, please, give General de Silva my very best regards, very best, mind."

Once outside the Embassy, Michael strolled slowly, head down, deep in thought. It was the sort of thing he had been expecting, but not such a challenging task. Looking for something that might not even exist. Still, if Stuart suspected it, there was a chance it was a real threat. He lifted his head and quickened his pace. He would make no plans until he had spoken to de Silva and found out what he had done, if the General was inclined to share with him. First, however, he would call on Roberta. Her house was on the way, more or less, to the General's headquarters, and she might give him a clue as to his current mood. It was even possible that she been involved in looking for Stuart's spies as one of de Silva's best agents, although de Silva had told him that she was giving that up in light of her forthcoming marriage. He also wanted to enquire of her about Catarina and now he had an excuse for calling.

Michael glanced around, an old habit, and slipped quietly down the narrow side street to the heavy door, studded with bolt heads, a small grill at head height, and set in a towering, windowless wall. He banged hard and waited, a smile on his face, expecting to see the face of Constanca, Roberta's maid, appear behind the grill. Nothing happened. He frowned and hammered again, with the same result. Disappointed, he turned back and walked on to de Silva's headquarters.

To Michael's relief he had no difficulty gaining admittance to see de Silva. The General was his usual welcoming self, calling for coffee even as he came from behind his desk to greet Michael.

"Captain Roberts! My congratulations on your promotion, it is a delight to see you again. Mister Stuart said you might be calling in." He seized Michael's hand and pumped it vigorously.

"Thank you, General, it is good to be back in Portugal."

"Excellent. Now, let us sit by the fire and we can talk in comfort."

A servant brought in coffee and cups, placed them on a table between the two men and silently withdrew. De Silva began to pour.

"So, when did you arrive in Lisbon?"

"Yesterday, sir, and I have just come straight from Mister Stuart. Well, almost straight."

"Almost?"

"Yes, sir. I called on Roberta, but got no answer."

"Ah, you won't. Senhor and Senhora da Rocha are at their home near Alcoentre."

"Oh!"

"Yes, I am afraid you missed their wedding," the General looked up from the coffee cups, "but perhaps that was for the best. Under the circumstances?"

"Yes, sir, probably."

"Although I gather that all is well between you and da Rocha?"

"Yes, sir. I think I may call him a friend."

"Indeed. But tell me, why did you call?"

"I wanted to ask Roberta about a mutual acquaintance."

"Hmm. I understand Wellington is still around Ciudad Rodrigo?"

The sudden change of topic surprised Michael. "Yes, sir, so I understand."

"And when you go to take up your duties your route will, no doubt, take you through Alcoentre?"

Michael realised the reason behind the General's questions. "Yes, sir, I suppose it will."

"Then take some advice, Captain, do not try to visit the da Rochas." He waved a hand. "I don't mean never, of course not, but they are recently married. It would be best for you to keep away for a while, perhaps, even, until you meet them back in Lisbon."

"Yes, sir, of course."

"Good, now, to the real reason for your visit." He smiled. "Mister Stuart's French spies."

"Yes, sir"

"I have to tell you, Captain, that I am far from convinced that they exist, far from convinced. However, Mister Stuart has his sources, and I must respect that. I also know that you seem to have a knack for winkling out and dealing with this sort of thing."

Michael nodded his acknowledgement of the compliment. "Thank you, sir, and Mister Stuart says he has complete confidence in you and your police, sir. He also sends his regards, sir."

"Hmm, he does, does he? Well, let me tell you that I have had a lot of questions asked, and a number of people have been very closely questioned." Michael knew what that meant. "Nobody knows anything. There is no trace of any intelligence gathering, nor of anything being communicated to Madrid." He took a drink of his coffee and Michael waited patiently for him to continue. "I fear that you will go over old ground with the same results. That is up to you. Mister Stuart is an important man and his wishes must be respected. I have only one request to ask of you." The General paused for a response.

"Of course, sir, if I can."

The General nodded. "Then, should you discover anything, I will be grateful if you allow me to deal with it. There are those who say we Portuguese defer too much to England. I am sure you understand?"

"Yes, of course, General. Mister Stuart instructed me that was to be the case. It matters not who deals with traitors, so long as they dealt with."

Michael and the General exchanged understanding smiles. "Excellent, then I shall wish you joy of your hunt." The General rose to his feet, Michael following suit, and held out his hand to Michael. As they shook, the General said, "Good luck, Captain Roberts. Remember, you may call upon me for help, and, please, do take my advice on the other matter."

"Thank you, sir, I shall."

Michael strolled thoughtfully back towards his house. His interview with de Silva had gone as well as he might have hoped. He had to admit to slightly mixed feelings about Roberta, but his happiness for her outweighed other considerations. As for asking her about Catarina, he suspected that he knew what she would say, that that particular boat had sailed. Perhaps it had, but he would continue to live in hope. There were no other sails on the horizon.

He turned his mind to Stuart's task. He would need help, that was certain, he didn't know Lisbon as well as he had running wild as a boy. He would turn to his boyhood friends, they had helped him before, and, he felt sure, would do so again, if they were in Lisbon.

Arriving back home he rapped on the heavy front door with the top of his cane. Moments later it swung open to reveal Frederico, who had clearly run up the stairs from the kitchen. Michael handed him his hat and cane and asked, "Do you know where Bernardo is?"

"I think he is down at the stables, Senhor. Senhor Bradley and Senhor Hall are exercising the horses, Senhor."

Michael found Bernardo leaning on the paddock fence watching Bradley and Hall as they walked

Robbie and Thor around, leading them without saddles. Michael nodded to him, "Hello, Bernardo."

"Senhor Miguel, hello!"

"Tell me, are Antonio and Carlos in town?"

Bernardo scratched his head. "Yes, Senhor, I think so. Carlos has been to Abrantes with his mules, but he was expected back last night, Senhor. Antonio is, well, Senhor, he is not away on a trip at the moment."

Michael laughed. "I'm not worried what Antonio gets up to as long as he doesn't get caught. Is Jorge still tailoring?"

"Yes, and he has married his employer's daughter."

"Has he? Then I shan't bother him, but Antonio and Carlos, can you find them? Tell them I have work for them. "He paused for a moment. "Tell them it's like before."

"Ah, I understand, Senhor."

"Tell them I'll meet them in the usual tavern on Black Horse Square, at eight o'clock this evening."

"Yes, Senhor. Do you want me to come as well?"

"Yes, I do, we can have a drink like old times, eh?" He turned to look at the horses, and called out, "Bradley, how are they all doing?"

Bradley led Robbie across and the horse stuck his nose into Michael. "No, lad, I've nothing for you," he laughed and rubbed Robbie's nose.

"Happen they're all right, another day or two and they'll be ready to be ridden." He reached up to scratch Robbie behind his ear.

"Good. We are likely to be in Lisbon for a few weeks, so there's plenty of time, all being well."

"Oh, aye, sir?"

"Yes. Nothing to be concerned about."

By the time Michael and Bernardo set out for Black Horse Square it had been dark for a while. Guttering oil lamps cast infrequent pools of light on the main throughfares. At the tavern they found Antonio and Carlos in a booth toward the back, a bottle and four glasses on the table between them. The greetings were effusive and the four old friends were soon comfortably settled.

"So, Captain," Antonio spoke, "what is it that you want us for? I hope that you don't want to go over the mountains again? It's not the best time of year for that."

Michael chuckled. "No, no, I don't think so, I certainly hope not." He grew serious. "There is a possibility that there are French spies in Lisbon communicating, somehow, with Madrid. General de Silva doubts it, the British Ambassador, Mister Stuart, suspects it. He has asked me to find out." He looked around the table. "And he has authorised me to pay any helpers."

Carlos and Bernardo grinned while Antonio laughed out loud and thumped Michael lightly on the shoulder. "Now you are talking" he exclaimed. "I have been a little bored, and in need of some diversion."

Carlos chipped in. "What he hasn't told you is that his mother died a few months ago, he needs something to distract him."

"What!" exclaimed Michael. "I didn't know, I am sorry, Antonio."

"Thank you, Miguel." He shrugged. "She is in a better place now." He crossed himself, and his friends followed suit. The four friends sat in silence for a minute, each lost in thoughts of lost loved ones. Michael thought of his parents, drowned fleeing Portugal and the French invasion, and of Elaine, shot down by Jean-Paul Renard. It was cold comfort to Michael that he had killed him, and now his father had tried to have Michael killed.

Antonio, appropriately, broke the awkward silence. "What do want us to do, Miguel?"

"To be honest, I am not sure. There are two questions, how is the agent, or agents, collecting the intelligence, and secondly, how are they getting it to Madrid?"

Antonio shrugged. "It is not so difficult to get to Madrid." He grinned. "Or so I am told."

Carlos grunted. "Ha, not with my mules!"

Michael asked, "How many do you have now?"

"Four."

"So, you will be getting paid five dollars a day?"

"Yes, when I have a job to do. There is not so much call for the smaller mule trains. It's the big ones of twenty or more that make the real money, when it gets paid, that is." He laughed. "Perhaps you can have a word with your Viscount Wellington, get us paid regularly."

"I don't think I can help there, but it does raise the issue of paying you for your time. I had been thinking two dollars a day, but that doesn't cover your mules."

"Don't worry about them. I can hire them to another muleteer."

"Are you sure?"

"Yes, and it's a bad time of year to be out with a mule train."

Michael turned to the other two, "Antonio, how does that sound to you?"

"It's good," he replied. "but what do you want us to do?"

"That's a bit harder to answer." Michael took a drink of his wine while the others waited. "I think the best thing for the two of you is to look for anyone making regular trips to Madrid, probably without a lot of smuggled goods. I'm sure the two of you can look into that better than de Silva's men. You could use an excuse of needing a courier for something."

"But what?" asked Carlos.

"That, of course, is a confidential matter." Michael tapped the side of his nose and the men all laughed.

"That should work," said Antonio, "secrecy is a given out there, or so I have heard." Carlos nodded his agreement, and then Antonio asked "What about Bernardo here? What would you have him do?"

Michael hesitated. He had been worrying about this moment. Bernardo was a good man, an old friend, a great gardener, but his twisted leg slowed him down. Bernardo himself supplied the answer.

"If someone is collecting information about the English army they must, surely, hang around the army here in Lisbon, collecting information without anyone noticing. Perhaps listening to officers in their hotels? I don't know, but I can hang around and look out for anyone like that."

Michael heaved a silent sigh of relief. "That's an excellent idea, and you will have the same pay as Antonio and Carlos while you do that. Now what do you say to another bottle?"

The following morning Michael woke late, with a thumping headache. He had discovered how his friends could drink, a change from when they were boys together. He swung his feet out of bed and groaned. Almost as if in response his door opened and White stuck his head into the room.

"Good morning, sir. I shall have some hot coffee and hot water for you in a few minutes, sir." He disappeared. Michael groaned again, stood up and moved slowly across to the window. Out on the Tagus he could see ships of the Royal Navy, merchant vessels, and numerous small boats busying themselves about between ships and docks. He pressed his forehead against the cold glass. He had agreed to meet his friends again in three days, in the same tavern at the same time. In the meantime he would carry on with the preparations to join the army and with some investigations of his own. But first, after breakfast, he would go to see his lawyer, Senhor Furtado. He would, he thought, also call on Senhor Rodrigues, Baron Quintela's chief clerk, and a very useful contact. He didn't want to cause offence by not calling.

His door opened and White appeared with coffee and shaving water. "Here you are, sir. Hall is down at the stables helping Bradley with the horses. Bradley reckons to start riding them tomorrow, sir."

"Thank you, White. My civilian clothes again today."

Michael was still a little thick headed as he left home for the day's business. Had he not been, he might have noticed that he was followed.

Palacio Quintela was the closest destination and he was soon being welcomed by Senhor Rodrigues. "Senhor Roberts, come in, come in. Tomas," he spoke to the porter who had brought Michael in, "coffee for both us. Please, please, sit down, and I hear you are to be congratulated on promotion to Captain?"

"Yes, that's right, thank you."

"No regrets on turning down the Baron's offer?

Michael laughed, "No Senhor, not at all."

Rodrigues shrugged. "Of course, I wrote to the Baron and told him. He was disappointed, but, I think, not entirely surprised. So, will you be in Lisbon for long?"

"I am not sure, Senhor. I have a little task to undertake and then I shall be rejoining the army."

"Please, no more spies in our company, I hope?" he laughed.

Michael smiled, hoping that was the case. "No, no, Senhor nothing for you to worry about, this is purely a social call."

The social call lasted the best part of an hour as they exchanged news and Rodrigues offered Michael any help that it was in his power to give. Michael finally made his farewells with promises to call again and that he would not hesitate to ask for assistance. Emerging from the Palacio he looked across to the square opposite and was pleased to see that old Priscila was still there, selling flowers.

His next call was on his lawyer, Senhor Furtado. After the usual pleasantries and the inevitable serving of coffee, they got down to business. Michael was primarily keen to hear about the quinta he had inherited. Furtado brought him up to date.

"Now, Senhor, the quinta. I received instructions from Mister Rutherford and I have subsequently concluded an agreement to rent the quinta to Senhorita Cardoso. In accordance with those instructions, I have refused to reveal the identity of the owner, although she has been quite persistent. In the end, I, ah, managed to give her the idea that the owner is currently resident in the Brasils. That has put an end to her enquiries. However, she has made it very clear that she is desirous of purchasing the quinta, for a fair price."

Michael broke in, "Has she suggested a sum?"

"Yes, Senhor. She has, of course, made much of the depredations caused by the French, and, I regret to say, much of the income from the rent has had to go on repairs and other remedial work. You are currently only receiving a small income, which is being paid into your bank here in Lisbon. To be frank, you might be better off selling and investing that money. Here are the figures." He handed Michael a sheet of paper covered with columns and figures.

"Any income is welcome, Senhor, and is more than I was getting."

"Indeed, Senhor, particularly taking into account the costs of your home, your servants and the work that has been carried out by Senhor Santiago. All of it quite justified. I have looked into it for you. And there are, of course, my own costs." He smiled apologetically. "However, at the moment, your income from the quinta is in slightly in excess of your expenditure on it and your house here, although it is a close thing."

"Hmm." Michael thought for a moment. "I still don't understand why my father bought it and, while I agree that selling would probably be the best option, I should like to see it first. So long as it isn't costing me money, I see no reason not to continue with the present arrangement."

There was little else of any importance to discuss and Michael was soon back outside. He consulted his watch. He had told Senhora Santiago that he did not know what time he would be home, so he would dine out. It was still a little early for dinner, so he strolled down to the dock area, to see if any troops or supplies were being landed and if anyone was taking an unusual interest.

A couple of American merchant ships were unloading cargoes of flour for the army, but they were a commonplace and regular sight. By late afternoon he gave up and went in search of dinner. He decided to try Lahmeyer's Hotel on Largo de San Paulo. It was popular with British officers staying in Lisbon and a short walk from his home. He was, perhaps not surprisingly, taken for a Portuguese gentleman. He enjoyed himself watching the officers flirting with the owner's daughter, smiling to himself at the remarks she shared with them in English and the other staff in Portuguese, they were quite different.

When he left it was quite dark and he strolled along slowly, carelessly, save for watching where he trod. He turned into the dark street that sloped upwards to his house. Gratefully, he reached the door to his home and pounded loudly upon it. After a few moments it opened to reveal Senhora Santiago, who beamed when she saw it was Michael.

"Ah, Miguel," she started to speak. And then her gaze moved over Michael's shoulder and her expression changed to one of puzzlement, concern. Michael spun on his heel to see what had caught her eye. As he did so, he moved slightly to one side, which was why the shot missed him. There was a flash, a bang and he heard a gasp from Senhora Santiago. He turned to her, just in time to catch her as she fell. He held her, felt her hand clutching at his arm and watched the light go out in her eyes.

"Hall, White, anyone!" he bellowed at the top of his voice and tried to look for the shooter. He thought he heard running footsteps and glimpsed someone disappearing up the street that ran at right angles to his own. Then steps thundered up the stairs from the kitchen and Hall and White appeared, followed by Fredrico and, last of all, Senhor Santiago.

"Bloody hell," exclaimed Hall, and then Santiago saw his wife and a long, loud, heart rending scream of "No!" filled the air.

Michael looked up at him as he grasped his baba to his chest and tears flowed down his face. "I am sorry, so very, very sorry."

Michael sat, hunched in a chair, staring at the fire in his drawing room. Opposite him sat General de Silva. An open bottle of brandy and two half empty glasses stood on a table between them. The last two hours had been a blur. Two of Lisbon's police officers had appeared and one had immediately gone to report to headquarters, resulting in de Silva's arrival an hour ago. Bernardo had returned from his investigations and had promptly been arrested, causing further confusion for a few minutes. Michael had carried Senhora Santiago up to her bedroom, where Senhora Pinheiro was taking care of the body. Bradley had been an unexpected rock. Perhaps calling on his own loss, and despite the language barrier, he had undertaken caring for Senhor Santiago, a man distraught with shock and grief. Michael himself was shattered. Having called for the brandy, de Silva sat silently, waiting for Michael to recover his wits.

Michael suddenly sat back and looked at de Silva. "Someone," he spoke deliberately, "is going to pay for this."

De Silva waited for a moment before he asked, "What do you think this is all about? It seems clear that you were the intended victim. Silhouetted against the open door you would have been a perfect target."

Michael gave a hollow, mirthless laugh. "Yes, if I hadn't turned to see what had caught the Senhora's attention..." He reached for his glass and emptied it. "And you are right, I was no doubt the intended victim, another assassination attempt."

"Another?" De Silva was shocked.

"Oh, yes," Michael's tone was bitter. "Twice in England, ordered by Renard."

De Silva was not a man given to blasphemy, but he swore under his breath at that. "Renard, isn't that the same name as..."

"Yes, it's his father. He is part of Buonaparte's police, he has responsibility for intelligence matters in Portugal and Spain. I have been a nuisance to him, apart from killing his son. He has decided that he wants me dead."

"That Renard! I have heard of him, naturally, but you have only been in Lisbon a few days! How could he know you were here?"

"My appointment to the staff was in the London Gazette, still, it has been quick work."

"Could it be connected to your task from Mister Stuart?"

Michael shook his head. "Only if there is a traitor in your office, or the Embassy."

De Silva hesitated before replying. "I suppose that is a possibility, although my instinct says not." He paused again. "I shall consider the possibility, make some discreet enquiries. Perhaps you might share your thought with Mister Stuart? Better you than me."

"What? Oh, Stuart. Yes, I shall have to see him."

"One thing seems clear to me, however." The General topped up the two glasses of brandy. "Mister Stuart is right, there are still French agents active in Lisbon, and your assassin is probably connected to them. Find the agents, find the assassin, or the other way round. And you may count on me for all the help you need, although I shall leave this to you for the moment. I looked and found nothing, there seems little point in my looking in all the same places again."

"Thank you, General, although I know exactly who is responsible and where they are, Renard, in Paris."

There was a subdued air about the house the following morning. The local priest had turned up and was looking after Senhor Santiago for a few hours while Hall and White saw to the horses with help from Bernardo and Bradley got a little sleep. Michael had barely seen Santiago, he wasn't sure he could face him yet as he felt responsible for Senhora Santiago's death. He would do whatever he could for Santiago. Frederico and his mother were busy in the kitchen and White brought Michael his breakfast in the dining room.

"White?"

"Yes, sir?"

"Your uncle told me that you can, as he put it, look after yourself. Did he mean what I think he meant?"

"Ah, well, a Whitechapel pub at closing time can get quite lively, sir, but no one has broken anything or marked me yet, sir."

"Hmm. You see, the thing is, after last night, I think it would be a sensible precaution for me to go about accompanied by someone who can, err, look after themselves. I'd get Hall to do it, but he needs to help Bradley with the horses. How do you feel about doing that?"

"Gladly, sir. I didn't know the Senhora like you did, sir, but she was a grand lady and if I can help I'll do it willingly."

"Thank you, White. The first thing is that I must go and see the Ambassador, we will leave in half an hour."

"Right you are, sir." He gave a positively evil smirk. "I've seen a nice stout walking stick as I think I shall borrow, sir."

Chapter 3

At the embassy a shocked Stuart listened to Michael's account of the previous evening. "Good grief, my dear fellow, that's awful. Thank God you are alright."

Michael snapped. "I have lost a very dear friend, Mister Stuart, Senhora Santiago was more than a servant. She was a second mother to me, and I cannot take any comfort in my escape."

"Forgive, me, sir, please. I didn't know."

Michael took a deep breath. "No, Mister Stuart, there is no reason why you should, please, forgive my outburst."

"Of course, sir, it is forgotten. But the question is, was this a chance attack, or a deliberate attempt on you specifically?"

"I think that we have to assume it was deliberate, sir."

"Yes, which would suggest that I am correct and there are still French agents at work in Lisbon."

"Yes, sir, and General de Silva now shares your view."

"Good, good. And you must take care, Captain."

"I have already taken steps, sir."

"Excellent, but, now, what to do?"

"Apart from carrying on as we were, sir? I don't think there is anything else. General de Silva has offered any help as it is needed." Michael shrugged. "At least we know we are not wasting our time, sir."

Senhora Santiago's funeral was held four days after her death. Senhor Santiago was a wreck and Michael walked with him, supporting him. The Catholic funeral was a new experience for Michael and he thought Senhor Santiago took some strength from it, as if being wrapped up in the ritual, the ceremony, somehow eased his pain. As for Michael, he felt his resolve to find the killer was strengthened. If there was a God, and some of the things Michael had seen made him wonder, then he hoped it was the God of the Old Testament.

The day after the funeral, as he was finishing his coffee after breakfast, Senhor Santiago came to him in the dining room. "Pardon, Senhor Miguel, but I must speak with you."

"Of course, Senhor, please, sit down."

"No, Senhor, thank you." Santiago took a deep breath. "Senhor, I must leave you and this house. I cannot stay. I keep thinking I hear Manuela's voice, I turn and expect to see her. Everywhere I look there are memories." Tears began to roll down his cheeks. "It is more than I can bear, Senhor."

Michael was taken by surprise, but the sight of the old man, his heart broken, told him he had no choice but to agree. "I understand, but I am sorry. Where will you go?"

"To my sister, Senhor. She and her husband have a small farm near Setubal. They were always writing to ask us to visit. We never did, so there will be no memories there to torment me."

Michael felt his own tears welling up. "Of course. And I will still pay you." He held up a hand as

Santiago began to protest. "There will be no argument. I was happy that you should live here for as long as you wished or God willed. I will speak to Senhor Furtado about making the arrangements. There will be someone he knows in Setubal who can make the payments to you." He rose from his chair and seized Santiago's hands in his own. "And I promise you that the man responsible for this will be brought to justice."

A few days later Santigo departed and with him went the last link to Michael's childhood. He still had his boyhood friends, although they were now men, not the youths of his memories. Time had broken even that link.

Michael had met his friends twice for progress reports, but they had come up with nothing. and it was beginning to feel like a waste of time. Then Michael received a letter from London. When he opened it he found a page covered in numbers, with a letter M at the bottom. Michael fetched his copy of de Laborde's 'View of Spain', shut himself away in his father's old study with pen and paper and began the task of decoding Musgrave's letter. It was short and to the point. Musgrave had learnt from his agent in Paris that orders had been sent to Lisbon for Michael's murder. A mirthless laugh escaped him. It was a bit late. He set about composing a reply. It was useful practice if nothing else.

Once the letter was finished he walked across to the British Embassy, accompanied by White, both of them alert for any attack. Stuart read the decoded letter.

"That would seem to confirm our belief that there are still French agents operating in Lisbon, pity we can't find 'em."

"I'm doing what I can, sir, but de Silva with all his resources couldn't find them."

"Yes, yes, I don't mean to criticise, no one who knows of your activities would doubt your ability to deal with French agents. What are you doing at the moment."

"I am meeting with the people working for me this evening, sir. If they have no news..." He grimaced. "Then I don't know what we can do, sir."

Carlos was already in the tavern with a bottle of wine and four glasses when Michael and Bernardo arrived. They slid into the booth and Michael asked, "No sign of Antonio yet?"

"No," replied Carlos, "I'm surprised he isn't here, still we can have a glass while we wait."

"Have you had any luck?"

Carlos poured the wine as he replied, "No, nothing."

"It's the same with me," Bernardo chipped in.

Michael took up his glass and sipped morosely. He was getting frustrated at the lack of progress.

Ten minutes later Antonio sauntered in, waved at them from the door and strolled over to join them.

"Any luck?" Michael repeated the question.

"No," replied Antonio. "At least, not until ten minutes ago." He took a swig of his wine and wiped his mouth with the back of his hand, looking rather pleased with himself.

"Come on, man, out with it, what do you mean ten minutes ago?" Michael demanded, snappishly.

"First of all I must ask you all to look at me, and whatever I say, do not look anywhere else."

"What?"

"Please, just do it."

"Oh, very well," Michael agreed, a hint of bad temper in his voice.

"Good, now, all of you, look here, at me. Michael, I am pretty sure that you are being followed. No, look at me!" Antonio snapped as Michael's head started to swivel. "If anyone looks around we shall lose him."

"Who?" demanded Michael.

"I saw you coming here, with Bernardo, caught a glimpse as you passed a lamp. Saw you turn a corner and then saw this other man. He was behind you, came to the corner, stopped and looked carefully around it before turning himself. It just looked suspicious. So, I hurried to the corner, and found that I was following him following you. I saw you come in, and he watched through a window. I watched him myself for a while, then came on in. He is still out there. And that's why I didn't want you to look round."

"What shall we do?" Carlos asked. Everyone looked at Michael, who was staring pointedly at the bottle of wine.

"I think," he said, slowly, "that first of all we should enjoy this bottle, and not too quickly." He looked around his friends. "Let's just talk and laugh and not look at the door or window. Let's not give any reason to scare him off. Now, we are looking very serious, so, we are all going to laugh as if I have just told a great story. Now!"

They all laughed and grinned and Carlos even slapped the table with his hand.

"Now," said Michael, "keep talking. Tell us all where you've been these last few days."

The conversation went around the table and Michael caught the attention of a waiter and called for another bottle. Eventually that bottle was almost empty.

"Now, listen," said Michael, pouring out the last of the wine, "this what we are going to do. You two," he indicated Carlos and Antonio, "are going to leave together, happy and cheerful, oblivious to all around you, and make yourselves scarce. Then in about a quarter of an hour, come back, very carefully, and get where you can see this fellow without him seeing you. In twenty minutes or so, Bernardo and I will get up and leave. We will walk to my house. Once we get there we will turn back. He should be in the street by then and you two can be at the bottom. There are no alleyways he can take, we should be able to seize him. I assume you are all carrying knives?" They all nodded. "Good. Once we have him, into my house with him and we can ask him some questions. Everyone understand? Yes? Good, then a toast to the prettiest woman in Lisbon!" They all laughed, emptied their glasses, and then Carlos and Antonio rose from their seats, and walked, still laughing, out of the tavern into the night.

"Are you alright, Bernardo?"

"Yes, Miguel, but another drink would help."

Michael laughed, caught the attention of a waiter, and ordered another bottle. For the next twenty minutes Michael asked Bernardo about where he had been in pursuit of his enquiries, and where he might go next.

"The only place I haven't been to and wandered around is the Palace out at Belem. I've been concentrating on the docks as that's where most troops land. And I would have thought that an odd character hanging around the army headquarters and main depot would be rather obvious."

"That's true," mused Michael, "but someone is getting information from somewhere and if Carlos and Antonio can't find anyone making regular trips between here and Madrid then the source of the information is our only chance. Anyway, it's time we were off." He drained his glass. "Ready?"

"Ready?" replied Bernardo, "I had almost forgotten what we are doing."

"Come on then," Michael laughed genuinely.

He called over a waiter and paid the bill. The two men stood and made for the door. Outside they could see little, coming from the relatively bright interior out into the dimly lit street. They strolled slowly along, looking neither left nor right, wending their way towards Michael's house. They turned the last corner and started up the dark slope towards Michael's. As they got around the corner, out of sight of any follower, Michael momentarily freed the blade from his cane, then pushed it back. Beside him he was aware of Bernardo slipping his knife into his hand.

Then there were only a few yards to go. "Ready?" Michael asked.

"Yes, Miguel."

They reached the front door. "Now!" Michael barked and the two men swung around. Some twenty five yards away a figure suddenly halted, hesitated, turned to run, and ran straight onto Carlos' fist.

"We have him, Michael!" Carlos and Antonio had him pinned to the ground and Antonio was searching for weapons. Antonio produced a knife, the sort many carried, but nothing else. As Michael and Bernardo ran back down the slope, Carlos and Antonio were pulling the man to his feet, each holding firmly to an arm.

"Very good, nice punch, Carlos. Let's get him into the house before anyone gets nosey or calls the police."

"I thought they were on our side," said Antonio as they dragged their captive along.

"Oh, they are, but I very much want a few words with this man myself." His tone was cold and grim.

Michael's thump on the door was answered when Frederico opened it. His eyes widened as the group entered, bundling their still slightly dazed captive with them.

"The ballroom, I think," Michael gave his orders, "Bernardo, you know where that is, show the way, take that candlestick from Frederico. Frederico, I want an old kitchen chair and a good length of rope.

Ask Hall to come up as well. And then bring in the candelabra from the dining room." He followed the others up the stairs and into the ballroom.

Within a few minutes their captive was bound securely to a chair that was placed in the middle of the ballroom floor. Four candelabra standing on the floor cast shadows and gave the whole room a slightly unworldly feel. In the light the man was revealed as a scruffy, black haired man in his mid thirties. He stared around with a look of fear on his face. Michael stood looking at him, assessing him. Hall had arrived, along with White and Bradley.

Michael stepped forward to stand a few feet in front of the man. "Who are you?" he asked quietly.

"Senhor," there was a note of panic and fear in the man's voice, "I have done nothing, why have you done this, please, let me go!"

Michael gave a slightly exaggerated sigh. "Please, Senhor, just answer my questions, it will be easier for everyone if you do." He paused for a beat, and then asked again, "Who are you?"

"Senhor, I am just a simple man, I do not know.."

"Enough", Michael shouted, stunning the man into silence. His knife was suddenly in his hand, he opened it and locked the blade. He changed to English. "I think that I shall just cut your throat." The look of incomprehension told him the man didn't speak English. "Hall?"

"Yes, sir?"

Michael continued in English. "Do you have your sharpening stone with you?"

"Yes, sir, always do."

"Good, take my knife," he passed it to Hall, "and make a good show of sharpening it, make sure our friend here can see you."

A silence fell, broken only by the sound of steel on stone. There was an atmosphere of tension, apprehension and the smell of fear coming from the captive. Sweat began to bead on his forehead. Michael waited.

When he thought the man was ready he said, "That should do it, Hall, thank you."

Hall passed the knife back to Michael who examined the blade, letting the candlelight catch it. "Now," he switched back to Portuguese, "Who are you?"

"Felipe Olmas, Senhor."

"There, that wasn't so difficult, was it?"

"No, Senhor." The man's eyes were rivetted to the knife blade.

"Why were you following me, Felipe?"

"Senhor, I wasn't, I swear!"

"On your life, Felipe?"

Olmas gulped, and very quietly said, "No, Senhor."

"You admit that you were following me?" Olmas just nodded. Michael stepped closer and held the blade so close to Olmas that he went cross eyed watching it. Michael asked, very quietly, very softly, "Why?"

Olmas cracked and began to sob, tears running down his face. "Please, Senhor, do not hurt me. I was only following you to see where it is that you go. I am a poor man and I was offered money to do it. I have never done anything like this before."

Michael heard Antonio mutter, "That's true."

"Who was paying you?"

"I don't know his name, Senhor. I was asking around one of the markets, looking for some work, and he just came up to me and asked if I would like to earn half a dollar a day. I said yes, and he gave a whole dollar straight away."

How long have you been following me?"

"Five days, Senhor. The man wanted to know if you went anywhere alone. I thought that was odd, but then I saw that you always have him with you." He nodded towards White.

That, thought Michael, meant it started after Senhora Santiago was killed. "Felipe?" Michael lowered the knife and the man looked up at him.

"Where do you meet this man?"

"A different time and place every time, Senhor, he tells me when and where each time."

"And the next time?"

"Tomorrow, Senhor, at eight o'clock, in a coffee house by the opera, Senhor, at the bottom of the steps to the west of the square."

Michael knew exactly the coffee house he meant. He had been there himself. Damn, he thought, one of the busier parts of Lisbon. "Is he there waiting for you?"

"No, Senhor, he always arrives a few minutes after I do, even if I am late."

Michael realised they were dealing with someone very skilled. No doubt he watched the meeting place to make sure that Olmas was alone. He turned to Frederico. "Frederico, go to the Police headquarters, tell them what has happened, tell them we have a prisoner for them. Bernardo, you had better go along as well. Keep your eyes open and be careful."

Michael put his knife away and went to sit in a chair against the wall. "White, do you think you can get coffee for everyone?" He looked at the others. "Make yourselves comfortable." He turned his mind to working out what to do with this new information.

It was nearly an hour before the police arrived, with them a senior officer who Michael knew from previous work with de Silva. Michael and he went to one end of the ballroom for a quiet talk.

"Begging you pardon, Senhor, but what has Olmas actually done?"

"I believe he is working for the man who tried to kill me and killed Senhora Santiago. He said he has been following me to see if I go anywhere alone, presumably so that the murderer can try again." He paused, and his face lit up. "And that gives me an idea!"

"Is there anything I can do, Senhor? The General has made it quite clear that we are to give you any help we can."

"Yes, the coffee house at the bottom of the steps by the opera house, do you know it?"

"Yes, Senhor."

"Can you find out if it has a back entrance?"

"Yes, Senhor, of course."

"Good, I shall be along to headquarters in the morning to see the General. What time does he normally arrive?"

The man smiled. "I would say nine o'clock when he hears about this."

"Then I shall be there."

At nine o'clock sharp, accompanied by White and Hall, who had insisted, Michael arrived and was shown in to where the General was waiting, coffee and rolls on the table.

"Captain Roberts! Coffee, and then tell me what your plan is?" he laughed at the expression on Michael's face. "Of course you have a plan, or I hope you do, for me to be here at this ungodly hour."

Michael smiled. "First of all, General, do you have four or five good men who can pass as gentlemen? Oh, and a few waiters would help."

At a quarter to eight that evening, Michael, alone, strolled slowly into the square in front of the opera house. It was relatively quiet as a performance was going on, and he was able to pause for a moment in the lights of the opera house. Quite casually he reached into his pocket for his cigar case, extracted one, and looked around for where he might get a light. His eyes lit upon the café, on the corner of the steps, but on a higher level than the square. He walked towards it, took the steps up two at a time, paused for a second at the top, then, his cigar in his mouth, he went in.

It was quiet, a couple of bored looking waiters, a pair of gentlemen at one table, three at another. He walked towards the back of the room, where one of the waiters opened a door for him and ushered him through. On the other side a plains clothes police officer guided him on until they merged on the street that crossed the top of the steps. A closed carriage was waiting, and Michael climbed in.

"Good evening, Captain."

"Good evening, General."

"I hope this works, we have several citizens very cross at being spirited out the coffee house and detained. However, they were mostly placated when they realised they were being detained in the Palacio Quintela." He waved at the rear entrance to the Palacio, just across the road. "It was good of Rodrigues to make it available."

"Well, General, if it doesn't work we are no worse off."

"Yes, anyway, I am glad you are alright, offering yourself as bait like that."

"Let's hope our man saw me and decides to see if it is me without waiting for Olmas." Somewhere a church clock struck eight o'clock. "We should know quite shortly, General."

They waited in silence.

Suddenly the carriage door opened and one of de Silva's men said, "We have him, General."

"Are you sure it's the right man?"

"Yes, General, he came in only a couple of minutes behind Captain Roberts, and stood looking around, looked a bit surprised. Just in case he was a genuine customer one of the waiters asked him to follow him and that it was a police matter. He tried to run for it and tried to pull this." He held out a long barrelled pistol. "It caught on his clothes and we overpowered him."

The General turned to Michael. "That looks like a very high quality and accurate pistol to me." He turned back, "And is he on his way to headquarters?"

"Yes, sir."

"Then I think we can return the coffee house to its owner and release our detainees, if we can get them to leave the hospitality of the Palacio. If you would see to that?" The man nodded and closed the carriage door. De Silva glanced over at Michael. "You realise, of course, that this will be all over Lisbon by the end of tomorrow?"

Michael shrugged. "It can't be helped."

The General banged on the roof with his cane and the carriage jerked into motion. "Then let us go and interrogate our prisoner."

At de Silva's headquarters four of his men were waiting in the hallway with the prisoner, his hands tightly bound behind him. and Michael got his first good look at him. He looked very ordinary, no distinguishing features at all. Shortish brown hair, brown eyes, an oval face, about the same height as Michael. The sort of man you could pass in the street and not remember or even notice. It was his air that marked him out, calm, collected, apparently unconcerned. He met Michael's gaze and seemed equally interested in him.

"What do you think, Captain Roberts, one of the cells or my office," de Silva asked.

It occurred to Michael that the usual interrogation methods of the Portuguese police would get nothing out of this man. Somehow he had to be thrown off balance. If this man was a professional assassin, like Rochambeau, he thought, then a professional approach would most likely fail. Michael lifted his cane slightly, pressed the catch, and slid a few inches of blade out. To Michael's great satisfaction he saw surprise and doubt flicker quickly across the man's face.

"Why bother." Michael's response surprised everyone, and, if anything, the prisoner looked even more keenly at him. "We know who he is, what he did. Untie him and let him try to make a run for it." Michael's face was a cold blank.

"Captain Roberts, are you mad?"

"Perhaps I am, General, but this man killed a very dear friend of mine, a harmless old lady, my baba, my second mother." Michael was gratified to see a flicker of uncertainty in the prisoner's eyes. He did not dare to look at the General, he hoped he would realise Michael was playing a game and play along. He did.

"I see your point, Captain, but we don't even know his name. Let us at least try to ascertain that."

"Victor Janardo." The man spoke without breaking eye contact with Michael. "General de Silva, I am your prisoner and I expect you to keep me safe from this man."

"My office," snapped the General, "and bring coffee."

The Police officers led the man away and the General raised his eyebrows to Michael, who answered with a little shrug and just the hint of a smile.

In the General's office de Silva ordered Janardo to be untied and directed him to a chair. Watched by four completely bemused officers, he and Michael settled themselves opposite him. Janardo was still watching Michael carefully, and Michael kept his face as expressionless as he could. In silence, coffee was brought in and de Silva poured three cups. Michael realised the General was stalling for time and had no idea how to play this further. Michael decided to push the issue.

"I wonder if Janardo's your real name?"

"Why should I lie? I know that you cannot prove in a court of law that I killed anyone and that is a very good reason not to lie."

"I don't need a court of law to know I want you dead. You can leave here, but I will find you and kill you." Michael suddenly thought he could see his way. A truth had occurred to him. "But I might as well smash your rather fine pistol as kill you. You are like that pistol, merely an instrument. You pulled the trigger, but you were not trying to kill me for any reason other than money." Michael saw that he had guessed right.

"In that case," mused Janardo, "what you really want is the man who paid me." It was a flat statement.

The General gave a little start at what was effectively an admission of guilt, but continued to sit quietly, reaching for his coffee to hide the movement.

Michael gave the slightest of nods in acknowledgment of Janardo's words.

Michael spoke. "The name for your life."

"You still have not proven that I did anything."

"No, but you just admitted it." Michael had to give him credit for being one of the most self-controlled people he had ever met. Barely a flicker of realisation showed. Then Janardo spoke.

"I suppose I did rather." He gave Michael a little bow. "But what sort of life, Captain, some sorts are not worth living."

"I don't care so long as I never see you again, because, if I do, I will kill you."

"I think you are a man of your word, Captain." For the first time since they had started talking he broke eye contact and turned to de Silva. "So, General, what sort of life can you offer me?"

De Silva stared at Janardo. "The Brasils."

"As a free man?"

De Silva glanced at Michael who gave an almost imperceptible nod.

"On arrival, and notified to my colleagues out there. One step out of line..."

Janardo bowed his acquiescence.

"And we will keep you in custody until the proof of your information and a ship can be arranged." He gave a mirthless little smile. "It will also keep you safe from Captain Roberts here. Who, I assure you, is a man of his word. Now, the name, and to show goodwill, a description."

Janardo replied, "I suppose a description is fair, as I have my doubts as to the veracity of the name. I know him as Senhor Loiro. My reason to doubt the name is that his hair is blond." Michael grunted, Loiro was Portuguese for blond. "He also has the most striking blue eyes that I think I have ever seen."

"Where did you meet him," asked de Silva.

"Now, General, I have told you what we agreed, however, he found me. I have no idea how to find him. If I did I might have bargained for more."

Michael gripped the arms of his chair and his knuckles whitened. "One last question. Have you already been paid?"

Janardo looked hard at Michael before he answered. "Yes."

"Take him away, guard him well," snapped de Silva.

In the doorway, Janardo turned for a moment. "General, one more thing."

"What?"

"Olmas is an innocent man. He had no idea what he was doing."

Once Janardo had been bundled away, Michael let out the breath he had been holding. It had taken all his self control not to have taken his knife and killed Janardo as he sat there. De Silva rose and walked across to a cabinet.

"I think we need something a little stronger than coffee after that." He poured two large glasses of brandy and handed one to Michael. "Best French, don't ask." He sank back into his chair. "That has to be the strangest interrogation I have ever witnessed."

Michael took a swig and sat silently.

"May I say, Captain that I admire your technique. But what was that question about him being paid?"

Michael was staring into his glass. "Nothing, just curiosity."

"Oh."

"I just hope it was the right thing to do. I hope Senhor Santiago will forgive me letting his wife's murderer go."

"Then don't tell him. If you must tell him anything, tell him you have the name of the man responsible. Sometimes one has to stretch and bend the truth. Anyway, I gather he has left Lisbon? There is no rush to tell him anything. Wait until this is all over."

"Yes, I suppose that you are right. And now we just need to find this Loiro, this blue eyed blond."

"It's a start Captain, it's a start."

"What will you do about Olmas?"

"Oh, hold him until all this is over and then let him go. Make sure he knows to keep his nose clean and his eyes and ears open and tell us if he hears anything, shall we say, unusual."

Michael emptied his glass. "That seems reasonable. Thank you, General, may I say you played your part well."

"Yes, well, next time, perhaps you might give me some warning?"

"Warning, General? I had no warning myself. And now I shall go home, I am tired and there are people who will want to hear all that has passed, twice, once in English and again in Portuguese."

De Silva chuckled. "And tomorrow we can start looking for Loiro. I'll send some men along with you, and I would urge you to keep up your precautions until we have him."

Michael had insisted on going to the rendezvous with Janardo on his own. He had not wanted to take the slightest chance of scaring him off. Back home, it was quite late by the time he had finished telling the evening's story, and arranged to start the hunt for Loiro in the morning. He said nothing of the deal with Janardo.

Chapter 4

The next morning Michael gathered everyone together in the dining room, save Senhora Pinheiro, who was out buying food to feed everyone. First, he gave his orders to Hall, White and Bradley. "White, I want you to continue keeping an eye on me when I am out and about. Hall, Bradley, you need to continue working with the horses, I know they're getting quite fit, but they can't be too fit for where we will be going. And when White isn't out with me, Bradley, try to make him a rider, will you." That got a laugh from the three Englishmen. "Now I'm going to instruct these three," he waved at Antonio, Carlos and Bernardo.

Michael spoke in Portuguese. "I don't see what we can do except carry on as before, perhaps speak to people again now that we have a description. But, be careful. This man is clever and ruthless. That is why I want you, Antonio, Carlos, to work together." They nodded to him. "Bernardo, you said the only place you haven't been to have a look around is out at Belem"

"Yes, Senhor."

"Then I think you should start there. You should be safe enough with so many soldiers around. I want you all back here just after dark to let me know how you have got on. Frederico?"

"Yes, Senhor?"

"I want you to sit at one of the upstairs front windows. Check whoever comes to the front door before you open it, and keep an eye open for anyone taking an interest in the house." Michael switched to English and spoke to Hall and Bradley. "While you are working with the horses, keep an eye on the back entrance for anyone being nosey, or trying to get in. If they're just looking, just remember them. If anyone tries to get in, then you can take them and hold them in the stables until I can see them." He looked around the table and then spoke twice, once in English, once in Portuguese and said the same thing both times. "Right, let's find this bastard." The expression on his face boded ill for Loiro.

At that moment there was a banging on the front door. Frederico skipped over to a window and looked down. "It is two police officers, Senhor."

Everyone followed Michael down the stairs to the hall, they were going their different ways. The two police officers stood back, a little surprised as Carlos, Antonio and Bernardo strolled out, Antonio with a grin and "Good morning, officers."

Michael led the two officers into the large reception room that opened off the hall. "Begging your pardon, Captain, but the General sent us. He said to tell you Janardo has escaped."

Michael barely raised his eyebrows, he wasn't entirely surprised. "How did it happen?"

"Early this morning, sir. The gaoler heard him groaning, checked and saw he was writhing in agony. He went in and got his neck broken for his trouble. Janardo took his keys and just walked out, sir. He knocked out another guard on his way. He's alright. The General is furious, sir!"

"Very well, tell the General thank you for letting me know."

Somewhat taken aback by Michael's calmness, they left. Michael closed the door behind them and walked across to what he still thought of as his father's study. He sat, listening to the silence of the house, thinking. After a while he went up to his bedroom and rummaged around until he found what he was looking for, a small, flat box. He opened it and took out the pair of pistols. He began his preparations.

Carlos and Antonio were first back, followed shortly by Bernardo. They had no news. Michael had been waiting for them in the study, told them to go down to the kitchen to eat, and to ask Senhora Pinheiro to send his dinner to the study. Michael was still there when Carlos and Antonio left and when Frederico secured the front doors and everyone else retired, with puzzled looks in his direction.

Once all was quiet, Michael took his candelabra across the hall to the reception room. Ten minutes or so later he returned, replaced all the candles in the candelabra with fresh ones, lit just one and placed it on a side table in the hall. Then he returned to the deep shadows of the reception room and settled down to wait. As he did he heard church bells strike midnight. He sat on the floor, between two windows, it wasn't the most uncomfortable watch he had kept.

The bells of Lisbon has just chimed two o'clock when the faintest of noises brought him fully alert. He watched the hall intently. There was the hint of a footstep on the stairs up from the kitchen. The slightest of drafts made the candle flicker and set the shadows dancing.

Michael called out, softly. "In here, Janardo."

For a moment there was no sound, no movement, then Michael heard a pistol being brought to full cock, then another. He waited.

Out in the hall Janardo readied himself. He was sure that Roberts was alone, otherwise he would already have been attacked. He was not entirely surprised that he was expected, or that Roberts was alone. What was between them was, after all, personal. The opening into where the voice had come from was wide, and the placing of the candelabra cast very little light into it. Clever, he thought, anyone stepping in would be clearly silhouetted. But it was still just enough to show what was in the room. Not so clever. Suddenly he launched himself across the opening, spinning from one side to the other and the protection of the wall. He had glimpsed a figure, standing by the inside wall, the little light from the single candle and from outside revealing a dark shape. He took a deep breath and stepped into the doorway, raising and firing one of his pistols at the figure as he did so. The answering shot came from low down, below the windows on the other side from the figure. The ball struck him high in his right shoulder, making him stagger. He tried to raise his second pistol, he couldn't see anything, the flash had blinded him. Damn, he's good, he thought. The second shot killed him.

Hall and White came crashing down the stairs almost together, White with his cudgel and Hall with his sabre. Michael was calmly lighting the rest of the candles. Janardo lay on his back, his sightless eyes staring up. Frederico and Bernardo appeared next.

"Bloody Hell," exclaimed White, then, "begging your pardon, sir"

"That's alright, White. Frederico," he switched to Portuguese, "open up the front doors and go with Senhor White, find a policeman, go to the headquarters if you have to." Back to English, "White go with Frederico, we need the police here." Back to Portuguese, "Bernardo, go and check the door in the kitchen, I think that's how he got in. Then go and check on Bradley." English again. "Hall, you know where the brandy is, get me a glass, and then, I have no doubt Senhora Pinheiro is awake, do you think you can try your Portuguese and ask her to make some coffee?"

General de Silva put down his coffee cup. "Captain Roberts, I begin to wonder if I should not move in here with you. It would save me being roused in the early hours and crossing Lisbon in the dark." He sat back in his chair in Michael's drawing room where he had listened to Michael's account of the attack. He had smiled when Michael explained about the cloak hung over a stool standing on a table to hint at a figure in the limited light. "But what I want to know is how you knew he would be coming?"

Michael finished pouring himself another coffee and answered. "He told me."

"What? Now, Captain, I was there, he did no such thing."

Michael smiled. "It was the money, he said he had been paid. He was a professional with a contract to honour. It had to be tonight because he needed to get out of Lisbon as soon as he could."

"Ah, yes, of course." De Silva nodded his understanding. "And you've had no luck in your search for Loiro?" Michael shook his head. De Silva went on, "I have had a number of complaints from fair haired men stopped and questioned in the street. However, I think we have no choice but to keep looking."

"No choice at all, General." Michael looked at his watch. "Would you care to stay for breakfast?"

Bernardo wandered slowly along the road outside the Royal Palace at Belem. With his limp it was easy for him to drift slowly along, no one gave him a second look. He was thinking about the events of the night and feeling rather tired with lack of sleep. He passed by a cart with a sleepy looking mule in the traces. The carter was half asleep in the back, but lifted the brim of his hat as Bernardo went by.

"Hello there, what brings you out here? You're a long way from home."

Bernardo spun round and recognised the carter who had brought Michael's baggage to the house. "Oh, yes, I remember you, that was a while back. Do you remember all your customers?"

"No, only the really regular ones, unless there's something odd to make it stick in my mind."

"Oh, so what was odd about Captain Roberts and his party?" Bernardo asked.

"Nothing at all. It was what happened the next day that was odd."

"And what was that?"

"Ah, now, there's a rough, vagrant type hangs about the Palace, he runs errands for officers and the like. Everyone calls him Mercurio, I don't understand it myself, some sort of English joke, but there you are. Anyway, the next day he comes and asks me about your officer. Asked me if I remembered where I'd taken him, I says, of course I do, and then he just wandered off."

"Is that it?" asked Bernardo, now wide awake and listening carefully.

"No, but you seem mightily interested. Is it anything to do with why you've been hanging around here? Is been, what, two days now? Oh, yes, don't look so innocent, I noticed you. So, what's it worth to tell you what happened next?"

"How about I go and get my officer and he comes down to ask you? Believe me, you don't want that."

"Alright, alright, no need to get nasty. Still, if it is worth something...?"

"I'll tell him how helpful you have been, there might be half a dollar in it for you."

"Fair enough, fair enough. Anyway, a few hours later this Mercurio comes back with this other fellow, and he asks me to show him where I took your officer, offers me a whole dollar." He shrugged, "So I did. Didn't go quite all the way. Had me point out the house, then he paid me and just walked away. Easiest dollar I ever made."

"What did he look like, the one that paid you?"

"Fair hair and really bright, blue eyes."

Bernardo stared at him for a moment and then made an offer. "How about you come with me and tell my officer what you just told me." He thought for a moment. "There's two dollars in it for you."

"Two? Right you are, climb on!"

Back at the house Michael listened to what the carter had to say. He asked him "How would I find this Mercurio?"

"He's usually sitting at the entrance to your headquarters, if he isn't running an errand for someone."

Michael vaguely recalled the presence of some disreputable looking man as he had arrived to see General Peacocke. He handed the carter two dollars and told Frederico to "Take our friend here down to the kitchen, get your mother to feed him well," and in an undertone, "try to keep him here as long as you can." Frederico nodded and led the carter away.

Next he said to Hall, "Get down to the stables, get your Billy and Johnny ready, and a saddle on Beau as well." White was next, "My uniform, now! I'll be up to change in a moment." Then, "Bernardo, well done, very well done. Now you are going to have to bother General de Silva again. Go and give him a message that we have a definite lead and I hope to be back here in, say two hours, with a suspect to question. Off you go."

The four miles out to Belem were quickly covered with Hall leading Beau. Michael led the way round to the extensive stables and got the horses put up, promising to be back for them very shortly. Then he led the way into the Palace, through a route from the stables. Eventually they emerged into the front entrance hall, where an orderly Sergeant jumped to attention and saluted as Michael appeared.

Michael returned the salute and beckoned him further in to the hall, away from the entrance. There he asked him, "Is that fellow Mercurio outside?"

"Yes, sir, do you want him for something."

"Yes, just call him in for me, Sergeant."

In answer to the Sergeant's shout, Mercurio appeared in the entrance and walked in. Then he saw Michael standing in the shadows and tried to retreat, only to find Hall in the way.

"Hello, Mercurio. There are people who want to talk to you."

The Sergeant coughed, "Err, I beg your pardon, sir, but what are you doing?"

"Making an arrest, Sergeant, and if you have a problem with that you can go and see General Peacocke and tell him Captain Roberts was acting on the instructions of Mister Stuart the Ambassador."

The return trip took twice as long as the ride out, Mercurio was no rider and they had to take a very slow pace. When they rode in to the stables Michael was not surprised to see de Silva's coach and half a dozen uniformed police officers. A police Sergeant told him the General was inside and detailed two of his men to take charge of Mercurio.

Mercurio was marched inside and was soon sitting on the chair that was still in the middle of the ballroom. There was a look of apprehension on his face. A look that turned to fear when de Silva came in. In his fear he could not answer the questions put to him fast enough. He told them all about his friend, Senhor Loiro, who was so interested in the comings and goings at the British headquarters, and the gossip he picked up. Within a very short space of time they knew exactly when and where they could find Loiro.

Michael and de Silva left Mercurio in the care of the police officers and retired to Michael's drawing room.

"I am not surprised we didn't find Loiro, that part of Lisbon is notorious and my officers don't go in if they can avoid it."

"What do you suggest?"

"I could arrange a raid with twenty or thirty officers, I wouldn't want to use fewer, frankly, but that might be seen coming. We would have to find the place, the right place, and even then we couldn't be sure to be able to cover the back exit, or any other ways out."

Michael unfastened his belt and laid his sword and sabretache on the floor. "What about a single man?"

De Silva gave him a sharp look. "What? Are you suggesting yourself?"

"Yes."

"That's not a good idea. How would you secure him and get him out?"

Michael met the General's gaze with his own cold, hard expression. "Would it be necessary to secure him and get him out?"

"What?"

"Say if you think me wrong, but he won't just surrender and come quietly. It would be my assumption that I would come out alone."

"No," de Silva protested, "I cannot agree to that, I must try to make an arrest and I will not take responsibility for you going alone. I shall arrange a raid, we will do the best that we can. From what this Mercurio has told us I think just before eight o'clock will be our best chance."

That night it rained, heavily, which suited Michael. After an early dinner he waited until all the other inhabitants of the house were taking their own dinner down in the kitchen. Then he went to his room and changed quickly into the rough old clothes he kept to hand. He put his knife in a pocket of his jacket and tucked a small pistol into the waist of his dirty breeches. It was the one Elizabeth had shot Rochambeau with. It seemed appropriate, and it was the right size to conceal easily. Small, but lethal. He wrapped himself in a disreputable looking cloak, pulled a broad brimmed hat down low over his face and, very quietly, slipped out into the night. It was just seven o'clock.

Half an hour later a hunched figure shuffled slowly down an alleyway. There was only one coffee house, Michael pushed open the door and went in. There were just two customers, deep in conversation, neither of them Loiro, and a waiter leaning nonchalantly in a doorway. The room was dark, only a few tallow candles guttered in sconces on the walls. He lowered himself slowly onto a bench in one of the booths, where he could see the front door and the door where the waiter stood. The waiter lazily pushed himself upright and came slowly over. Michael feigned a coughing fit, bringing his hand up to hide his scar. In a voice rough from coughing he ordered a coffee. It arrived, a foul smelling brew in a chipped cup. While the waiter stood by his booth, he slowly and carefully counted out a few vintines for him. His hands were filthy and the waiter picked up the coins reluctantly before leaving him. Michael sipped at his coffee, it tasted worse than it smelt. He settled down to wait.

Ten minutes or so later, the door opened and Loiro came in. There was no mistaking him, his blue eyes were clear even in the dim light. He glanced around the room and as his eyes fell on Michael, Michael feigned another coughing fit with his hand covering his scar. Loiro seemed satisfied and sat down in booth in the darkest corner of the room. He was clearly a regular, as his coffee appeared without an order.

The waiter disappeared through door on some errand. Michael finished off his coffee and rose to leave, his cloak wrapped around him. He took a couple of shuffling steps and stumbled over a stool, staggering towards Loiro. Then he straightened, another two steps took him to beside Loiro, who looked up in alarm. He caught sight of Michael's scar and he started to rise, reaching for something under his coat, but Michael caught his arm, pulled Loiro across the table towards him, and then drove his knife up, under the man's jaw and deep into his throat. A strangled gurgle came from Loiro who fell back into the shadows of the booth, clutching his throat.

"I beg your pardon, Senhor," Michael muttered as he backed towards the door. The two men in their booth had seen nothing except someone stumbling over a stool. He was half way through the front door before a shout came from behind him, "Hey, you, stop!"

Michael turned, producing the pistol, the two customers hadn't moved, it was the waiter who had shouted, but at the sight of the pistol he backed away. Then Michael was out, into the rain and hurrying away down the alley, into the street and around corners.

He hadn't gone far when he heard shouts from the direction of the coffee house. It sounded as if de Silva's raid was on time. He smiled grimly and hurried home, where he managed to slip in unnoticed.

Michael was sitting in his drawing room, in front of a good fire, drinking decent coffee and with the rain hammering on the windows. Then there was a pounding on the front door, and a few moments later White showed in General de Silva.

Michael rose, smiling, "Good evening General, White, take the General's cloak, it's soaking, then get another cup for the General. Have you been successful? Did you get him?"

"Yes, we got him, but he was dead!"

"What?"

De Silva looked hard at him. "I suppose you have been here all evening?"

Michael laughed. "Of course. And very glad not to be out in this rain. But, tell me, what happened? You say Loiro is dead?"

"Yes, somebody knifed him just before the raid went in."

"Any witnesses?"

"No, not a one. The place was completely deserted, except for Loiro."

"Hmm. Where was he stabbed?"

"In the throat, why?"

"Oh, no reason, but it sounds to me as if someone wanted him silenced. Very symbolic, a knife to the throat. Anyway, I can't say that I am sorry. I can tell Senhor Santiago that the man who killed his wife is dead, and tell Mister Stuart that the French spies have been dealt with."

"Humph! I suppose you can. Does this mean you will be leaving Lisbon?"

"I do hope so, General." Michael beamed at him.

Over the next few days preparations to march to join the army were completed. With help from Juan Moreno, Michael acquired a pair of baggage ponies. Mister Stuart expressed his satisfaction with the outcome of Michael's investigations and said that he would write to Wellington and tell him, said he would write to Musgrave as well. He happily reimbursed Michael what he had paid his friends. Furtado undertook to make the arrangements for paying Santiago. To Senhora Pinheiro's relief he decided to leave Frederico in Lisbon. There would be enough to do looking after the house without the Santiagos.

The day before they were due to leave, Michael got a message from General de Silva, asking him to call in. He did, and it transpired that after much effort they had discovered where Loiro had been living.

"We didn't find much, but there was this, I thought you might like to have it." De Silva handed across a scruffy sheet of paper. It was an order from Paris instructing Loiro to have Michael killed. It was signed Renard.

"Thank you, General. Any idea how it got here from Paris?"

"None at all, I'm afraid."

.   .   .

In Paris Renard was reading Loiro's report that Captain Roberts had arrived in Lisbon and that steps were being taken to kill him. The report had reached him quite quickly. Loiro had simply put it in the post for Falmouth. It had travelled by packet. There it had been collected and passed on to one of the smugglers who made regular runs to France. It had then entered the official postal system and arrived on Renard's desk. Renard found that amusing.

Renard was happily anticipating Loiro's next report when one of his clerks came in.

"I beg your pardon, Monsieur, but the Duke wishes to see you."

"What, oh, very well."

"He said you should bring your hat and cloak, Monsieur"

A short walk brought him to the office of the Duke of Rovigo, Rene Savary, who ran the secret police for the Emperor.

"You sent for me, your Grace?"

"Ah, Renard, good, come along, we have been summoned to see the Emperor."

It was not a comfortable audience for Renard. Napoleon expressed considerable dismay at the lack of intelligence success in Spain. He was annoyed that his brother, Joseph, King of Spain, was using this to excuse his failures. Something needed to be done, so he was sending Renard to Madrid to take direct control of the intelligence war in Spain and Portugal. The real sting came when the Emperor informed Renard that if he was so keen to see some obscure English cavalry officer killed he could go and do it himself. Renard had been shocked to realise the Emperor knew about his personal vendetta, and had tried to explain to the Emperor about Michael's counter intelligence successes against them. The Emperor's reaction to that was that it was all the more reason for Renard to go and finish this man. He told him he could have three weeks to prepare for his journey and settle matters in Paris.

Renard was subdued on the return journey, but inside he was seething. His hatred for Michael Roberts had just been enhanced. It wasn't enough that Roberts had killed his only son, oh, no, he had also thwarted French intelligence efforts in Portugal, leading to his embarrassment in front of the Emperor. And he was being forced to leave Paris and all its comforts, like his mistress, Françoise. He wasn't looking forward to telling her, she would not be happy, there would be tears. Still, he told himself, he had heard a lot of praise for the ladies of Madrid. He didn't expect it would be long before he found fresh comforts. He was also confident that once he was on the spot he would be able to shake things up for King Joseph.

There might be honours and rewards in it for him, and the Emperor was quite right, it would put him in a better position to finish Roberts once and for all. He cheered up a little.

Chapter 5

It was a glorious, early spring day when Michael and his party left Lisbon. Trees everywhere were beginning to blossom, the sky was blue and the wind light. Spirits were high as they waved goodbye to Senhora Pinheiro, Frederico and Bernardo who had all come down to the stables to see them off. Michael led on Johnny, the horse feeling fit and back to his best under him. To his left rode Hall on Billy, leading Thor. Behind came Bradley on Jasper, leading Robbie and one of the baggage ponies, with White on Beau leading the other pony.

They made their way slowly through Lisbon's busy streets, but once clear of the city the pace picked up. Michael was intending to ride through Santarem, Abrantes, Sabugal and on to Wellington's headquarters at Freineda, some two hundred miles and more. He was keeping away from Alcoentre. He expected to take at least a week. At the end of the third day, however, they found Abrantes occupied by the 1st Division. They were on their way to Badajoz and had called in to collect new uniforms. Michael learnt from a harassed division quartermaster that the entire army was on the move and that Wellington was expected at Nisa in a day or two. He managed to extract three days rations for his party, but the town was full and they had to push on, crossing the river by its bridge of boats and then heading further east.

At the end of a long day they found shelter in a barn with the horses. This was a new experience for all except Michael, who had had far worse accommodation. It was at least dry, and they managed to obtain a reasonable amount of fodder for the horses. Bradley was already beginning to see the problems that lay ahead when it came to keeping the horses fed, let alone fit. White was a little taken aback by the complete absence of any amenities. A thirty mile ride the next day brough them to Nisa, where Michael learnt that Wellington was expected the next day. Quarters had already been allocated for headquarters and Michael got in by waving his orders in the face of a young lieutenant, who advised Michael that if The Peer didn't like it, it would be on his, Michael's, head.

"The Peer?" Michael asked him.

"Yes, Wellington. Gets new honours so often it's easiest just to call him The Peer. Did you know he is now the Earl of Wellington?"

"Is he? No, I must have missed that while I was in Lisbon."

"Not to worry, the news has only just reached us here. Oh, and the Spanish have made him a Duke. Duke of Ciudad Rodrigo would you believe? Damned confusing, frankly."

Late in the afternoon, Wellington rode in, as usual outstripping most of his staff. In the hustle and bustle of the arrival of the cavalcade, Wellington was accompanied by a dozen or so officers and an escort of Portuguese Dragoons, and all this was followed at intervals by servants and batmen and orderlies, with a mule train bringing up the rear. A staff officer saw Michael watching from a doorway and rode over.

"I say, who are you?"

"Captain Roberts, Sixteenth Light Dragoons, reporting as ordered."

The officer saluted. "Beg your pardon, sir, Lieutenant Hook, in charge of billeting. I've been expecting you to turn up somewhere."

Michael returned the salute. "That's quite alright, Mister Hook. I see you have your hands full. I have my party in here, myself, a batman, two servants and eight horses. I hope that's acceptable."

"Yes, yes, but I shall probably have to put a few others in with you. I say, do you know Major Krauchenburg?"

"First German Hussars?" Hook nodded. "Yes, I do."

"Splendid, I'll put him in with you. Now, if you'll excuse me?" Michael nodded, they exchanged salutes and Hook rode off.

It wasn't long before Krauchenburg arrived. "Ach, Mister Roberts, how are you?"

And so began a convivial evening with the two exchanging reminiscences of the retreat from Buçaco to the Lines. Krauchenburg had fully recovered from his wound, and they congratulated each other on their promotions. Krauchenburg's three servants arrived and they were, all in all, quite comfortable.

Night had barely fallen when an orderly sergeant arrived. "Captain Roberts, sir? Begging your pardon, sir, but the Earl of Wellington wants to see you."

Wellington was seated at a small table in his quarters, writing letters, when Michael was shown in by

Wellington's secretary, Lieutenant Colonel Lord Fitzroy Somerset.

"Beg your pardon, my Lord, Captain Roberts for you, sir."

Wellington looked up. "Thank you, Somerset, that will be all. Captain Roberts, pleased to see you."

"Thank you, my Lord." Behind Michael, Somerset closed the door, leaving them alone.

"Yes, Captain, eh? And still in the Sixteenth. You got what you wanted after all."

"Err..."

"Come now, Roberts. You've got your Captaincy, and well deserved."

"Thank you, my Lord."

"Yes, I understand the Duke of York was particularly impressed by your activities as it made it easier for him to grant my wishes, and so I have also got I want, which is to have you on hand for that special line of work at which you seem so adept. And it is the situation here, in Portugal and Spain that must now take priority, not anything you might have been involved in for Musgrave."

"Yes, sir."

"I have heard from Mister Stuart, by the bye, spoke very highly of you over this recent business in Lisbon."

"Thank you, sir."

"Now, you will be joining Sir Stapleton as an extra Aide, I would rather have you with me, but, as you know, Murray has gone home, and his replacement, Gordon, is not a political ally, writes letters behind my back and they end up in the London papers. Then Napoleon reads it all a few days later. Man's not competent. Of course, you heard none of that from me, but it's as well you understand that all intelligence matters are now managed by myself and no one else, and why. Do I make myself clear?"

"Yes, sir."

"Good, I don't want him knowing about tasks I might give you. Attaching you to Sir Stapleton keeps you out of his view, but close enough at hand. And Sir Stapleton knows about your intelligence work, which makes everything easier. D'ye see?"

"Yes, sir, I understand."

"Good, and now I shall bid you goodnight."

On his way back to his billet Michael came across a few officers he knew a little, a little because they were all senior to him. Then a voice hailed him. "Hello! Roberts!"

He turned and peered at an officer standing in an open doorway. He recognised Major Scovell, walked over, saluted and greeted him. "Hello, sir, it's good to see you again."

"And you, Roberts, it's been a while. I gather you are joining Sir Stapleton."

"Yes, sir, as an extra Aide de Camp."

"Come in, I've got some coffee just ready."

Inside, Scovell's billet was a single small room, a bed made up to one side and a chest acting as a table, another as a bench. There was no other furniture. "Sit you down," Scovell pointed Michael to the bench, lowered himself carefully on to his bed and poured Michael a cup of coffee. Scattered on the chest between them were various scraps of paper and a small notebook. So far as Michael could see they were all covered in a combination of writing and numbers. He realised Scovell was watching him.

"Know what those are, do you?" Scovell asked.

"They, err, look like coded messages, sir."

"Yes, exactly, and I'm trying to decipher them. They're French, mostly acquired by your old friend Don Julien Sanchez."

"Do you have the book the French are using?" Michael asked.

Scovell looked puzzled for a moment. "Oh, you mean the type where each person has the same book and uses page and word numbers? Know about that do you?"

"Yes, sir."

"I suppose it looks a bit similar, but no. The French use numbers to represent words, individual letters and common groups of letters. It's the devil's own work, but I make progress, slowly. I have a go whenever I have some spare time." He had been staring at the bits of paper and now looked at Michael. "The simple fact is that the more messages I can get hold of, the more I can decipher. It would be good to get a copy of the cipher itself." He paused, thoughtfully. "Perhaps, one day, who knows, except that then they would just change it and we, I would be back to square one. But you are just back from England, how was it there?" And the conversation became general.

The following morning Wellington was on the move again, to Portalegre, with Michael and his people following along behind. Colonel Campbell, who ran the headquarters, told Michael that they would be moving on to Elvas the day after, that Sir Stapleton should be there and he could join his staff immediately.

Elvas was a fortified town just inside the Portuguese border with Spain. A mere ten miles or so to the east lay the strongly fortified Spanish town of Badajoz. Wellington had already been forced to give up one attempt to take it, but take it he must, it was the key to Spain in the south as Ciudad Rodrigo was in the north. With both in his possession he could choose where to attack and know that the main routes into Portugal were blocked and protected. Sir Stapleton and his staff had been billeted in a number of fine town houses just off the main square. When Michael and his party arrived he was greeted by an infantry captain, who introduced himself as William Campbell, Sir Stapleton's quartermaster.

Michael dismounted and shook hands with him. "Pleased to meet you, Campbell. Roberts, reporting for duty."

"Yes, we've been expecting you. Got you a fair billet, but we are all rather cramped, what with the whole army being hereabouts. Let's see, you, your dragoon, two servants and, what, eight horses?"

"Yes, that's right."

"Hmm, I think I can get you all in." He smiled. "The lot of a quartermaster, never enough of anything. If you come this way, I'll show you where you are." He led them a little way down the street to a three story house. "Here we are, you're sharing with Captain von der Decken, First Hussars. Perhaps you know him?"

"No, I don't think so, I know a few of the First, but not him, so far as I can recall."

"Well, Sir Stapleton thinks very highly of him, he saved the General from being captured up at Rodrigo last September." He pointed to a narrow alleyway, "The stabling, such as it is, is down there. Decken's establishment is smaller than yours, just a batman, a valet and one spare horse for himself. I expect he will welcome some company." He pulled out his watch. "We shall be dining in an hour, best come and report to Sir Stapleton in forty-five minutes. I'll let him know."

Michael got himself and his people installed. Decken was, according to his Portuguese valet, with Sir Stapleton. Once again they were snug quarters, but he and Decken had their own rooms and the stabling was just adequate even if Bradley had sucked his teeth at the sight of them. Forty-five minutes later he entered the building that housed Sir Stapleton and his closest staff. As he walked in a German Hussar officer was just coming out of a room, but stopped when he saw Michael.

"Ach! You must be Captain Roberts! I am von der Decken." He came forward to shake Michael's hand. "Do you snore? I hope not, the walls in our billet are quite thin." He gave a small chuckle. "Now, this way, our General is in here, expecting you."

He turned back to the door he had emerged from, stuck his head in and said, "Captain Roberts for you, Sir Stapleton."

"Excellent," Michael heard the General's voice, "show him in, show him in."

Sir Stapleton Cotton was a striking figure. He was wearing the full dress uniform of a Lieutenant Colonel of the Sixteenth, which he was, as well as being a Major General. He was well known for preferring the more flamboyant uniform, rather than the simpler redcoat with gold braid of a general. It was, superficially, the same uniform that Michael was wearing, but instead of Michel's travel stained overalls, Sir Stapleton was wearing immaculate white pantaloons tucked into highly polished hessian boots. His blue dolman with its silver lace was spotless and his ivory hilted, mameluke style sabre leant in a corner, with a full dress belt and sabretache of red Morrocco leather and silver lace. He rose to meet Michael.

"Good to see you again, Roberts, and congratulations on your Captaincy."

"Thank you, Sir Stapleton."

Sir Stapleton sank back onto his chair and waved Michael to another.

"Now then, Roberts, tell me, how are things in England?"

Michael briefly ran over matters at the depot, although Sir Stapleton was aware of most that had happened recently. There was a knock at the door and an orderly peered in. "Dinner is ready, sir," he said before closing the door.

As both men rose, Sir Stapleton said, "you can ride with me tomorrow, get to know your way around a bit, d'ye know, we've fourteen cavalry regiments here, to say nothing of Alten's up near Rodrigo. Takes a bit of handling, I can tell you."

Dinner was a relaxed and convivial affair. Michael had already met Campbell and von der Decken and now he was introduced to Colonel Elley, Sir Stapleton's Adjutant General and Captain White, Campbell's assistant. It was Sir Stapleton's rule that business was not discussed at dinner and Michael found himself giving a full account of the horse fair in Howden. As they broke up to go their separate ways, Sir Stapleton spoke to Michael.

"Just a moment, Roberts, sit down, there's something I need to say, I forgot earlier." Puzzled, Michael did as he was bid and, once they were alone, Sir Stapleton went on. "Yes, it was your talking about your new batman that reminded me. I know exactly why you are here, Wellington was good enough to take me into his confidence. Of course, it's no great surprise, seen you at work myself. However, it seems to me that you should have an orderly as well as your batman. I know he's a new man, no experience to speak of, an experienced man who can watch your back would be good. It wouldn't appear unusual, there're orderlies everywhere, and damn useful they are too. It also struck me that it should probably be a man of our own, from the Sixteenth, keep it the family as it were. NCOs are usual, corporals particularly. I've already had a word with Colonel Archer, and he has no objection if the man is willing." Sir Stapleton smiled at him. "Can you think of anyone?"

Michael returned Sir Stapleton's smile. "Indeed, I can, sir."

"Excellent. The Regiment's up at Avis at the moment, that's the best part of fifty miles, but will be down to join us shortly. Then you can pay a visit, renew old acquaintances, eh?"

"Yes, sir, thank you."

"There's one other thing you should know."

"Yes, sir?"

"Yes, Colonel Archer is retiring, but I am not sure quite when he will be leaving us. As you know, Hay is now a Major, since Stanhope went. I expect Major Pelly will get the Lieutenant Colonelcy, and then join from England to take command. I have spoken to Major Hay as well, explained one or two things about your promotion and your attachment to the staff, he is quite happy about it, and agrees with Archer about the orderly question."

"Thank you, sir."

"Yes, of course, the Earl of Wellington's and the Duke of York's views do help." He smiled. "Major Hay isn't going to do other than accept that, however, as it is, he is in fact quite keen on your role, feels it reflects well on the Regiment."

For the next few days Michael familiarised himself with the area around Elvas and the locations of all the brigades and Regiments of cavalry. He met the brigade and regimental commanders and became known as one of Sir Stapleton's Aides de Camp, a man with the General's authority behind him. He rode each of his horses in strict rotation, while Bradley did his best to keep them in condition, something that became easier as the coming of spring improved the supply of green forage. Something that also heralded campaigning becoming possible again.

Everyone knew that it was Wellington's intention to lay siege to the Spanish fortified town of Badajoz, and in mid-March the army did exactly that. To prevent French interference with the siege operations a force of three infantry divisions and two cavalry brigades under General Graham marched to the southeast to block any such attempts. Sir Stapleton went with the cavalry accompanied by all his staff.

The next two weeks saw a lot of marches, counter marches, night marches and attempts to surprise inferior French forces, all of which failed, but did keep the French well away from Badajoz as the siege progressed. At the end of the first week it began to rain. For Michael it was nothing new, and Hall had some experience to call on from the training in England. Bradley was used to working out in all weathers with horses, he cheerfully claimed Yorkshire in winter was worse. White struggled. City born and bred he found day after day in heavy rain, with no real chance to get dry, to be hard. The cheery readiness he had displayed when he had accompanied Michael around Lisbon with his cudgel had gradually worn away.

Finally, the Earl of Wellington decided that Graham and Sir Stapleton had done all they could, and the force was recalled, the cavalry going to Villafranca and the surrounding area. Sir Stapleton Cotton and his staff were already comfortably billeted in Villafranca when the Fourteenth and Sixteenth Light Dragoons rode in. The sound of the approaching cavalry attracted the attention of Sir Stapleton and he was standing in the doorway to his billet as the two Regiments rode past. Michael watched from an upstairs window as the long column of horsemen, riding in threes, passed by. The Fourteenth, by dint of their seniority, led, paying Sir Stapleton the compliments due to him. Then came the Sixteenth, Colonel Archer at their head, followed by the three squadrons, each about a hundred strong. Michael knew all the officers, Major Hay, Captains Lygon and Murray leading their squadrons, he saw Persse, now with a troop of his own, Alexander, Tomkinson, Penrice and George Keating amongst others. He saw Lloyd, two corporal's chevrons on his sleeve. Finally the Regiment's baggage went past, Pedro Moreno and his friend Rafael Martins amongst the servants, and Michael caught a glimpse of Maggie Lloyd sitting on a mule like a queen. Michael went down to where Sir Stapleton was standing.

"Ah, Roberts," the General turned and spoke as he heard Michael on the stairs. "Cut along and find Colonel Archer, ask him to call here as soon as he can, tell him if he gets here in the hour he can join us for dinner. And you need not rush back, I'm sure you have some greetings to exchange."

"Yes, sir, thank you, sir," and Michael shot off after his Regiment.

The two streets where the Sixteenth was being billeted were a scene of apparent chaos as officers and NCOs got their men distributed between the houses, arranged stabling and forage for the horses and organised the hundred and one matters that went with billeting in a strange town. He came across Keating and Penrice, who greeted him with exaggerated salutes and congratulations on his promotion. Many hands were shaken before he found Colonel Archer, standing in the middle of the street with Mister Barra, the Adjutant, and Regimental Sergeant Major Williams.

Michael saluted Colonel Archer and greeted him, "Hello, sir, I have a message for you from Sir Stapleton."

Archer returned the salute and said "Thank you, Roberts, it's good to see you looking so well. Now, what does our good General want?"

Michael gave the message and Archer replied, "Very well, I shall go along shortly. I saw Sir Stapleton as we rode in, I can find my own way. I expect you will want to renew old acquaintances, no need to stand on ceremony, Captain, you are one of us."

"Thank you, sir, I will just take a stroll along."

He saluted and started to turn away when Archer, returning the salute, commented, "Lloyd's in Captain Persse's Troop, they're in the next street over."

Michael made his way through the busy streets and found Persse. "Hello, Captain Persse. Congratulations on your Troop."

"And congratulations to you, but no Troop, eh?" They shook hands.

"No, 'fraid not, it's more of a staff appointment," he smiled and shrugged, "one day, perhaps."

"Well, it's quite alright with me. If you'd got a Troop I would still be a Lieutenant."

"Look," said Michael, "I won't detain you, I know you are busy just now, but can you tell me where I can find Corporal Lloyd?"

"Ah!" Persse grimaced. "Tell me you haven't come to take him from me? He's good man and a genius with the horses." Michael began to stammer a response, but Persse forestalled him. "Don't worry, Colonel Archer mentioned the other day that you might come calling. Said he'd let me have first choice from the next batch of remounts if Lloyd goes. I think you'll find him in a shed down that alleyway over there." He pointed to an arched opening between two houses. "As far as I am aware nothing has been said to him."

"Thank you Persse, that's very good of you."

"Yes, well, get along before I change my mind. Just let me know, will you?"

The alleyway led to a yard with a large shed at the back of it. As he approached the doorway, the sound of singing reached Michael. It was a song he knew, it was Lloyd. What was it called? It came back to him, Suo Gan. He stood just outside for a moment, listening to the soft tenor voice and the restful sounds of the Welsh lullaby. Two dragoons appeared, leaving the shed, and they came to attention and saluted at the sight of Michael. The singing stopped.

Michael returned the salutes, adding "Carry on." Then he stepped into the shed. In the gloom he saw Lloyd, jacket off, a straw wisp in one hand, the other resting on Rodrigo's neck. Seeing Michael, he came to attention and saluted.

Michael returned the salute and suddenly felt very awkward. "Hello, Lloyd, it's good to see you. Rodrigo looks well."

"Diolch yn fawr, Captain, and, begging your pardon, sir, how is Johnny?"

"Oh, he's well enough, Lloyd, well enough. I've two more as well now, and a new groom."

"Oh! May I ask, sir, what happened to Parra?"

"When I was ordered to England he decided to go home to the Douro."

Lloyd nodded at his information and a silence fell.

"I understand," Michael began, "that congratulations are in order."

A slight smile appeared on Lloyd's face, "Yes, sir, diolch." The smile went and Lloyd looked at Michael for a second before he continued. "That's why I took the rank and didn't come after you, sir."

"Yes, I know, Colonel Archer explained it all to me. It's quite alright, I am pleased for you and look forward to congratulating Mrs Lloyd." He smiled. "I trust that she is keeping you on the straight and narrow?"

Lloyd grinned back, "Duw, she is that, sir. Barely a drop passes these lips nowadays, sir. You'll be having a new batman then, sir?"

"Yes, a Dorset lad, Hall, he was a poacher, good with a sabre, rides well, but he's not the horseman that you are."

"Diolch, Captain, and is your new groom a good man with the horses, sir?"

"Bradley. Yes, he is. He's a Yorkshireman, hired him at the horse fair in Howden."

"I've heard of it, sir, is it as big as they say?"

Michael laughed. "Oh, yes. Earl Harcourt sent me to buy horses, I must have looked at a thousand, bought twenty."

Lloyd raised his eyebrows at that. "Now there's something I should like to see."

"But you might meet Bradley yourself."

"No doubt I might, sir, run into most people sooner or later."

"I was thinking of something more certain."

"Oh, aye, sir?"

"Yes." Michael hesitated for a moment. "You will know that I have a place on Sir Stapleton's staff?"

"Yes, sir."

"Well, the thing is, Lloyd, he has told me that I can have an orderly dragoon, a corporal for choice." Lloyd remained silent. "Frankly, I'd like to have you." He waited for a moment for a response, but got none. He pressed on. "Colonel Archer approves. And there's another reason why I would like you, I'm here to be on hand for, err, special duties. Like we did before, and I would like someone with me I can rely on."

Something flickered across Lloyd's face, realisation, interest, Michael wasn't sure.

Lloyd shifted, slightly uncomfortably. "That's a very fine offer, sir, diolch yn fawr, but, err, it's Mrs Lloyd, sir."

"Yes, of course, you must speak to her. It would take you away from the Regiment."

"Yes, well, you see, sir, the thing is, sir, she's expecting." Lloyd looked very uncomfortable and stared at the floor.

"Oh" was all Michael could find to say for a moment. "My congratulations," he added. Then a thought struck him. "Look, if you like, she could go to my house in Lisbon!" Lloyd looked up, sharply. "But I've some bad news there."

Quietly, Michael told Lloyd about Senhora Santiago, told him that the man responsible was now dead, at which Lloyd gave a satisfied nod. He told him about Senhor Santiago, Senhora Pinheiro and Frederico and Bernardo. "So, there's plenty of room, company, and, frankly, Senhora Pinheiro would probably be glad of some help. As and when Mrs Lloyd could, of course. I can't say that I know much about this sort of thing."

"No, sir, no more do I."

"Well then, what do you say? Speak to Mrs Lloyd, first, of course."

"Aye, sir, but we're a ways from Lisbon, sir."

Another thought struck Michael. "I can send White with her!"

"Who, sir?"

"My other servant, a very handy young man, but, between ourselves, I don't think he is entirely taking to life on campaign. I had been wondering what to do about him, and now I have an answer. He can go to Lisbon and help look after the house for me. I can get by perfectly well with Hall." Michael beamed.

"Well now, sir," Lloyd began, slowly, "that is all very tempting, sir, but I should need to speak to Mrs Lloyd, sir."

"Yes, of course you do. You do that when you can and if the answer is yes, I will see Colonel Archer and we will make all the arrangements."

"Yes, sir, diolch yn fawr."

The two men stood in silence again. Michael spoke, "Then I shall leave you to Rodrigo." He started to turn away, paused, and started to speak, "Lloyd..." he tailed off.

"Yes, sir?"

"Look, if you prefer to stay with the Regiment, I will quite understand. Go after those sergeant's stripes, eh?" Lloyd remained silent. "And if you like, Mrs Lloyd can still go to Lisbon."

"Duw, diolch yn fawr, sir, that's very good of you."

"Damn it, Lloyd, it's the least I can do, all things considered. Just let me know, please?" And Michael spun on his heels and walked quickly away. All in all he felt he had made a complete mess of things. He was angry with himself, but what had he expected? Lloyd had his corporal's stripes and was probably in line for the next step to sergeant. Maggie Lloyd was amongst friends, why would she want to go to Lisbon to be amongst strangers?

He walked away in the opposite direction to that he had come by. He was passing through Captain Lygon's troop when he saw another person he recognised, Sergeant Butler, the man whose arm he had broken way back in Dover, a lifetime ago, it seemed, and who had tried to bully Hall in Radipole. No, there was a stripe missing, Corporal Butler, somehow Michael wasn't surprised. At the same time Butler saw Michael. Butler was some distance away, too far to be expected to salute, and the two stood for a moment, looking at each other. Michael saw something unpleasant in Butler's gaze, saw the hint of a sneer. Michael felt the stirring of anger, pushed it down, knowing it would not serve at the moment. Instead, he allowed himself a slight, mocking smile. Then Butler turned away, spitting on the ground as he did. Michael knew rank insubordination when he saw it, hatred as well. There's trouble he thought to himself, and went on his way.

Colonel Archer joined Sir Stapleton and his staff for dinner. It was a quiet affair, it was clear to all that Archer was not well, that he was a tired, worn out man and the evening broke up early. Conversation had been desultory, but as he left Archer did ask Michael if had found Lloyd and what the outcome had been.

"I am not sure, sir. He said he will talk to Mrs Lloyd about it. I have offered to have Mrs Lloyd at my house in Lisbon, what ever he decides, it seemed the right thing to do."

"Yes, indeed," Archer replied. "For myself, I think it is an excellent idea. I've seen to much of the perils of motherhood when following a regiment." He shook his head sadly. "It all too usually ends badly. I am glad my wife is safe in Wimbledon. Well, good night to you, Roberts."

"Good night, Colonel."

Chapter 6

Michael was roused early by Hall with coffee and bread. He was followed by White with hot water for shaving. Shaved and refreshed, half an hour later he was climbing into the saddle on Thor as Bradley held the horse's head and then checked the girth. In the small yard of their billet, Sir Stapleton Cotton, resplendent in his uniform despite the early start, and his staff gathered in the last chilly hour before dawn. Captain Cocks of the Sixteenth had been newly promoted to Major, in an infantry regiment, but for the moment had permission to stay with the Sixteenth as a Major. Sir Stapleton was making full use of this, and had sent him forward to Ribero with a squadron each of the Fourteenth and Sixteenth to act as a guard against any French advance. Sir Stapleton wanted to be with him when it got light, to get the earliest warning of any French movement.

It was a difficult ride as much of the countryside was covered in woods that added to the darkness. Fortunately it was no great distance, a little over five miles, and the road was familiar to most of the riders. As it was they could have stayed in bed. There was no sign of any French advance, but Tomkinson, with the squadron from the Sixteenth, had patrolled further ahead and come across small French patrols that had retreated when they saw Tomkinson's patrol. He returned to Ribero to report and with all seemingly quiet, Sir Stapleton returned to Villafranca with his staff.

As they clattered their way into the stable yard of the billet, batmen and grooms appeared to take charge of the horses. Bradley and Hall both came to Michael's assistance. Half an hour later Michael was drinking coffee and talking to von der Decken when they were interrupted by White.

"Beggin' your pardon, sir, but there's a Corporal and a lady 'ere askin' for you, sir. 'E says you're expecting 'im."

Michael's hopes rose and he leapt to his feet. "I beg your pardon, von der Decken, if this is who I hope, then I must see them."

"Ach, so, I will give you the room, I must check on my horses, my man is not so good with them."

"Thank you! White, show them in."

White opened the door and in came Corporal Lloyd, tarleton and sabre tucked under one arm, his other held by a lady Michael recognised. Lloyd came to attention and von der Decken gave the lady a slight nod as he passed out of the room.

"Thank you, White, that will be all." Michael paused until the door was shut. "Lloyd, Mrs Lloyd, I haven't yet had the opportunity, but let me congratulate you on your marriage."

Lloyd smiled, as did Mrs Lloyd who bobbed a small curtsey and it was her who answered. "Thank you, Captain, that's good of you, and so is your offer to my husband, and to me, sir."

Michael smiled, and was about to speak when, nervously, she rushed on. "But, and begging your pardon, sir, I know 'e was your batman afore, and you was often away from the Regiment, sir, but I dunno what you and he did when you were off together, sir, I 'eard the rumours, sir, like everyone else in the

Regiment, but 'e won't tell me nothing, sir." She paused, glanced at Lloyd who stood, his face a blank, and took a breath. "The truth is, sir, I'm afeared for 'im. I've lost one 'usband, I've no wish to lose another doing gawd knows what, sir."

"I see," said Michael, "and I would hazard that you would like to know a little, before he goes off with me again?"

"Yes, sir, I would. You see, I knows soldiering, sir, or I thought I did, and I suppose it must be soldiering as you does, sir, but it ain't no soldiering as I know, and I should like to know what my husband is a doing, sir, begging your pardon."

Michael studied her. She was black haired, somewhere in her twenties, her face tanned and weather beaten, her clothes were old and patched, but well cared for, she was neither tall nor short, she looked whip cord tough and her dark eyes were penetrating. She had a fearsome reputation in the Sixteenth as the person who really managed the baggage.

"Very well, Mrs Lloyd, I think I can give you an indication, and I admire your husband for resisting your questions. Please, forgive him, it is my doing, and I must also ask you to keep to yourself what I tell you."

"Of course, sir."

"Thank you. Now, as to what we will be doing, most of the time I expect to be engaged on run of the mill staff work for Sir Stapleton, however, from time to time there might be other work to be done, and, put simply, that is hunting for French spies."

Maggie Lloyd's mouth formed a soundless "oh".

Michael went on. "And that is what we were about when away, Mrs Lloyd. I think I should add that your husband's role in these activities has been to act as my covering file, much as he did on the field at Talavera. I say this because you should understand that it is a different form of soldiering, but no more dangerous and, in many ways, more important." Michael addressed Lloyd who had stood silent all the while. "Is that a fair way to put it?"

Lloyd answered him, "Yes, sir, chwarae teg, I would say it is."

Michael nodded and turned back to Mrs Lloyd. "One more thing before you and Lloyd give me your yea or nay, I meant what I said about sending you to my house in Lisbon, and that holds whether Lloyd takes up my offer or no. I, err, think it would be good, given your, err condition." Michael felt his ears redden. "You will have all the help you need there. I will ensure that."

"I see, sir. Thank you, that's very generous of you. Lloyd has told me about your house, and about Senhora Santiago. I am sorry about that, sir."

"Thank you."

"Now, sir, you have put my mind at rest, and you can be sure that I will be as quiet as Lloyd about your soldiering, sir. So, yes, sir, I am content."

Michael looked at Lloyd questioningly.

"Duw, well, sir, it looks like I am going to be your orderly, sir." He grinned. "Might I ask you to tell the Colonel and Captain Persse, sir?"

After Corporal and Mrs Lloyd had left, Michael went up to his room, where White was busy with his laundry.

"Ah, White, I'm glad you're here, there's something I want to discuss with you."

"Yes, sir? I hope everything is alright, sir?"

"Yes, well, and no." White looked worried. "No, don't worry," Michel went on, "your work has been first class. The thing is, I have noticed that you are uncomfortable with our way of life."

White looked uncomfortable. "Well, sir, yes. I'm sorry, sir, but I'm not sure that I'm cut out for this work, sir. It's not so bad in quarters like this, sir, but even then there's no real chance to get settled, and those barns and sheds and even out in the open all night, sir, I don't like it, sir. But, sir, I don't want to let you down, sir, not to get sent 'ome sir. Or just turned off, sir."

"I appreciate your honesty." Michael smiled. "Then you might be pleased to hear that I have a solution."

"You do, sir?" White's face filled with hope and relief.

"Yes, indeed I do. Corporal Lloyd has just agreed to become my orderly, and I have offered to send Mrs Lloyd to my house in Lisbon, she is, um, expecting a child. And with only Senhora Pinheiro, her son and Bernardo to look after the place I am concerned that it might be too much for them. I thought that you might prefer to go with Mrs Lloyd and become one of my staff in the house. What do you say?"

White positively beamed with pleasure and relief. "Yes, sir!" he exclaimed emphatically. "I should like that very much, and I can certainly look after your house for you, sir!" Then his face dropped a little. "But you, sir, who will look after you, sir?"

Michael chuckled. "I managed well enough with just Lloyd as my batman, I am sure I shall manage well enough with Hall and Bradley and Lloyd."

"Oh, yes, sir, I reckon as you will."

"Good, then that's settled."

The next few hours were spent moving Corporal and Mrs Lloyd into the billets of the cavalry headquarters. Captain Campbell managed to find them a room to themselves, tiny, and with no glass in the window, but it was a huge improvement on a blanket as a curtain to give them some privacy that was the usual arrangement in the other ranks' billets. Sir Stapleton already knew Lloyd and was charming to Mrs Lloyd and asked her about laundering his linen. He seemed genuinely disappointed to learn that, while she would do so gladly, for the usual rates, she would soon be departing for Lisbon.

When Lloyd appeared with Rodrigo, Michael went with him, knowing full well that Hall and Bradley were in the stables and that much would depend on how they all got on. He knew that Hall had already heard much about Corporal Lloyd, both in England and since arriving in Portugal. Hall also knew that Lloyd had been with Michael on some of his more unusual duties. That did not worry him. It was the meeting of Bradley and Lloyd that concerned him, two men from very different backgrounds, but both remarkable horsemen. He hoped there would not be any competition or disharmony between the two. Bradley was rubbing down Johnny, who happened to be in the stall nearest the entrance. Bradley had turned Johhny around to work on his fore legs, neck, chest and withers. The horse caught sight of Lloyd and his head went up, his ears pricked forwards and he gave a little stamp. Bradley spun round to see what had attracted Johnny's attention so markedly. He saw Michael with a dragoon corporal, on the short side, slight, but wiry, not thin, with black hair and the typically tanned face of a veteran. He was leading in a very fine looking dark bay.

"Bradley, this is Corporal Lloyd who is joining us as my orderly, Lloyd, Bradley."

The two men looked at each other and then Johnny gave a little wicker and stamped his foot again. Lloyd looked at him and said something. Bradley didn't understand a word except "Johnny". Bradley cast a glance over Lloyd's bay. He had become aware of how difficult it was to keep a horse in any sort of condition in the present season, with forage and feed in short supply, but the bay looked well, very well. He had, of course, heard about Lloyd being the best mounted dragoon in the brigade, and now he could believe it. As for Lloyd, Johnny had given him the excuse to cast his eye over the horse. Considering he had been on a horse transport and then ridden across Portugal and Spain in a poor season he looked well, very well.

Both men started to speak, "Johnny's looking well...", "That's a fine looking...". They grinned at each other. Then they shook hands.

Michael relaxed. "I shall leave you to get acquainted", he said, and left them to it.

Going back inside he found White and Mrs Lloyd going over his spare linen and clothes and White eagerly telling her all about Michael's house and who was now there. It had all worked out rather well. He touched the wood of the door frame and wondered how long it would last.

White's observation about never being able to get settled anywhere proved prophetic. It had not been dark for an hour when Michael was summoned to the dining room. Sir Stapleton was there as were all his staff. He did not beat about the bush.

"Gentlemen, we are moving, now. It has become clear that the French are pushing on to attempt the relief of Badajoz. General Graham is retiring with the infantry to take up a blocking position at Albuera. We are to fall back slowly, delaying the French, but without getting too tangled up with them. Get yourselves and your people ready. Captain von der Decken, Colonel Elley has orders for you to take to Ponsonby and the Twelfth at Los Santos, I want them to retire across the Guadajira and on to the high ground overlooking Villalba. Roberts, get along, find Archer and get the Sixteenth moving, they're to march on Villalba as well. From there we can watch all the crossing points the French might try. Then find Colonel Hervey and tell him I want the Fourteenth to march to Fuente del Maestre to cover that road. Very good, carry on."

On his way out Michael shouted for Hall and told him to get everyone packed and get Johnny ready, they were moving. He found the Sixteenth's headquarters where Archer had his billet along with the Regimental staff. Archer's batman informed him the Colonel was in bed. Then Major Hay appeared with Lieutenant Barra and asked Michael, "What is it, Roberts?"

"Orders to move immediately, I'm afraid, sir, I was looking for Colonel Archer."

Hay and Barra exchanged a look. "The Colonel's not well," Hay informed him, "he's in bed. You'd better tell me."

"Yes, sir. We are falling back to the high ground behind Villalba, sir."

"Right now?"

"Yes, sir, I've just this minute come from Sir Stapleton and I've got to find Colonel Hervey next, sir."

"Very well." Hay paused for a moment. "Look, Roberts, I shall get the Regiment moving, leave the Colonel to rest while we can. I'd appreciate it if you didn't mention this to anyone. Keep it in the Regiment."

"No, sir, of course not." Michael wanted to ask how bad the Colonel was, but realised this was not the time.

"Very good, Roberts, thank you."

Michael found Hervey a street away. He was up and about, cursed at the orders, thanked Michael and set about rousing out his Regiment and calling for his batman to help him dress. He had lost his right arm in an action after the crossing of the Douro in '09, but didn't let that stop him commanding his Regiment in the field.

Fortunately the night was dry and clear and the regiments got away with little fuss and bother. It was not a long march, ten miles or so from Villafranca and the Sixteenth arrived at the new position a couple of hours before the Twelfth. As dawn broke, Michael was sitting on Johnny with Sir Stapleton, his staff and Colonel Ponsonby of the Twelfth looking down at Villalba, a mile or so away with its mediaeval castle towering over the low roofs of the houses huddled around it. Behind them were Lloyd, Hall, and four other batmen and orderlies. Half a dozen pickets had been sent out and were covering all the crossing points for miles in either direction. Their own position gave them a good view for miles over the rolling landscape across the river. Somewhere out there was Major Cocks with his two squadrons. Sir Stapleton became impatient.

"Damn it. Where is Cocks?" He turned in his saddle. "Ponsonby, I'm going forward. Elley, you and your people stay here. Von der Decken, Roberts, bring your people." With that he put his horse into a trot and set off towards Villalba. They passed through the town, trotted past the picket on the bridge, and headed back towards Villafranca. They found Cocks and his squadrons formed behind a small stream a couple of miles short of the town. Their arrival coincided with Tomkinson and his patrol galloping in to report that the French were advancing on Villafranca.

The French soon appeared, in some strength and emerging from the town began to form to attack. Sir Stapleton did not wait. "Cocks, take the Fourteenth's squadron to Fuente, join the Fourteenth, tell Hervey to retire slowly on Villalba. I'll take the Sixteenth's back with me." As the French began their advance the two squadrons turned and retired, quickly losing the French in the woods and then parting company.

They returned unmolested to where the rest of the brigade was. Then, in the late afternoon the Fourteenth joined them, having been pushed back from Fuente after several hours of skirmishing. Sir Stapleton waited until it was dark and then marched the whole brigade back to Santa Marta, leaving a line of pickets to watch the Guadajira. In the dark Major Hay's horse tripped and fell, breaking the Major's arm. Archer sent him with the baggage, on its way to join the infantry under Graham in anticipation of falling back to them at Albuera. The departure of the baggage meant the departure of White, Bradley and Michael's spare horses. He decided to ride Robbie who had good stamina and it could be several days before he could change horses.

In the morning news started to arrive that Badajoz had fallen during the previous night. As the sun rose and the day got hotter it became clear that the taking of Badajoz had been a bloody affair and had come close to ending in failure. A commissary arriving with supplies brought news of the casualties. He claimed that upwards of three thousand men had been killed or wounded, but no one was sure as the troops who had got into the town had gone on the rampage, killing, looting, raping and drinking. A dragoon might have more to do than an infantry man, with his horse to care for and feed as well as himself, but at times like this they were thankful that their horses kept them out of such work.

The Brigade spent the day on the hill behind Santa Marta, exposed to the cruel heat. The dragoons sat on the ground in rank and file, each man holding his horse's reins. The only break in the tedium came with brief excursions, a troop at a time, to a stream just behind their position, to water the horses and the men. Some talked quietly, others stretched out and tried to get what sleep the heat allowed them. In the afternoon, during the worst heat of the day, they were moved into the town and took advantage of the shade offered in buildings, and barns. It didn't last. A report came that the French were advancing on the town and the whole brigade came tumbling out in disorder to take up position once again on the hill. It was a false alarm, its origin never discovered.

Sir Stapleton, impatient as always, rode forward again with his staff to the picket line watching the other side of the Guadajira. From the high ground behind Villalba they could clearly see formations of French cavalry, but none attempted to cross. Michael watched them as intently as anyone. They had been expected to press on towards Badajoz and the view of Sir Stapleton was that news of the town's capture had reached them, halting their advance more effectively than any defeat in battle. Indeed, as the day passed it seemed to the watchers that the numbers of French slowly, but steadily, decreased.

Late in the afternoon it became clear that there would be no French advance that day, particularly as no infantry appeared. Leaving the picket line in place, Sir Stapleton rode slowly back to the brigade as they all enjoyed the cooler air that came with the onset of night. The cold of the night that followed was not so welcome. Fires were not allowed in order to hide their position from the French. Bread and water was all the food available and then they tried to get a few hours of restless sleep under cloaks, each man holding his horse's reins as they were kept saddled and ready to be mounted. The brigade was roused before dawn and stood to, dragoons shivering by their horses heads, waiting for the order to mount if the French came.

Once again Sir Stapleton led his staff forward before dawn. The picket on the bridge at Villalba reported no sign of the French all night. Sir Stapleton led his staff south, along the bank of the Guadajira. An hour later and the day was again warming up. They rode cautiously and, as they got closer to Fuente del Maestre, Sir Stapleton ordered Michael, with Lloyd and Hall, to ride ahead. Riding slowly and quietly they were moving through a small copse on the river bank when Hall reined in.

"I can smell tobacco smoke, sir," he whispered.

Michael sniffed the air, but detected nothing. "Are you sure?" he asked quietly. Hall just nodded. "Do you think you can get closer, see what it is?"

In answer, Hall silently dismounted, and passed his reins to Lloyd. He took off his sabre and his tarleton, took out his knife and disappeared into the trees. A few anxious minutes passed before he reappeared.

"There's a Spaniard fishing, sir, he's on the far bank. Smoking a foul cigar."

"Any sign of French?"

"Not a trace, sir."

"Can we get across without him seeing us?"

"I reckons as we might, sir. We'm down stream, so 'e'll not see any mud if we crosses. There's a bit of a bend and more trees, should be right, sir."

"Very good, get mounted and lead the way."

A few minutes later the Spaniard was terrified when he heard a hoof clip a stone. He spun round, dropping his cigar in the stream, and found himself face to face with three horsemen. He hesitated, looked as if might try to run, then, hesitantly, he asked "English?"

"Yes, Señor, and we will not harm you." Michael smiled encouragingly and turned to Hall. "Hall, take yourself up the hill a bit, see if you can see anything, be careful, try not to be seen."

Hall grinned, "Right you are, sir," and set off.

"Now, Señor, Have you seen any French this morning?"

The man grinned. "No, Señor, they have all gone!"

"Gone?" Michael exclaimed.

"Yes, Señor, they left Fuente during the night, Señor"

"Are you quite sure?"

"Oh, yes, Señor."

"So you would be quite happy to guide us there?"

"Yes, Señor."

"Lloyd, did you follow that?"

"I think so, sir, he said there's no French in Fuente, left last night?"

"That's right. Ride back and tell Sir Stapleton, I shall wait here with our new friend."

Less than an hour later Sir Stapleton led his staff into the town. They rode a short distance into a main square dominated by an imposing church. "Well, Roberts, it appears our friend here is correct." He looked around. "Any idea who has the picket watching the town?" Heads were shaken. "Hmm. Roberts, take your men and go and find out. Whoever it is, give them my compliments tell them it is quite safe here, and if they have finished their nap they might care to join us. Now, where can the rest of us find some refreshment?"

Michael, Lloyd and Hall had a short ride before they found the picket, under the command of Lieutenant Alexander of the Sixteenth. He was somewhat surprised to see them approach from the direction of the enemy.

"Captain Roberts, sir, are you out on patrol, sir?"

"Err, not exactly. Um, Sir Stapleton presents his compliments and said to tell you that Fuente is empty of French, and if you have finished your nap it is quite safe to join him."

Alexander's face paled. "Oh," was all he could manage.

The brigade moved into Fuente del Maestre that evening. Patrols were sent out and established that the French rearguard was some twenty miles away. With a picket under Tomkinson established in Los Santos, halfway towards the French, it mean that they could all relax a little. Sir Stapleton approved the recall of the baggage. Then, in all the excitement of the retreat of the French, a rumour went around that the Spanish General Ballesteros had captured Seville. Firing was heard from the direction of Los Santos and the brigade was about to be roused and stood to when a messenger came in from Tomkinson saying it was only the Spanish celebrating the news.

In the morning, the Sixteenth, with Sir Stapleton, made a short march of less than ten miles to Zafra while the other two regiments marched back to Villafranca and Cocks was once more out in front with two squadrons at Ribero. The residents of Zafra declared that they would hold a bull fight to celebrate the capture of Seville and give a ball in the evening.

It was midday when an orderly dragoon came in with orders for Sir Stapleton from General Graham. After consultation with Wellington it had been decided that the cavalry should 'press a little' on the French rearguard. The intention was to suggest that Wellington was moving south when he was, in fact, moving north. Sir Stapleton gathered together his staff and told them the news.

"I am going to ride out to Bienvenida, see what we can see. Elley, you had better come with me, the rest of you can stay here, enjoy the bullfight." He gave a mirthless laugh. "Damned unsporting if you ask me, but there you are. Who is at Bienvenida?"

"Lieutenant Penrice, sir, with half a dozen dragoons." It was Michael who was able to answer. "I gather you can see for miles from the church steeple, sir, see as far as Llerena."

"Very good. I intend to be back in time for the ball, however, if I see an opportunity to press the French rearguard, I shall take it."

As the day went on an arena of sorts took shape in the town's Grand Plaza, formed from farm carts. The windows and balconies all around were full of the ladies of the town, of all classes and types. There was much boasting from the men of the town who promised a spectacle like they had never seen. Michael, along with most of the officers of the Sixteenth was sitting under a colonnaded walk, enjoying a glass or two of wine, and some fresh cooked food. Everyone was in good humour, even Alexander who had been ribbed mercilessly about the incident with Sir Stapleton. It was a pleasant enough way to pass an afternoon and there was much speculation about that evening's ball.

Eventually, however, questions began to be asked about when the bullfight might begin. Captain Murray, the senior officer present, Archer was again resting, called to Michael. "Roberts, you've the best Spanish of any of us, see if you can discover what's happening."

Michael strolled across to the arena where he could see a man he recognised as the town Alcalde, the Mayor, in earnest conversation with two other men. There was a lot of arm waving and it all looked a bit heated. "Señor," he began. Immediately the conversation fell silent and the Alcalde looked very uncomfortable. "Señor," Michael began again, "can you tell me when the bullfight will begin?" There were glances exchanged between the men and Michael realised that all was not well. "Señor, is there some difficulty?"

The Alcalde looked for help to the other two, and got none. "Señor, I do not know how to say it, it is a matter of great shame for me, for our town, for our country."

Michael was taken aback. "Señor, please, tell me, perhaps I can help?"

A little hope flickered in the Alcalde's expression. "Señor," he said, "we have no bull."

Michael stared at him for a second, and then began to laugh. He laughed until the tears ran down his face. He was still laughing when he returned to his comrades. They were equally amused, and then Persse said "I've got an idea!" and disappeared, taking Alexander and Penrice with him. They reappeared half an hour later, with a commissary officer and a couple of Spanish peasants driving a bullock before them. More laughter erupted as the officers realised this was one of the bullocks driven along to provide rations for the army.

To the sound of cheers from the assembled towns people and dragoons the bullock was driven into the arena, where it stood gazing around and looking more like falling over than making any dramatic charges. The clamour that had greeted the bullock died away to an expectant hush, but nothing else happened. Michael and his fellow officers had climbed up on the carts that formed the arena. He saw the Alcalde a few carts away and called to him.

"Señor Alcalde, why is there a delay?"

Once again the man looked as if he wished the ground would swallow him up. "Señor, we have no matadors."

Michael groaned and passed on the news to his comrades. Just then, one of the Regiment's farriers, who had clearly partaken of a quantity of wine, jumped down into the arena, staggered a little, and began waving his leather apron like a cape. The bullock turned its head and stared at him without moving. Three more dragoons leapt into the arena, cheered on by men and officers alike. They tried to prod the bullock into action, poking at it with their sabres, but it soon became clear it was having none of it and just walked away from them. The cheers turned to boos and whistles, the towns people began to drift unhappily away, embarrassed. Laughing the men and officers of the Sixteenth dispersed in search of food and drink. In the end the commissary recovered his bullock, which was led away, slaughtered and distributed to the men of the Regiment.

Shortly before the ball was due to start, the Brigade's baggage appeared. Lloyd was reunited with Maggie, Michael with White and his best uniform, and with Bradley with Johnny and Thor. The return of the horses was welcome, he wanted to change from Robbie who had been carrying him for several long days. The return of White and his best unform raised his hopes of cutting a dash at the ball and with the Señoritas. He was soon dressed in clean, white pantaloons and polished hessians instead of dirty overalls and, above all, a clean shirt.

The ball started off well. There was a good number of the better off citizens of the town, and a lot of Señoritas. One in particular caught Michael's eye. He realised she was looking at him, staring, almost, at his cheek, at, he realised, his scar, which stood out white against his deeply tanned face. She realised that he had noticed and blushed delightfully, raising her fan to cover her confusion. Her confusion deepened when she looked his way again and saw that he was now standing a foot or so from her. Her eyes widened when he addressed her in his passable Spanish.

"Señorita, may I have the pleasure of the next dance?"

An older lady suddenly intervened. "You, Señor, who are you? You have not been introduced."

Michael gave her a little bow. "Señora, please forgive me. Captain Roberts, at your service." He bowed again. The older woman seemed placated. She gave a little curtsey.

"Señor, I am Señora Escudero and this is my niece, Señorita Larosa."

"Charmed, Señora. Señorita Larosa, may I have this dance?" She gave a little bob of agreement and smiled delightfully. Michael turned to Señora Escudero, "Señora, my comrades," he waved vaguely around the room where his comrades stood watching the dancing, "do not have the benefit of my familiarity with your beautiful language. I wonder, might I prevail upon you to introduce some Señoritas to them, with the approval of their parents and chaperones, of course."

Señora Escudero looked thoroughly flattered and charmed, "But of course, Señor," she gushed, and rushed off.

Michael danced with the Señorita as the ice was gradually broken and the ball livened up for the officers of the Sixteenth.

It was all going very well when he saw Sir Stapleton had returned and was in discussion with Captain Murray near the entrance to the ballroom. Something told him that it was a serious conversation. As he watched, Murray broke off and started to walk around, speaking to the officers of the Sixteenth, they looked startled, and a few of them left the ballroom hurriedly. Sir Stapleton saw him looking and, as he was between dances, waved to him to come over.

"Good evening, sir."

"Evening, Roberts. We are moving against the French. They have a force of cavalry at Villagarcia. It's unsupported by any infantry and begging to be attacked. So we'll oblige them. Ponsonby is moving the Twelfth and Fourteenth up to Usagre and then will advance on Villagarcia at dawn. Le Marchant is marching on Bienvenida and I'm going with him. I understand from Murray that the Regiment is still having rations issued. As soon as that is done you will guide them to Bienvenida. You know the ground after all our recent toing and froing and that business at Llerena, Murray doesn't. He says he should be ready to move soon after midnight. Don't get lost."

Chapter 7

Michael slipped away from the ball and made his way back to his billet. He found preparations to march already underway. Hall was packing Michael's valise with essentials, as well as packing his own. Maggie was packing Lloyd's valise and White was packing everything else. Michael looked at him quizzically, but it was Maggie who explained.

"Best be prepared, sir. Going forwards, going back, 'tis good to be ready. And stay put, 'tis no problem to unpack, sir."

"Err, yes, no harm, I suppose."

"No, sir. Lloyd is with the horses, sir, with Mister Bradley. 'E said as you would prob'ly be wanting Johnny, sir. And they's taking care of Billy for Hall 'ere, sir."

"Ah, good, I'll, err, go and see them. White, I'll change into my overalls and old jacket later, a little after midnight, I think. We should be marching at about one o'clock."

Down in the stables there was a considerable amount of activity as batmen got horses and tack ready. The horses were still standing in their stalls with everything needed being carefully laid out to be put on at the last moment. Lloyd saw Michael and saluted.

"Evening, sir, I thought you'd be wanting Johnny, sir, if there's to be a fight."

"Yes, how is he?"

"Very fair, sir," it was Bradley who replied, "Happen as how I managed to find a good amount of feed while you were away, sir, and a bit of a rest has helped. Thor's fit an all, sir, if'n you want him."

"Very good. I understand Captain Murray plans to move at about one o'clock. Have the horses ready a quarter hour before that. Lloyd, I'll be guiding the Regiment, you and Hall should stay close." Michael looked around and then consulted his watch. "I shall go and see about another dance or two. I think I've time."

Señorita Larosa seemed pleased to see him. She hid her face behind her fan, but the corners of her eyes crinkled, hinting at a smile. He claimed another dance from her. As they danced he explained, in fragments of speech when they were close enough, that he very much regretted that he would have to leave just before midnight. He was going on duty, but hoped that he might, perhaps, be lucky enough to see her again on his return. She blushed and said nothing.

At the end of the dance, Michael glared at Lieutenant Alexander who appeared to be approaching to ask for the next dance. Alexander swerved away towards another Señorita and Michael danced again with Señorita Larosa. He hoped neither she nor her aunt would get the wrong idea, but if they did he it wasn't as it he would see them again. All too soon the dance ended, Michael noticed other officers quietly leaving the ball. He led the Señorita back to her aunt, to whom he bowed.

"Señora Escudero, thank you for allowing me to dance with your niece. Señorita Larosa my thanks for your elegant dancing and pleasant company. Now, I apologise, but I must go." He bowed to both ladies, who looked genuinely disappointed, then he turned and walked out into the night.

Outside their quarters, Lloyd and Hall were already mounted. Lloyd was leaning down, out of his saddle, to hold Maggie's hand as they talked to each other in low voices. Bradley stood holding Johnny's reins and talking to Hall and White. White had Michael's old jacket, overalls and ankle boots ready and Michael changed quickly in the hall. Then he took Johnny's reins and climbed up into the saddle. He returned the salutes from Hall and Lloyd, then turned to White, standing in the doorway.

"White, if you have to move, let yourself be led by Mrs Lloyd, she has a lot experience. Mrs Lloyd, I trust you to keep an eye young White and our baggage." He paused. "I rather hope we shall be back tomorrow, I mean, later today." The were a few quiet chuckles. "Corporal Lloyd, Hall, stick close."

With that he wheeled Johnny round and set off down the street to find Captain Murray. The streets were filled with the regiment, the troops forming their ranks and files and then combining into their squadrons. It seemed chaotic, with horses shuffling and barging, dragoons swearing and Sergeants shouting. Then, suddenly, the scene changed and the Regiment stood, formed, everyone in their place and silently waiting for orders. Michael found Murray at the extreme right of the Regiment.

"Ah, there you are, Roberts, unless you have any knowledge that suggests otherwise, we shall march right in front, and a three man front."

"Yes, sir, I know no reason not to."

"Good. You lead on and I shall follow with the Regiment." Murray raised his voice. "Sixteenth! Threes right, march" The order was repeated by the three squadron commanders, Lygon, McIntosh and Persse, and the Regiment became a column six wide, facing down the street. Murray called out again. "Sixteenth! March!" and seconds later, "Rear rank, left incline and cover!" and the six man front became three.

Michael, Lloyd and Hall rode side by side, a few lengths ahead of Murray and led the way through the dark streets of Zafra and out into the countryside, heading south-east for Bienvenida. It was a straight, flat road of some fifteen miles that took them a comfortable four hours. The sun was beginning to climb above the horizon as Michael led the way into the small town and on into the square by the church with its high, commanding tower. Sir Stapleton was waiting for them with a handful of riders, staff and orderlies.

"Come on," he shouted, "follow me," and he wheeled his horse around and led them out of the town.

A mile or two beyond the town they found Le Marchant's brigade drawn up, the men of the three regiments of redcoated heavy dragoons dismounted and resting. Sir Stapleton reined in and turned to face the Sixteenth. Murray brought the column to a halt as Sir Stapleton rode up to him.

"Well done, Murray. Your men can have a quarter hour, then we will be off and I doubt there will be another chance to rest for a while. Come and join me with Le Marchant as soon as you can. Roberts, you've five minutes, then join me."

Once they were all gathered together again with Le Marchant, Colonel Elley also present, Sir Stapleton gave his orders quickly. "We are about six miles from Villagarcia. It's light, so we must move quickly, we will advance at the trot. Murray, you lead. Once close to the town we will halt briefly, let the men and horses get their wind and I'll give you your final orders then." He looked round the small group. "Very good, gentlemen, on we go."

Forty minutes later Sir Stapleton led the column off the road and halted it. Murray, accompanied by Michael, and Le Marchant rode to join him where he sat looking at the long, open slope rising gently in front. As they gathered they realised they could hear distant, sporadic gunfire.

"It would appear that Ponsonby is already in action, just skirmishing from the sound of it. Le Marchant, Elley will guide you around on to the flank of the French, their rear if you can mange it." He pointed away to the right where a tree covered ridge ran away from them. "That high ground should hide your advance, as quick as you can please." Le Marchant and Elley rode rapidly away. "Murray, straight on up that rise and join Ponsonby, you should come up on his right flank. I am going to join him now. Good luck, gentlemen." With only two riders accompanying him Sir Stapleton put spurs to his horse and galloped off towards the firing.

Murray turned to Michael. "I'll bring the Regiment on, but I'd like to know what is on the other side of that rise." He gave Michael a grim smile. "Go and find out, if you please."

Murray turned to the Regiment, which was still dismounted, Michael waved to Lloyd and Hall to join him and set off at the canter for the distant ridge. Far away to his left the top of the ruin of the castle at Villagarcia came into view and gave him his bearings. Then he reached the crest of the bare ridge. He stared as Lloyd and Hall caught up with him. He heard Lloyd swear. Away to his left he could see both the Fourteenth and Twelfth in line, the six hundred or so men of the two regiments facing what looked like three or four times their number of French cavalry. Between the two were skirmishers, popping away at each other with carbines, little clouds of smoke appearing, followed by the crack of the discharge. The smoke hung in the still, clear morning air, but was not enough to obscure the picture of what was happening. Ponsonby's command was being slowly forced back onto Villagarcia by the weight of the French. They had a regiment of brown jacketed Hussars in front who were engaged with the light dragoons. Behind the Hussars, in two columns, on either side of the road to Llerena, were two regiments of French dragoons in their green coats with the sun reflecting off their brass helmets.

Immediately to Michael's front the ground sloped gently down to the road about half a mile away and the French hussars deployed on either side of it. He glanced to his right and could see Le Marchant's brigade hurrying along and disappearing behind a line of low hills that ran parallel to the Llerena road. Turning his attention back to the scene before him he cast his eyes over the ground between the ridge and the French. Then he saw it. A low wall ran right across the hillside, about halfway between where he sat and where the French were.

Michael spoke, "Lloyd, what do you make of that wall?"

Lloyd looked a moment and replied, "Duw, not a lot, sir."

"Hall?"

"I reckons as Billy could take it, sir."

"Good, let's get back."

Murray was bringing on the Regiment at the trot, in column of squadrons over the beautifully open countryside. As Michael rode to him he halted the column. "Well, Roberts?"

"This line is perfect, sir, it will bring you in to the right of the brigade, sir, partly on the front of the French, they've hussars in line, in front, and partly on the flank of a column of dragoons behind the hussars, sir. The only difficulty is that there's a wall, runs right across the line of advance, about half way down the slope to the French, sir."

"Damn! Do you think we can take it?"

"Yes, sir, I know I could and Lloyd and Hall reckon they could as well."

"Very good, Captain Roberts." He turned and gave the order to the Regiment to deploy into line. "I am sure you would like to join us, Roberts. Ride along and warn the squadrons about the wall, they can open up a little then close again as soon as they're over. Take it at the trot, d'ye think?"

"Yes, sir."

"Then tell them that and then choose your place, Roberts, choose your place."

"Yes, sir. Lloyd, Hall, did you hear that?"

Both answered with a "Yes, sir."

"Lloyd, tell Captain McIntosh, Hall, tell Captain Lygon, then join me between the centre and left squadrons, quickly!"

Within a few minutes that seemed to stretch forever the Regiment deployed, Michael managed a quick word with Persse leading the centre squadron, told him about the wall, wished him luck and joined Lloyd and Hall in the twenty yard gap between the two squadrons, Lloyd on Michael's left, Hall to his right. Then they saw Murray draw his sabre and every man followed suit. There was a moment's pause, then Murray put his horse into a walk. The squadron commanders shouted their orders and seconds later the Regiment started to walk up the slope to the crest of the ridge. Michael looked left and right and felt a surge of pride. In a perfect line the three squadrons moved forward, each about a hundred men in a two deep line, their commanders in front, Murray a little ahead of them.

A few yards short of cresting the ridge, Murray went into a trot, and the squadrons followed suit. All together they broke the skyline and saw the scene in front of them. It had changed a little in the last quarter hour, the Fourteenth and Twelfth were now even closer to Villagarcia, dangerously close to stone walls where they could get boxed in, unable to manoeuvre. Michael caught a glimpse of a regiment of Le Marchant's brigade emerging from amongst olive groves far away to the right, and then his attention was taken up by the wall.

It was an old wall, irregular in height, getting on for three feet high in places, and very solid looking. It suddenly occurred to Michael that the French might assume their advance would be blocked by the wall. They certainly made no move to turn any troops to face them. They must have seen them by now. Then the wall was coming up, now just a hundred yards away, fifty, twenty five, ten, there was a slight forward surge as dragoons urged their mounts at the wall. Michael felt Johnny quicken slightly, collect himself, and then they sailed over the wall to land safely on the other side.

Michael glanced left and right, Lloyd and Hall were with him, he saw no sign of any fallers or confusion in the ranks, he grinned in exultation as officers and NCOs shouted to tighten up the formation after the jump. Now the French were three hundred yards away. Murray quickened the pace to a canter, the Regiment surged forward after him and the gap began to close rapidly. Michael felt Johnny stretch himself, his canter comfortable and collected. He could see that the squadron to his left would catch the end of the line of French Hussars. The one on the right would take the head of the nearest column of French Dragoons in the flank, just as Le Marchant's dragoons would also hit them in flank. It looked as if the centre squadron would pass between the Hussars, across the front of the nearer column, and take the head of the further column in flank.

Fifty yards to go and Murray put spurs to his horse, which broke into a gallop. A cheer went up from the

Regiment, and the whole line accelerated forward in the charge. Johnny threw up his head for a split second and then went effortlessly into a flat out gallop, hurtling across the rapidly diminishing gap to the French. Michael saw a Hussar NCO a few yards behind their line, and rode at him. So did Lloyd. They came in on either side of him, he tried desperately to fend off both, Lloyd's sabre took him across the face, sending him reeling, and then they were past. Michael now only had eyes for the dragoon officer out in front of the far column. He urged Johnny on and flew at him. His sabre whirled as he came, his arm straight, aimed at the man's face, the cuts following one after the other, forcing the Frenchman to defend himself, his longer sword now a disadvantage. Then he missed a parry and Michael's sabre cut upwards through his jaw, taking him clear off his horse.

The French dragoons were stationary when the Sixteenth's centre squadron tore into them, the front rank a line of whirling sabre blades. The leading dragoons recoiled, some went down, others tried to turn and run. Michael saw Hall engage with a trumpeter, cutting his bridle arm, forcing the man to surrender to him. Then Michael and Lloyd plunged into the confused mass of French, the light dragoons of the centre squadron hacking and cutting to left and right, driving the leading French physically back on to the rest of the column.

Michael became aware that French Hussars were streaming past and saw men of the Twelfth in amongst them and close behind. He looked around for his two dragoons, saw them a few yards away, looking for more French cavalry. Clouds of dust were thrown up by the hundreds of horses galloping and milling around. He shouted at the top of his voice, "Lloyd, Hall, to me!" Twice, three times he yelled out before they responded and came over to him, Hall driving his prisoner before him.

"I need to find Sir Stapleton, he might need help." More dragoons from the Twelfth rode past, mixing with the Sixteenth as they continued to drive the French back. "This way!" he shouted and started to ride on across what had been the French line before it had disintegrated under the assault of four British regiments. They came across a dismounted man of the Twelfth.

"Can you take care of this prisoner?" Michael called out to him.

The dragoon hurried across, "Aye, that I can, sir, lost my horse, this'n'll do nicely. Right Monsewer, off you get, lively now."

Leaving the man to his prisoner and new mount, they rode on, trotting steadily after the whirling, running fight, blinking in the dust. At last Michael caught a glimpse of Sir Stapleton in the middle of the fight and pushed up to him. Sir Stapleton was breathing heavily, sabre in hand, a gleam in his eye and a grin on his face.

"Ah, Roberts, good man! What do you think? We showed 'em eh?" He was looking around, assessing the situation. "We must keep 'em running, not let them rally. Find Le Marchant, tell him to follow up close with his other two regiments. If you see Murray, tell him to keep pushing on. Lively now."

Michael turned in the direction he hoped he might find Le Marchant, followed by Lloyd and Hall. Small parties of British dragoons were escorting prisoners to the rear, many of them wounded and bleeding from faces and arms where razor sharp sabre blades had sliced through. Riderless horses, mostly French, ran around in confusion, many bleeding from sword cuts. Turning to follow the confused mass of men and horses heading towards Llerena, he saw Le Marchant's two unengaged regiments coming up and also turning towards Llerena. He squeezed slightly and put Johnny into a canter, passing by the redcoated dragoons and reaching their front. Of Le Marchant there was no sign. The closest regiment was the Fourth Dragoons and he saw their commander, Lord Edward Somerset, leading them and Michael rode across to him.

"My Lord," he saluted, "do you know where I can find General Le Marchant."

Somerset returned Michael's salute as he and his regiment walked steadily on. He pointed ahead. "Up there somewhere with the Dragoon Guards. Thought we should probably follow on."

"Yes, sir, Sir Stapleton wishes you to follow up closely, he is concerned they might rally."

"Very good, Captain, I shall let Major Clowes know. Like me he will be disappointed we were not able to get our regiments up in time to charge, any opportunity to be of service will be most welcome."

"Thank you, sir."

"If you do find our general you might let him know where his other two regiments are."

A mile further down the road to Llerena Michael first found Captain Murray. He was desperately trying to get two of the Sixteenth's squadrons into some sort of order. Michael passed on Sir Stapleton's order.

"Damn it, Roberts, what does he think I'm trying to do? The right squadron is up the road with Le Marchant and the Dragoon Guards. We shall be along presently, as soon as we have some sort of order." He turned to shout at some dragoons milling around and Michael took the opportunity to push on further after Le Marchant.

It was only five miles from Villagarcia to Llerena, and half way between the two a stream in a deep ditch cut across the road. Here the French attempted to rally, the ditch providing a pause in the pursuit. Temporarily thwarted, the Sixteenth's right squadron was endeavouring to form. Around them the three squadrons of the Dragoon guards were doing the same, under the watchful eye of General Le Marchant.

Michael managed to reach the General. "Sir! Sir Stapleton wishes you follow up closely, and the Third and Fourth are doing that, sir, I took the liberty of informing Lord Somerset. They should be up shortly, sir."

"Thank you, Captain, but I see Sir Stapleton coming now." He nodded over Michael's shoulder. Advancing on either side of the road came the two squadrons of the Sixteenth in line and next to them the Twelfth, its three squadrons also in line and followed by the Fourteenth. Just visible through the dust, behind them were the two regiments of redcoated heavy dragoons. In front of all rode Sir Stapleton. It was a magnificent sight, eighteen hundred blue and red coated British cavalry advancing irresistibly.

Le Marchant watched for a moment. "I think, Captain, that we would be well advised to move. I believe Sir Stapleton is going to charge."

As Le Marchant spoke the squadrons of the Sixteenth and Twelfth started to trot. They swept past the still reforming dragoons, went to canter, and then charged straight at the ditch and the French. As the British Light Dragoons leapt the ditch and charged on the French broke, turned and ran. The Fourteenth followed close behind.

Le Marchant spoke to Michael. I think you should go after Sir Stapleton, tell him I shall bring up the Third and Fourth."

"Yes, sir," Michael answered, saluted and turned a hot and sweaty Johnny to follow the charge.

Along with the faithfully following Lloyd and Hall, Michael got as far as the ditch when he realised that Sir Stapleton was standing on the far side. They jumped the ditch and Michael saw that Sir Stapleton's prize charger was laying on the ground, trying to rise, but failing.

Lloyd saw the problem immediately. "Duw, he's dislocated his shoulder, sir. There's no curing that."

Sir Stapleton looked up from his horse as they rode up. "Roberts, would you be good enough to lend me one of your pistols?"

Without a word Michael drew his pistol and passed it to the General. A moment later and the deed was done.

"Thank you, Roberts." He passed the pistol back to Michael and looked sadly at the dead horse. "Damn fine horse that, best I ever had." He was silent for a moment, then looked at Lloyd.

"Corporal Lloyd, I fear that I must ask you the loan of that rather fine animal of yours."

"Yes, sir, but 'tis Captain Roberts' horse, sir, not mine." Lloyd answered even as he dismounted and handed the reins over.

"Really?" Sir Stapleton swung into the saddle. "That's not what Wellington told me, and he had it from Don Julian Sanchez himself. But fear not, I shall return him, and Captain Roberts can ride with me to protect this fine animal. Perhaps you would be so good as to guard my horse furniture for me? Come along Roberts."

Together Michael and Sir Stapleton, followed by Hall, trotted after the pursuing cavalry. Another mile and the pursuit came to an end as the French force formed outside Llerena opened fire with artillery. The shots flew clear overhead, the British and French were still too mixed together to allow the artillery to fire properly, but the message was clear. This far and no further.

Sir Stapleton reined in Rodrigo. "Well, that would seem to be that. Do you go after the Lights and get them turned around for Villagarcia, I shall see to Le Marchant and the Heavies myself."

Slowly the regiments returned. As they marched they gathered up prisoners, wounded dragoons and horses, and men who had simply got separated rejoined the ranks. The withdrawal was protected by the Third and Fourth Dragoons who had not been engaged at all. At the fateful ditch they found Lloyd who had stripped the tack and furniture from the dead horse. A passing French dragoon prisoner was dispossessed of his horse, its tack unceremoniously dumped and replaced with Sir Stapletons. Lloyd eagerly reclaimed Rodrigo.

Sir Stapleton commented, "I suppose it will get me home. Can't go keeping another man's horse," without suggesting which man he was talking about. Lloyd looked at Michael who merely shrugged, and started the long walk back on a horse that, like all the horses, was tired and sweated up.

Le Marchant and his brigade, the Sixteenth and Sir Stapleton and his staff retired that evening to Bienvenida. The Twelfth and Fourteenth went to Usagre while Cocks stayed at Villagarcia with two squadrons to watch the road from Llerena.

Everyone was tired after marching through the previous night and then fighting a running battle over four or five miles of Spanish countryside, but on reaching Bienvenida the first thing that happened was the horses being cared for. They were rubbed down, fed and watered, some were stitched up where swords had inflicted cuts. The prisoners were shut up in the church and their horses looked over by the veterinary surgeons. The horses that got a clean bill of health were kept well away from the British horses, quarantined in case of disease. Others were considered unfit and were shot. The prisoners, over a hundred and thirty with as many horses, included a Lieutenant Colonel and three junior officers. The Lieutenant Colonel was invited to dine with Sir Stapleton. The surgeons were busy through the night. A lot of the French were badly cut up, some were not expected to survive. British casualties were light, mostly amongst the Fifth Dragoon Guards who had some three dozen killed and wounded. The Light Dragoons, perhaps as a result of their longer experience, had only six casualties. French dead were estimated at over fifty.

An awkward moment arose in the evening when Colonel Archer rode in from Zafra. He had risen from his bed and insisted on joining the Regiment. He was an extremely distressed man, having missed the opportunity to lead his Regiment in one of the great cavalry victories of the war. He and Sir Stapleton spent half an hour together in private. No one knew what was said, but Archer looked better when he emerged.

Chapter 8

The day after the fight was a hard one. The excitement had drained away leaving exhausted men looking after equally exhausted horses. There was feed and forage to find, wounds to be kept clean, equipment to clean and repair and there was always the possibility of the French striking back. That threat was alleviated when, early in the morning, a messenger came in from Cocks at Villagarcia. Before dawn he had patrolled to Llerena, and found the French had gone, marching back towards Seville. Seville, apparently, had not been captured after all. Sir Stapleton put his staff to work. He decided they should all return to their old quarters until orders came from Wellington.

Michael was kept busy arranging affairs for the prisoners. He felt sure it was because of his grasp of French. The six British cavalry regiments each provided half a dozen men as an escort and they sent the dejected French on their way to Badajoz. The wounded were loaded on to ox carts, which departed to the accompaniment of their screaming axles. Michael was glad to see the back of them, particularly as one of the men from the Sixteenth was Butler.

Le Marchant's brigade marched away, back to Santa Marta, the Twelfth and Fourteenth went back to Villafranca. At midday Sir Stapleton and his staff led the Sixteenth on the road back to Zafra. It was a short march of fifteen miles and it was good to get back to familiar quarters and faces. In the stables of the headquarters billet Bradley was waiting anxiously when they rode in.

"By 'eck, sir, it's reyt good to see yer all back and safe, sir, and t'osses."

Michael dropped down off Johnny. "Thank you, Bradley, it's been hard on them"

Lloyd joined them. "It has that, sir, and I reckon that Billy is struggling a fair bit, sir."

They all turned to look where Hall was fussing over Billy, holding his head, stroking his face and ears and talking quietly to him. The horse looked worn and tired.

"It's bad enough for a horse in the ranks, but all the riding we were doing is a lot more demanding." Michael thought for a moment. "We will rest Billy, Hall can ride Thor for a day or two, then we might look for a better horse for him." He turned to Lloyd. "After all, there is a precedent, and I notice that Sir Stapleton's orderlies are quite well mounted."

Dinner with Sir Stapleton and the staff was a frugal affair. There had been little time for the servants to do any more. It was not enough for Sir Stapleton. He leant back in his chair and looked around the table. "Damn it, it's not good enough." Silence fell at this outburst. "We gave the French a damn good lickin' and what do we get? A cold dinner." He paused. "Day after tomorrow, I shall give a ball. Say thank you. Get as many officers in as can be spared from their regiments. We know Zafra can put on a ball when they've a mind. Let's show 'em what we can do." The rest of the evening was spent in planning.

Planning of a different sort began the next day when orders arrived from Wellington for Sir Stapleton to bring the cavalry north, following the army. Sir

Stapleton would not be thwarted. "We can march at dawn after the ball," was his response. Michael had mixed feelings. He had enjoyed his time dancing with Señorita Larosa, but he had no wish for any complications, particularly when they would be leaving after the ball. He also had to make arrangements for White and Maggie Lloyd to leave for Lisbon. He consulted Lloyd.

"Lloyd, I am concerned about Mrs Lloyd and White travelling to Lisbon. Do you have thoughts on the matter?"

"Diolch yn fawr for asking, sir, but I think they will be alright, sir. It's a fair distance, to be sure, sir, but Mag..., I mean, Mrs Lloyd, has seen a fair bit of marching, sir, and her Portuguese is good and her Spanish passable. I reckon as young White can look after himself as well. So, it might take them a fair while, but they'll get there, sir."

"I'm relieved by your confidence, Lloyd." A thought struck him. "And what about Mrs Lloyd's mule and White's Beau?"

"Mrs Lloyd is as good a hand with horses as many a dragoon, sir, she's been around them long enough. She can tell White what needs doing."

"And when they get to Lisbon?"

"I think her idea is to sell the mule, sir. I told her to try Senhor Moreno, sir. Might as well sell him Beau, sir. Won't be any need of him in Lisbon, sir."

"You're right there, Lloyd. Very well, that's what I shall tell White to do."

Michael wrote a letter for Senhor Furtado, explaining about Maggie and White's return to Lisbon, and authorising any expenditure he thought necessary for the care of Maggie during her confinement. He quietly hoped that Maggie and Senhora Pinheiro would get on. It would have been so much easier if Senhora Santiago had still been there. The thought was painful.

The following day was busy as the preparations for marching north and the ball continued. By the day's end all the baggage was packed save a few essentials, the horses were as well as could be expected, although it was decided that it would still be as well for Hall to ride Thor and lead Billy for a few days. Michael would be more than adequately served on a march by alternating Johnny and Robbie. Half an hour before the ball was due to commence Michael changed out of his overalls and old jacket into his still white pantaloons, hessian boots and best jacket.

He was not surprised when, on entering the ballroom, he came almost immediately face to face with Señorita Larosa and her aunt. He bowed to the two ladies who bobbed little curtsies back. Señorita Larosa covered her face with her fan, but her aunt spoke to Michael.

"Captain, we understand that you are leaving us?"

"Señora Escudero, that is, unfortunately, true."

"And when do you think you might return?"

"I am afraid Señora that I cannot say, such things are not in my power." When, he thought?

"Of course, it is the war, but, after the war, you will, of course, return to us, to my niece. Or will you be kept occupied elsewhere? I hear you have a splendid house in Lisbon and a quinta?"

"How in God's name did she discover that?" were the unspoken words in Michael's head. Out loud he answered. "That is quite possible, Señora, but the war is not yet over and we have yet to beat the French."

"But you surely will, and then, of course, you can return to our little town, my niece and I will be expecting you!" The Señora smiled while, behind her fan, the Señorita blushed.

Michael forced a smile. "Who knows what may come to pass, Señora?" He turned to the Señorita before a reply came. "Señorita, may I have the next dance?"

He was damned if he was ever going to return to Zafra. He supposed he had no one to blame but himself for the assumptions that had been made, however, in the meantime, he would take what he could of the pleasures on offer. He danced several times with the Señorita, he danced with others and she danced with several other officers, but kept returning to him. He escorted her to supper, and danced again afterwards. He noticed Colonel Archer looking very subdued and watching the proceedings. After a short while he had disappeared. Sir Stapleton was enjoying himself, cutting a very fine figure in his immaculate dress uniform. Just after midnight the officers from other regiments started to disappear. An hour before dawn the sound of trumpets reached into the ballroom. There were now few officers left, all from the Sixteenth and Sir Stapleton's staff. There was one last dance, Señorita Larosa seeming to know this, gripped his hand tightly. Then the music ended and Sir Stapleton addressed the remaining townspeople.

"Señors, Señoras and Señoritas, my deepest gratitude for a wonderful evening, but now, I fear, duty calls. Gentlemen, to your duty, please." He bowed to the assembly and left the room followed by every last officer. Michael did not look back as he made a resolve to be more restrained around Señoritas in the future.

Michael hurried to the billet. All the staff horses and servants were ready to move and he rushed in to where White was waiting. A few minutes later he emerged, dressed in his overalls, White with a bundle of his best uniform that was quickly secured to one of the ponies. Bradley was sitting on Jasper the reins of Johnny in his hand. Taking them from him, Michael swung up into the saddle and with a clatter they followed Sir Stapleton and the staff out of Zafra and onto the road north.

Sir Stapleton pushed on fast, leaving the Sixteenth behind. They passed by Badajoz and paused for the night at Elvas. There they found the men who had been escorting prisoners, Butler amongst them. They were told to wait for their regiments that were only a day or less behind. Sir Stapleton pushed on and another hard day saw them arrive at Nisa. Here Maggie and White were to separate from them and go on their way to Lisbon. A convoy of wounded was travelling the same road, and Michael persuaded a young infantry subaltern to accept the addition of Maggie and Lloyd to his charge. No one saw anything of Lloyd or Maggie that night.

In the cold light of dawn, waiting for Sir Stapleton to appear, Michael and Lloyd sat side by side on their horses and watched the convoy depart.

"Everything well with you and Mrs Lloyd?" asked Michael.

Lloyd's eyes remained rivetted on the receding convoy. "Yes, sir, diolch yn fawr. It's a fair thing you have done for us, sir."

"My pleasure, Lloyd, my pleasure."

Nothing else remained to be said.

.   .   .

Madrid in mid-April was pleasantly warm and, above all, dry. Matthieu Renard stared down at the inner courtyard of the Royal Palace, half of it bathed in sunlight. Not his side. His department was tucked away under the roof, a walk of several minutes from the fine apartments where Marshal Jourdan conducted the military affairs of King Joseph. His personal quarters were also tucked away under the roof of the Palace. He had not expected to be welcomed with open arms, but the coldness of his reception had surprised him, until he realised that it was generally believed that he had been sent by the Emperor to spy on his brother Joseph.

As if his personal circumstances were not bad enough, he had been shocked by what he had learnt of current intelligence operations. To all intents and purposes there were none. What was more, having been sent from Paris to take care of that aspect of the war, both the King and Marshal Jourdan seemed to expect him to work miracles overnight. He pondered on the latest setback. A longstanding and effective agent in Lisbon who had supplied regular and useful updates on the comings and goings of the British army through Lisbon had suddenly gone silent. What was more the silence had fallen almost immediately after he had reported the arrival in Lisbon of Captain Michael Roberts. Renard had no evidence, but he could not believe the two events were not connected.

He turned away from the window, crossed his office and passed into the office occupied by his clerks. They were, he thought, a poor lot, but then no one of any competence would wash up in this God forsaken country. Silently, he laughed ironically. God forsaken? He had never seen so many priests. They were everywhere, like a flock of carrion crows. He despised them, even the solitary priest who, it seemed, was actually useful. A genuine afrancesado. He had yet to meet him, but according to his senior clerk, who had had many dealings with him, he was a tireless worker in the cause of the Bonapartes and no lover of the Bourbons. He didn't understand it, but he was not one to look a gift a horse in the mouth, and just at the moment he needed all the help he could get. Even keeping Madrid acquiescent was a challenge.

The four clerks had paused in whatever they were doing when he entered.

"I am going to see Jourdan. Is there anything new I should know before I go?"

The clerks looked at each other, nervously. Then one of them spoke. "Err, no, Monsieur."

"Now why does that not surprise me? No, no, don't try to answer. Just," his voice rose to a shout, "find out what happened to Loiro in Lisbon." His voice dropped back to a normal level, but dripped with sarcasm. "If it's not too much trouble, gentlemen?"

Jourdan listened without interruption to Renard's account of the current state of the intelligence services. When he had finished, Jourdan sat in silence for a moment, toying with a quill pen on his desk. Then he spoke.

"It seems to me that much of your departments difficulties arise from the actions of a single British officer, if your assessment is accurate." Renard made to protest, but a raised hand from Jourdan stopped him. "You will note, Monsieur, that I say your department's difficulties, not your difficulties, although I could do so quite justifiably. You have not long been here, Paris is a long way away and it may have been hard for you to understand the situation here and to manage affairs effectively at such a distance." He paused and stared coldly at Renard. The implied criticism was clear. "But now, Monsieur, you are here, distance is no longer an explanation and I can assure you that His Majesty expects an improvement in the situation. All of which begs one immediate question. What are you going to do about this British officer?" Renard opened his mouth to speak, but Jourdan raised his hand again. "Secondly, what are you going to do about restoring some sort of supply of intelligence about what the British intend to do? The last I heard was that they had taken Badajoz and were marching on Seville. I have heard nothing from Soult to confirm or contradict that. As for the rest of my brother Marshals, they also tell me nothing. This has to change and I look to you for assistance in that particular matter. I want a plan detailing your answers to these problems on my desk tomorrow morning, before I have my usual audience with His Majesty. You may go."

Back in his office, Renard called in his clerks. "I need information. One, do we have anyone who can be sent after the British officer, Roberts? He is a menace and a danger and I want him dead. Two, do we have anyone in Lisbon that we can contact, or, failing that, someone new we can send? Three, who do we have in the other armies in Spain who can tell us what is going on and why are they not telling us? Get to work on it now, Jourdan wants answers tomorrow, I want them in an hour."

.   .   .

Three weeks after the fall of Badajoz Viscount Wellington arrived in the small Spanish village of Fuenteguinaldo, a mere ten miles from the border with Portugal and some fifteen miles from Ciudad Rodrigo. His quarters were in a smart house adjacent to the church. Sir Stapleton and his staff caught up and arrived in the mid afternoon of the following day. A nearby, slightly smaller house, was marked up as being for them. Campbell allocated rooms, and Michael found himself sharing a room with von der Decken again. Lloyd and Hall were given space in a garret with other servants while Bradley was with other grooms in a loft over the stables.

Sir Stapleton was invited to dine with Wellington and the rest of the staff made the best they could of cold rations washed down with the local wine. They were sitting around, chatting, drinking and smoking foul smelling cigars, a habit that Michael had eventually succumbed to, there was a general belief it helped to keep insect life at bay. The door to the dining room opened and Lloyd looked in. Michael didn't see him at first and he called across the room.

"Beg your pardon, Captain Roberts, sir!" Michael looked up. "There's an orderly from the Earl of Wellington, says you're wanted over the way, sir."

Michael groaned while his comrades speculated on what he was wanted for. "Probably wants you to haggle with some merchant for more wine," was one of the few repeatable suggestions. There was much sympathetic laughter as he left the room. Outside, the orderly, an infantry sergeant was apologetic.

"Sorry to drag you out, sir, but the Earl of Wellington wants you, sir."

"Very good. Lloyd, no need for you to come as well, wait here for me. I hope I won't be long."

The orderly led the way across the square to Wellington's headquarters, past the sentries and showed Michael into a small room. Gathered around a table he found Viscount Wellington, Sir Stapleton and Major Scovell. Wellington looked up.

"Ah, Roberts, come in, come in. Come and look at what Scovell has here."

Michael stepped over to the table on which were several sheets of paper and some tiny scraps with miniscule numbers on them. "More coded messages, my Lord?"

"Ah, yes, Scovell said he'd shown you some, but these are different. Tell him Scovell."

"Yes, my Lord. The thing is Roberts, the messages I showed you before were in the cipher used in the

Army of Portugal. That cipher has only a hundred and fifty characters, or numbers. With the French being careless in their ciphering and leaving too much in plain language, not in cipher, it has not been too difficult to work out the content of their messages. Recently, however, we have intercepted a number of dispatches in a new cipher. As far as I have been able to tell, so far, it has over a thousand, perhaps as many as a thousand and four or five hundred. It's very, very difficult."

Michael was stunned. He had got some idea of what Scovell was doing when they had talked. This sounded far, far more complicated. "Why so many ciphers?"

Scovel answered. "Some numbers represent people or places, some whole words, some parts of words, one word, particularly a common word, might have a number of ciphers, to stop it being guessed at by frequency, by repetition." He paused, staring at the scraps of paper. "These, just the four of them, are all the examples we have managed to get. Two were taken from one of Marshal Soult's Aides de Camp heading for Paris. This one is from Marshal Marmont, also going to Paris. This one was going to Madrid. That's all we have."

Wellington spoke, "Three of these came to us from your friend Don Julian Sanchez. His men swarm around the roads from Madrid and Salamanca to Paris. Scovell tells me that the more messages he has the greater his likelihood of success in deciphering the messages, which is how he broke the other, simpler cipher. Is that not so?"

"Yes, my Lord," from Scovell.

"This is where you can be helpful, Roberts."

"My Lord?"

"Yes, this is exactly the sort of work I wanted you on hand for. Don Julian's lancers are under my command, and, as cavalry, under Sir Stapleton's command. It would not seem out of the ordinary for one of Sir Stapleton's staff officers to communicate with Don Julian, so it is fortuitous that you are on the staff of the cavalry, and that you know Don Julian. You, Captain Roberts, are to join Don Julian, encourage him in his intercepting of dispatches and make sure they get to Scovell here. You can expect to have to spend a few weeks with him. In order to maintain the propriety of your mission, it is Sir Stapleton who will give you your formal orders, which will amount to maintaining liaison and coordination with Don Julian. There are a few of Don Julian's men here, they brought the last of these. They will take you to him. He is up in the mountains south of Salamanca somewhere." Wellington waved his hand over the papers on the table. "We need more of these, Captain, and we need the intelligence they contain as much as we need more men."

"Yes, my Lord."

"Then I shall leave Sir Stapleton to issue your final orders. Goodnight, gentlemen."

Back at their house, Sir Stapleton sat with Michael in the room that served him as office, drawing room and bedroom. "Campbell will introduce you to Don Julian's men tomorrow. They have already been told that they are taking someone back with them. You had better take all your baggage, horses, Lloyd, of course, and your batman and groom. You could be with Don Julian for a month or more. That will depend on Wellington's plans, and no one knows what those are. I don't think anything will happen until we have finished resupplying and the grass has grown a bit more. It may even be that any dispatches you capture will help decide him on a plan. I understand that the paymaster will issue you with funds, see him tomorrow, you might need it, but best not advertise you have it. Now, anything else?"

"Yes, sir, I should like all my horses and baggage animals reshod before we leave."

"Yes, that's sensible. Best plan to leave the day after tomorrow."

Chapter 9

Early the following morning Campbell took Michael to find Sanchez's men. They were busy grooming their horses. They might look villainous, thought Michael, running an eye over the six men and assessing the condition of their horses, but they are horsemen. They glanced up as Michael and Campbell approached, then one of them, a sergeant, looked again and grinned.

"Señor Roberts!" He turned to his comrades, "Hey, it's Señor Roberts who rode out of Ciudad Rodrigo with us!" he turned back to Michael, "Lieutenant, it is good to see you. You probably don't remember me, there were a few of us that rode out, and it was at night." He laughed. "But we all know how you distracted the French pickets for us."

Michael didn't know the man, but two hundred men had cut their way out of Ciudad Rodrigo that night, so it wasn't surprising. "Thank you, Sergeant, but it's Captain Roberts now."

"Ah, Captain, forgive me. And Don Julian is now a Brigadier!"

He smiled. "Yes, I had heard. That was a night, and now I understand that you are a lot more than two hundred?"

The man's grin widened. "Yes, Señor, we are nearly a thousand, and in two regiments. And we also have infantry and artillery."

"Then I shall look forward to seeing them."

Realisation dawned on the man. "Then it is you Wellington wishes us to take to Don Julian?"

"It is. Can you tell me how long a ride it is?"

"About thirty leagues, but it is a rough road, through the mountains, two days' journey. We should leave at dawn, if not before."

"Then shall we say an hour before dawn tomorrow? We can meet you in front of the church. There will be four of us, and six horses, with two more ponies for our baggage."

"That will be good, Señor."

The two days started easily enough, the road from Fuenteguinaldo passing across a rolling landscape, before it began to climb up into the mountains. The road followed the contours and twisted and turned through dense woods. Occasionally there was a panoramic view, revealing the spread of the mountains all around them. Further into the mountains the road became little more than a stoney track, forcing them to ride in single file, but always with one of the lancers scouting ahead. They spent the night in a small village tucked away in a fold in the mountains.

On the second day they came out of the mountains along the side of a steep valley and then rode across rolling moorland. Small villages were ridden through without stopping, curious villagers watching them go. Around midday they crossed the river Tormes and as the day was ending they rode into Sanchez's headquarters in a small town nestling on the edge of the mountains. Michael noted that there were two small cannon facing the road from the north and the narrow streets of the little town were full of men in the blue uniforms of Sanchez's lancers. Not just lancers he realised, infantry as well.

They were all very glad to dismount in front of one of the larger houses in the village. Michael was stretching himself when a voice called out, "Is that Señor Roberts? I believe it is. Strenuwitz, see who is come visiting."

Michael looked towards the sound to see Sanchez striding towards him, a huge smile on his face, and behind him the Bohemian, Strenuwitz. Sanchez's greeting was effusive, while Strenuwitz, with a smile, gave Michael a small bow. Michael was surprised when Sanchez said "I believe congratulations are in order, Captain!" He laughed at Michael's surprise. "Ha! We do get all the army orders, the Gazette and so on. It is one of the many benefits of being part of the British army."

"Thank you, sir," Michael answered, "and I believe you are also to be congratulated, Brigadier."

"Haha, and Strenuwitz, who is now a Major. He should be a Lieutenant Colonel, but he is not Spanish. Still, he is my right hand. Now, come in, come in and tell me what brings you here? Strenuwitz, find that good for nothing servant and order some coffee for us. No, on second thoughts, some of the fine French brandy we captured last week."

"Don Julian!" Michael interrupted. "thank you, but my men, my horses..." He gestured behind him.

"Yes, of course." He looked at the small group now standing at their horse's heads. "We must see to you all." He turned back to address Michael. "With servants and baggage I am thinking this is not a flying visit? Perhaps you will be here for a while?"

Michael nodded. "Indeed, Don Julian, the Earl of Wellington wishes me to work with you for a while, perhaps a month or more."

Sanchez gave him a shrewd look. "A month or more? Then there must be something very important? Very well, you can tell me all later." He turned to Strenuwitz. "Now, what are we going to do with our guests. We must find them a good house close by if they are to be our guests for a while." Turning back to Michael he explained, "My little band of lancers has grown and this place is not really big enough, but we get by. It helps that a lot of the lancers are out on patrol at any time.

Strenuwitz looked thoughtful for a moment. "I suppose there is the widow Martinez. Her house has no one billeted in it."

"Because no one can stand the dragon," roared Sanchez. "However, it is a nice house and close by. Señora Martinez has refused to have anyone in her house who is not a gentleman," he explained to Michael, "But a Captain in the British army! How can she refuse? And I know she has stabling enough for your party. Come, we will go and see her and you must be charming. Your men had better wait here."

Sanchez led the way along the street to a house just on the edge of the town square. Michael wondered what sort of harridan he was about to meet who could refuse to billet Sanchez's men. A partial answer was volunteered by Sanchez.

"Señora Martinez has a very nice house, I believe she inherited it from her father. She came here from near Salamanca to escape the French who killed her husband. He was an important cattle farmer, and she is not without influence, even in times like these. That is why I put up with her, her, ah, you will see what I mean." Sanchez stopped in front of what looked to be one of the few two floored houses in the village. "The Señora lives with just a maid and a cook." He shrugged. "Not that she could not have more servants if she wished." He hammered on the door of the house.

A few moments passed and the door opened to reveal a woman in her thirties, apparently, from her dress, Señora Matinez's maid. She said nothing.

"Is Señora Martinez able to receive visitors?" asked Sanchez.

The maid seemed to consider the question for a moment, and then she opened the door wide. "If you will be so good as to wait in the drawing room, I shall ask the Señora."

Sanchez knew the way and took Michael into a small room with a few comfortable chairs, a couple of side tables and a fireplace with no fire. The door was closed behind them and the two men stood in silence. Michael glanced at Sanchez, who merely shrugged, again, and turned to look out of the window.

At a sound from the door, they both turned to face it as it swung open. A woman entered. Black hair carefully arranged, deep brown eyes, fine features, a fine figure in a well cut, black, silk dress, and, Michael guessed, of a similar age to himself. She was, he thought in his surprise, a rare beauty. Her eyes lighted upon Michael's, and stayed there.

Sanchez bowed to the lady, for such she clearly was. "Señora Martinez, may I present Captain Roberts of His Britannic Majesty's Sixteenth Light Dragoons?" Without breaking her gaze she gave a slight nod to Sanchez, who turned to Michael. "Captain Roberts, Señora Martinez."

Michael gave her a slight bow, which was returned and then she spoke. "Don Julian, a pleasure as always, to what do I owe the honour of this visit and introduction?"

"Señora, Captain Roberts is going to be with us for a few weeks." He paused, but before he was able to go on Señora Martinez spoke.

"And you are hoping that you might be able to prevail upon me to offer the Captain the hospitality of my house?"

"Señora," Sanchez began, only to be silenced by a gesture.

Señora Martinez regarded Michael searchingly. "You have ridden far, Captain?"

"From Fuenteguinaldo, Señora, two day's ride."

"Your Spanish is very passable."

"Thank you, my Portuguese is better, my French less so." She raised her eyebrows quizzically at this. "I am English, Señora, but born and raised in Lisbon."

"Ah, I see." She thought for a moment. "And why do you think I should acquiesce to Don Julian's request and put myself, my maid and my cook at the mercy of you and your men? I assume you have servants?"

"I do, Señora, two dragoons and a groom. As for your personal safety, Señora, I am a gentleman and I give you my word that you and your servants would be quite safe while we were in your house." He smiled. "Also, we are not the French, Señora, and if I were to transgress on your hospitality Wellington would have me hanged."

For a moment Michael thought he had blundered. Then Señora Martinez laughed. "A gentleman and an honest man! A rare combination Captain." Michael acknowledged this with a bow of his head and a wry smile. "Don Julian, the Captain and his men are welcome to the hospitality of my house." She swung her attention back to Michael. To his surprise she addressed him in English. "As you can hear, I shall have no difficulty understanding anything you or your men might say, or speaking to your men, should it be necessary."

"Señora Martinez," Sanchez spoke, "I am grateful to you. Perhaps you would care to join me for Captain Roberts' first dinner with us? I am sure the Captain would be glad to escort you." Michael gave a nod of agreement. "But first he and I need to talk. I shall send his men and horses over with Major Strenuwitz, if that meets with your approval, Señora?"

Señora Martinez smiled at Sanchez. "I should be delighted, Don Julian, and of course the Major may bring the Captain's men over."

As Michael and Sanchez walked back to where Michael's party was waiting, Sanchez expressed his surprise. "I must say that I thought that would be a lot harder. She is not an easy woman to get on with. We have been here a month, and tonight will be only the second time I have persuaded her to dine." He laughed. "You bring us hope, Captain, that time will bring success. Now, come and tell me why you are here."

The two men sat in silence while a servant poured the brandy. Strenuwitz was temporarily absent from Sanchez's side as he took care of Michael's men and horses. As the glasses were filled, Sanchez asked, "So, Captain, tell me all."

Michael gave a meaningful glance in the direction of the servant and Sanchez told him to leave them. Once the door had closed behind him, Michael began. "Don Julian, it is those messages that you have captured and sent to Wellington."

"What? Those meaningless numbers? I nearly didn't bother, it was Strenuwitz who urged me to send them. He said he thought they might be secret messages."

"He was quite correct, Señor, they are and they are proving very informative. There is a man on the staff who has had considerable success decoding, deciphering them. What he needs are more messages, not just for the information in them, but he says that the more he has, the easier it becomes. However, there is a new cipher that has begun to appear, far more complex than the first and so far it has not been possible to make anything of it, but, again, the more examples we have, the more likely it is that some success will be achieved."

"I see, so Wellington has sent you to encourage me to intercept more messages and make sure they get to him in Fuenteguinaldo?"

"Yes, Señor, but my orders are to assist with communications with headquarters, to help maintain liaison and coordination with you, in my role as one of Sir Stapleton Cotton's staff officers. It will be of no surprise to anyone." He took a little sip of the very fine brandy. "Wellington thinks I have a nose for this sort of work."

Sanchez almost choked on his brandy. "He thinks you have a nose! Oh, now that is funny!"

Michael chuckled. "My apologies, Don Julian, I would not have you waste this fine brandy."

Sanchez got his breath back. "Yes, it is too good." He took a deep breath. "And that is why you are here?"

"Yes, but there is one thing more."

"What?"

"It is important that the French do not learn of our interest in these messages, or that we can decipher any of them. If that caused them to change the ciphers we would lose a useful source of intelligence and be forced to start again."

"Yes, yes, I see." Sanchez sat pensively for a moment, staring into his glass, before he looked up and said, "Then we must show you how we do things, how efficient and well organised we are, so that you can report back to the Earl of Wellington that Don Julian's men are to be relied on. At the same time you can be on hand to see any intercepted couriers and messages for yourself. Between us, you and I, I think we can carry out Wellington's wishes."

"Thank you, Señor."

"Then we shall start the day after tomorrow. You can rest and settle in tomorrow and I shall organise a party to go out with you." Michael nodded his agreement. "But first, tonight, we shall dine with Señora Martinez, so there is much to prepare if we are to make a good impression, eh, Captain?" he looked at his watch. "And we have only two hours!"

A little under two hours later, Michael was standing in Señora Martinez' drawing room. He was in his best jacket, pantaloons, highly polished Hessian boots with his dress sword belt and cartouche belt and box. His tarleton, its bearskin crest freshly brushed and its silver trim polished, was under his arm. He was about to check his watch when the door opened and Señora Martinez entered.

Her black hair was now artfully piled on her head, ringlets and curls falling around her face, and all covered with a fine, black lace mantilla. Her dress was a midnight blue silk, with puffed shoulders, silver lace embellishments and a line of white lace across the top edge, emphasising her decolletage and white skin. White gloves stretched to above her elbows and she carried a fan of matching midnight blue lace.

Michael was momentarily lost for words. Then he bowed and said, "Señora, you look magnificent."

She flipped her fan open across her lower face, but not before Michael caught a glimpse of a smile and flashing white teeth. "Captain, you are very gallant. Shall we go?"

Dinner was a pleasant surprise to Michael, Sanchez appeared not to stint himself on his comforts. But then, thought Michael, nor did Sir Stapleton or any brigade or division commander, not if it could be avoided. Sanchez's local connections clearly helped him obtain both provisions and servants. The current situation, the war, was a subject mostly avoided, although, when Señora Martinez asked how Captain Roberts came to be acquainted with Sanchez and Major Strenuwitz, Sanchez gave a rather colourful account of the break out from Ciudad Rodrigo and Michael's part in it. He explained how Lloyd came to be so well mounted. He made no mention of the spy they had hunted and caught. Instead the evening was a round of tales of childhood and pre-war fun. It was clear that Señora Martinez was from a wealthy background and well educated. That in itself was unusual among Spanish women. From what she said it seemed that she was an accomplished horsewoman and had learnt a degree of competence with the lance used to herd the cattle. The lance that became the weapon of Sanchez's men. It also became apparent that most of the men from her husband's cattle farm had joined Sanchez's lancers and that she had more than a little influence. Michael was curious about her and determined to learn more if he could.

The dinner broke up quite late and Michael was glad not to be starting out before dawn as had become all too common. He escorted the Señora back to the house, through the cool of the late spring evening. On the way he offered his arm, but she chose not to see the offer. They walked in silence to the house where she rapped on the door, which was almost immediately opened by her maid. Once inside she simply turned to face Michael, thanked him for a pleasant evening and disappeared up the stairs with her maid.

Michael was left bemused and at a loss. Then Hall appeared from the back of the house. "Good evening, sir. We are all settled in, the horses are fine, if you want to take a look, sir. Corporal Lloyd and Mister Bradley are with them now, sir. I thought I'd just wait to show you your quarters, sir."

"Just as well, Hall, I'm not sure where I am and it wouldn't do to blunder into the wrong room." As he spoke he removed his tarleton and sword belt, laying them on a side table. "But let's look at the stables first. Lead on Hall, lead on."

Lloyd and Bradley were waiting. The stables were snug, but adequate. Michael made a fuss of his horses and asked if everything was well with them. Bradley answered, "Aye, sir, champion."

"And your own quarters?"

It was apparently Lloyd's turn to answer. "Very good, sir, we've a nice big room up there," he pointed above the stables, "so we're nice and handy, sir. Gave our rations to the cook, Señora Noriega, sir, and she did us a grand dinner, sir."

"Grand?" Michael laughed. "You're spending too much time with Mister Bradley, Corporal." There was laughter all round. "Very good. Hall, show me where my room is. I shall want coffee and hot water to shave as soon as it's light. We aren't doing much tomorrow, so it's a chance to make sure all our accoutrements are in in good repair. I want everything checked, all the tack, everything. As soon as it's all done you can have a look around."

The three men all nodded their understanding with a "Right you are, sir," from Lloyd.

Hall led Michael back into the house and showed him up to his room towards the back of the house. It was comfortably if sparsely furnished, but the bed looked comfortable. A bed! A luxury.

Hall volunteered information, "The maid and the cook 'as a room up in the roof, sir, sort of a garret by all accounts. The Señora is at the front of the 'ouse, sir. Down the corridor, right 'and door."

Michael looked at him closely by the light of the lantern he was carrying. His face was expressionless. "Very good, light me a candle and help me off with these boots, then you can go."

Once Hall had gone, Michael finished undressing and got himself into the bed. It was comfortable, and he lay there quietly enjoying it. It had been an interesting day. It had been good to see Sanchez and Strenuwitz again. Sanchez's account had brought back the tension and nervous excitement of the breakout, the mad fight in the dark and Señora Fraile shooting a French dragoon. He wondered about Señora Martinez. She had been pleasant enough company, but there had been a barrier, an aloofness, he was sure she hadn't relaxed for a moment. Ah, well, he wasn't concerned. He expected to see little of her and then never to see her again once his job was done. He snuffed the candle, turned over and went to sleep.

The morning passed quickly and busily. Michael joined in caring for the horses, grooming Johnny himself. The black horse was in a playful mood and kept nudging him, looking for treats. Then they walked them all around the village for a quarter hour, leading two each. Forage was acquired, plenty of it and good quality. Local connections, Michael assumed. He had slept extremely well and working with the horses only increased his feeling of well being.

He left Lloyd, Hall and Bradley checking over all the saddles, tack and accoutrements and strolled to the house occupied by Sanchez to ask about the arrangements for the following day. A sentry, one of the infantry, gave him a sloppy salute and opened the door for him. Sanchez was in his office talking to a lancer who had his back to the door. Michael began to apologise for intruding when the man turned and grinned.

"You will remember Sergeant Fraile, Captain?" said Sanchez, "Although it's Lieutenant Fraile now."

Michael was delighted to see him again. "Yes, yes of course I do. How are you, Lieutenant, and your Señora?"

"Very well, Señor, as is my wife, although she is not here, she is up in the mountains with our little boy."

"My congratulations, Lieutenant. I am sorry I will not see her."

Sanchez chimed in. "Captain Roberts, if you are to see my lancers in action, I thought I should show you personally. We will leave at dawn tomorrow with a squadron of a hundred lancers. I thought a familiar face would be good, so Lieutenant Fraile will be your personal escort with a dozen lancers."

"Thank you, Don Julian, that's very good of you. Lloyd will be pleased as well, to see Lieutenant Fraile again. You remember my man, Lieutenant, and the horse he took?"

"Yes, Señor, of course," Fraile answered.

"We called the horse Rodrigo," Michael told him with a smile.

Sanchez laughed. "That is a splendid name for a splendid horse."

They talked for few more minutes about horses and then Michael excused himself to go and start to prepare for the trip. He found Lloyd and Bradley in the stables, grooming the horses.

"Is all well with them?" Michael asked as he walked in.

"Aye, grand, no problems, sir," answered Bradley. "Do you know who you'll be taking tomorrow, sir?"

"Yes, I'll ride Thor, a few days work will do him good. Lloyd, you come along, but I'll leave Hall here with you, Bradley. I'm not sure about the condition of Billy for the sort of work we might be doing. It's rough country and a long ride."

"Right you are, sir!" answered Lloyd.

He left them to carry on with the horses and walked into the back of the house and almost into Señora Martinez' maid.

"Oh, Señor, I beg your pardon. The Señora asks if you will dine here tonight?"

Michael was gratified by the invitation. "Yes, of course, please thank the Señora for me, but tell her I will be leaving at dawn for a few days."

Dinner was a brief affair. Señora Marinez was back in the black silk dress she had worn when they first met, her hair less formal without a mantilla and Michael was in his old jacket and overalls. The conversation was enjoyable. Mchael was able to give her his undivided attention and he found that not only was she an attractive woman, but intelligent and well educated.

"I must say, Señor," she said after the last plates had been cleared and the maid had left them, "that your company has been most enjoyable. Unfortunately most of Don Julian's men are ill-mannered peasants. There is no company fit for a lady, the sole exception is Major Strenuwitz, and I include Don Julian. An undoubted patriot and a brave man, but no gentleman. Some have ideas above their station and can be tiresome, which is one reason I keep myself apart from them." She smiled, a little winsomely and very prettily, thought Michael.

"Perhaps you might permit me to offer myself as acceptable company for a lady?" he offered tentatively, letting his voice communicate his hesitation. He was to be disappointed.

She frowned at him. "No, Señor, you are a guest in my house because of the chances of war, otherwise we should never have met, our worlds are different. I accept that you are a gentleman, Señor, but you are also a soldier, and soldiers are notoriously unreliable, through no fault of their own. No, Señor, it would not do for me, to say nothing of the impropriety of such behaviour." She paused before adding, "But I thank you, Señor, you are most gallant. And now, I think it would be well for me to retire, but, please, finish your wine."

Up in her room Señora Martinez was helped by her maid, who been with her for many years and was as much a companion as a servant. "So, Señora," she asked, "how was the Captain?"

"Pleasant enough company, Silvia." She paused in her undressing for a thoughtful moment. "Handsome enough, intelligent, a gentlemen and a pleasant change from Sanchez' savages."

"And?"

"And nothing. As I said, he is handsome and intelligent and probably has many women into the bargain. No doubt he will be gone in a few weeks, never to be seen again." She paused again. "And there is something about him that is a little frightening. I sense a coldness for all his manners and good humour." She shrugged. "But it's of no importance."

As the sky lightened Michael and Lloyd rode up to Sanchez's quarters. He was just mounting his horse and was accompanied by Lieutenant Frail, Strenuwitz stood in the doorway, watching the departure.

"Good morning, Don Julian."

"Captain Roberts, good morning to you. You shall ride with me, Lieutenant Frail will follow with your escort. The squadron is waiting just outside the village."

Michael watched with interest as a dozen men were dispatched ahead of the small force, clearly, even at this distance, Sanchez and his men were taking no chance of running into a French force. They were followed by the bulk of the squadron, then Michael and Sanchez with their escort, finally another twenty lancers brought up the rear.

The day grew brighter and warmer and Sanchez struck up a conversation with Michael.

"So, Captain, what do you make of Señora Martinez?"

Michel was taken aback by the blunt question. "Err, she is a very fine lady," he offered.

"Oh, yes, no doubt. But you, Captain, what did you think of her. Attractive, no?"

"Indeed, Señor, but I think she has little interest in a humble light dragoon captain."

"Ah ha!" Sanchez grinned at him. "So you have tested the waters and found them cold?"

Michael shrugged.

"You are not alone, Captain. She has been a widow for three years or so and has rejected all advances that I am aware of. All she wants is to recover her farm and rebuild it. She also seems rather set against soldiers."

"Really? But I shall be gone in a few weeks at most and unlikely ever to be back, so it is a matter of no importance."

As the day progressed they rode out of the mountains and the landscape became one of gently rolling hills and woodland. They halted every hour for five minutes, and made good, steady progress northwards.

In the middle of the afternoon they stopped one more time, but this time the lancers gave every impression that this halt would be a longer one, as they dismounted and eased giths and dropped bits out of their horse's mouths. Sanchez turned to Michael.

"We will ride on a little. There is a view from the other side of that wood." He pointed up a long slope to a wooded hilltop. "Lieutenant Frail, make sure you keep the escort out of sight. Now, Captain, come along."

Minutes later they were walking their horses quietly through the wood. At the edge was a lancer who saluted and said "All is clear, sir." Sanchez returned the salute and beckoned to Michael to follow him. They halted at the very edge of the wood, amongst the last trees, just under the canopy of branches. Sanchez pointed down the slope to a dusty, winding, rough road that passed in front of them.

"There you are, Captain, the road to Madrid." He looked at he road and snorted. "Not very impressive is it? Still, it goes to our capital that way," he pointed east, "and that way to Salamanca." He started to back his horse into the trees. "Now we hide and wait."

They rode back to the main body and as they went Sanchez explained matters to Michael. "Once the men are rested we will send out parties of twenty to look out for couriers or anyone else trying to travel but avoiding the main road. Sometimes we are lucky and find individuals or small parties we can engage. Sometimes the enemy are just too many and we stay hidden."

The rest of the day passed without incident and they dined on cold rations and slept wrapped in cloaks. No fires were kindled and it was a cold night. Just before dawn Michael was shaken awake by Sanchez himself.

"Come along Captain, a little brandy, a little bread and we shall see what the new day brings."

In the late morning it brought a single rider, trotting along on a mule in the direction of Madrid. Before he could do anything about it the man was surrounded by a dozen lancers and escorted quickly off the road and into the trees. Warned by the lancers watching, Michael and Sanchez arrived in the wood at the same time as the captive. The man looked terrified and was sweating profusely.

"Search him," was Sanchez's curt order.

Michael and Lloyd exchanged glances as they watched the man being stripped naked and his clothes minutely examined. His mule was completely untacked and his baggage and tack similarly searched. While that was going on Sanchez questioned the man, asking who he was, what he was doing on the road, where he had come from, where he was going. The man stammered his answers, pleading that he was a simple farmer, going to visit relatives some twenty leagues further on.

Then one of the lancers called out, "Don Julian, there's another rider coming! It looks like a French cavalry officer."

Swiftly the lancers sprang into action and two parties of half a dozen galloped out from opposite ends of the wood. The officer saw them, turned his horse and put it to a gallop away from the wood. Then a third group of lancers appeared from the far side of the wood. Seeing them the officer turned his horse in the direction of Madrid, drew his sabre and charged headlong at the lancers blocking his road in that direction. They killed him.

Lloyd swore. "Duw, there's brave, but he didn't stand a chance, sir."

Michael watched in silence as the body was thrown over the officer's horse and brought to where they waited in the wood. There the lancers searched him, and quickly found a bundle of dispatches in his sabretache. They were handed to Sanchez who handed them on to Michael.

"Is this what Wellington wants?"

Michael opened the package and found five dispatches, all bar one in a mixture of French and cipher numbers. The exception concerned a captured British officer.

"Yes, Don Julian, this is exactly what he wants."

"Then we had better get you on your way to him. If you set out now and push hard you should make Fuenteguinaldo sometime the day after tomorrow. I'll provide you with a small escort. If Wellington is happy then we shall hunt for more."

A lancer spoke up, indicating the naked man. "Don Julian, what about this fellow?"

Sanchez glanced at him. "Send him on his way!"

Chapter 10

Madrid's weather in early May was, to Renard's relief, much like Paris. He harboured no illusion, however, that it would not be hotter in the summer, much hotter. He was also feeling quite pleased with the progress he had made since arriving little more than two weeks ago. One of his clerks, who seemed a little sharper and brighter than the rest, had managed to find a man who was willing to travel to Lisbon and find out what had happened to Loiro. He had left a week ago, but it would be at least another two weeks before he could expect anything from that investigation.

He had also managed to open communications with the staff of all the French armies in Spain. He smiled wryly, he had made much of having been dispatched to Spain by the Emperor personally to address intelligence shortcomings. They might distrust, dislike and even hate each other, but Napoleon's Marshals were all in thrall to him and Renard's communiques had produced some results, even if only an improved flow of information to Madrid.

The afrancesado priest had proved useful, but in a different way. He had his own, private network of contacts throughout the city, and heard all the gossip as he sat in salons sipping coffee. Thanks to him, Renard had already surprised the incompetent chief of police with his knowledge, leaving the man somewhat in awe of him. The security of Madrid was not, however, his main concern, frankly he was happy to leave that to the police and the army.

No, his main concern and the subject of much thought was Lisbon. He did not expect good news where

Loiro was concerned, if he ever heard anything. Lisbon seemed to be a bottomless pit into which agents simply disappeared. All supplies and reinforcements for the British passed through Lisbon and it would be of considerable help to know what did pass. He needed to rebuild a network of agents there, and, he believed, that also meant dealing with what he considered the main threat to such endeavours, Roberts. What was more, that gave official cover to Renard's private mission, to kill Roberts for killing his son, Jean-Paul.

He sat down at his desk and rang his handbell. A moment later a clerk appeared. "I want a cold drink, lemonade if possible." The man disappeared and Renard reached for sheet of paper. Taking up his pen he began to draft a letter to his contacts in the French armies in Spain. He was going to set them watching out for the Sixteenth Light Dragoons and any sign of Captain Roberts on the British army staff. Shamelessly he would invoke the name of the Emperor, after all, had not Napoleon himself said that Roberts needed to be dealt with?

He paused for a moment, to consider how he might deal with Roberts if he was found with the army. A report that he had barely glanced at came to his mind. Something about the British hiring Spanish muleteers to supply the army now their lines of supply stretched into Spain. He rang the bell again.

The door opened and the clerk began to apologise, "Forgive me, sir, your lemonade will be here soon."

"What? Oh, very good. Send in young Faucher."

A moment later the young man came in and stood nervously in front of Renard. Renard looked up from his letter. "Sit down, Faucher." He pointed to the chair in front of his desk. "Now, I was impressed by the way you found a man to send to Lisbon."

"Thank you, sir."

"But one man is not enough." Faucher's face dropped. "And since you seem to have an aptitude, I want you to recruit more men to go, men of intelligence, men who will not cheat us of funds, men who can be trusted. We must know what is happening in Lisbon. You can devote yourself solely to that task. I am relying on you Faucher. I need a right hand man who I can rely on, and that could be you. Do I make myself clear?"

"Yes, sir. Thank you, sir."

"Good. There is one other matter. The problem of the British officer, Roberts."

"Yes, sir"

"As no one has told me anything I can only assume that he has not yet been located?"

"No, sir."

"Then any men we send to Lisbon must be instructed to be on the lookout for him. He is extremely dangerous."

"Yes, sir."

"I suspect, however, that he will not be found in Lisbon, that he is with the British army, which would make him difficult to get to. However, I have had an idea. I understand the British are beginning to hire Spanish muleteers to transport supplies?"

"Yes, sir."

"Then you should also look for a man who can pass as a muleteer, perhaps is a muleteer, it would make his task easier. A man who would be willing to kill Roberts for us. His reward would be considerable."

The enormity of the request dawned on Faucher. "Err, ah, yes, sir."

"Can you do that?"

Faucher braced himself, this was his chance. "Yes, sir, I believe I can."

"Then see to it."

Faucher left the room, a new spring in his step. Renard watched him go. It would be the making or breaking of the young man. He wondered, briefly, if Faucher considered the price of failure. He did not care, he turned back to his letter. He would have to use the local cipher, the cipher for Paris was not widely available, still, the British had not broken it, it was secure.

Once out of Renard's office, Faucher rolled his eyes at his fellow clerks. Renard was becoming obsessed, he thought, and this scheme was just impractical madness. He wasn't going to try too hard.

. . .

It was getting dark when Michael, on Johnny, and Lloyd, on Robbie, rode into Fuenteguinaldo. Thor and Rodrigo had been left to recover after their exertions, and the escort had also been changed, Fraile also staying behind. Wearily they dismounted outside Wellington's headquarters and Michael passed Johnny's reins to Lloyd.

"I don't know how long I shall be. Find Captain Campbell or Captain White, let them know we will probably be here just tonight, perhaps tomorrow night as well, and ask him on my behalf to find somewhere for our escort."

"Right you are, sir."

Michael made his way past the sentries, exchanging salutes with them, and into Wellington's headquarters. Inside an orderly was standing outside the dining room door and he came smartly to attention when he saw Michael.

"Good evening, Captain Roberts."

"Evening. Is the Earl at dinner?"

"Yes, sir, can I pass him a message?"

"Yes, my compliments and I have some dispatches for Major Scovell."

"Beg pardon, sir, but Major Scovell ain't in there, sir."

"Never mind, that's the message."

The orderly gave Michael a puzzled look and slipped into the room. A buzz of conversation and laughter rose through the open door. A few moments later the man was back, with Colonel Lord Fitzroy Somerset, Wellington's secretary.

"Hello Roberts, dinner is just breaking up and his Lordship will meet us in his office shortly." He turned to the orderly who had followed him out. "Go and fetch Major Scovell, tell him it's urgent."

"Yes, sir" and the man scurried off.

Somerset led the way to Wellington's office where the man himself joined them a few minutes later.

"Roberts, you've been successful already?" Wellington barked as he came in.

"Yes, My Lord. Don Julian was very keen to help and his men are pretty adept at taking messengers. I watched them intercept one."

"What happened to the messenger?"

"Dead, my Lord, a French cavalry officer, he tried to make a run for it and the lancers killed him."

"Hmm."

The door opened and Scovell came in. "My Lord, you sent for me?"

"Indeed, Captain Roberts says he has something for you. Now, let's have a look, Roberts."

The dispatches were soon laid out on the table and Scovell was poring over them.

"This one is in the new cipher, my Lord, it appears to be from Marmont to Jourdan. Some of it is not ciphered. The others are in the usual cipher and I should be able to get the gist of them easily enough. This last isn't in cipher, it's about Colonel Grant, sir, it looks like they are moving him to France."

"Damn," exclaimed Wellington. "We shall have to see if any of our guerilla friends can free him. As to the rest, do your best, Scovell, let me know as soon as you have anything."

"Yes, my Lord." Scovell left the room.

Wellington spoke to Michael. "D'ye know Grant?"

"No, my Lord."

"Damn good intelligence officer, rides all over Spain and brings me excellent information. At least they ain't shot him. Now, Roberts, this is exactly the sort of thing we need, you take a day's rest and then get back to Don Julian, you must give him my very best personal thanks, d'ye understand?"

"Yes, my Lord."

"Then get yourself off and refreshed. Well done Roberts, well done."

Michael felt rather cheerful as he made his way to Sir Stapleton's headquarters. There, Lloyd was waiting for him. "Got the horses away, sir, rubbed down and some nice forage for them. You're in with Captain von der Decken again, I've taken your valise up. Got a billet for the lancers all arranged as well. Oh, and there's a letter for you, Colonel Elley has it, he's in with Sir Stapleton just now, sir.

"Thank you, Lloyd. Lord Wellington has said we can leave the day after tomorrow, give the horses a rest. Have you found anything to eat?"

"Just going to, sir, diolch, Captain von der Decken's lads have something for me."

"Excellent. Ask them if they can rustle me up some hot water in the morning, will you."

"Right you are, sir."

Michael knocked on Sir Stapleton's door and entered when he heard a gruff "Come."

"Hello, Sir Stapleton, Colonel Elley."

"Ah, Roberts, heard you were back. Been successful have you?"

"Yes, sir, Lord Wellington seems pleased."

"Got a letter for you somewhere," said Elley, "yes, here it is." He passed it to Michael.

Michael opened it and muttered "Bloody hell!"

"What is it, Roberts, not bad news, I hope," Sir Stapleton asked.

"Err, I don't know, sir, I think it's from Mister Musgrave, it's in code, sir."

"Is it, by God? And just what can you do about that?"

"Fortunately I have what I need to decode it in my valise, sir, safest place for it."

"Best get on with it then. You can use the table here, I'll get some food sent in for you as well."

"Thank you, sir."

When Michael returned with his copy of de Laborde's 'View of Spain' the room was empty and he settled down to decode the letter. He had just finished when the door opened abruptly and the Earl of Wellington strode in.

"Ah, Roberts, do you know where Sir Stapleton is?" His eyes fell on Michael's letter. "What the devil is that, sir?"

"Err, a letter, my Lord, from Mister Musgrave."

"Is it, by God. I'm not sure that I like my officers getting coded letters from government servants. I've enough damn trouble with some of the letters my officers write to people in London. Perhaps you will be good enough to put my mind at rest by telling me what Mister Musgrave wants with you now? I seem to recall telling you that it is affairs out here that matter to you now?"

"Yes, my Lord, you did, and this is relevant, my Lord."

"Then enlighten me, Captain."

"There's a man called Renard, he has responsibility for French intelligence matters in Portugal and Spain, my Lord."

"Yes, yes, I know of the man. In Paris."

"Begging your pardon, my Lord, but no, Mister Musgrave writes to tell me that Renard has been sent to Madrid."

"Has he now." Wellington looked thoughtful. "A dangerous man, I believe?"

"Oh, yes, my Lord, very. He, err, he has tried to have me killed, my Lord, three times, twice in England and once in Lisbon just after I had arrived."

Wellington's expression was one of surprise and incredulity. "Has he now. And does Mister Musgrave offer any advice?"

"Yes, my Lord. He suggests it would be a good thing if this particular fox was accounted for, his words, my Lord."

Wellington harrumphed. "He does, does he. I don't suppose he says how you can bring about this desirable state of affairs?"

"No, my Lord."

"No, I thought not." He turned and put a hand on the door knob, then paused. "How dangerous do you think this man, Renard, is?"

"I would think very dangerous, my Lord. He has risen high in the French intelligence services."

"Yes, he has, and now he's in Spain." Wellington turned to look at Michael. "I think I concur with Mister Musgrave's assessment, it would indeed be desirable for this fox to be accounted for. Like Mister Musgrave, I have no suggestions as to how that might be achieved. Perhaps the opportunity will arise, Captain, and if it does, take it." He nodded at Michael to emphasis his words and left the room.

Michael took a deep breath, that had been a bit harrowing, and he was mightily relieved by Wellington's support for Musgrave's view, one wholeheartedly shared by Michael. If the occasion should arise to account for this particular fox, he would unhesitatingly seize it.

Three days later, Michael, Lloyd and their escort rode into the village housing Sanchez's force. He thanked the escort, six men under a sergeant, and passed the sergeant some money to treat them all to some wine. They rode off happily and Michael slipped down from Johnny, passing the reins to Lloyd.

"I don't expect this will take long, if Don Julian is here. Tell Hall I want some coffee, some food, some wine and some hot water to shave." He rubbed the stubble on his chin and grinned at Lloyd, "you're no better either."

"No, sir. Shall I tell the Señora you will be in for dinner, sir?"

The idea of dinner with Señora Martinez suddenly struck Michael as a very pleasant prospect. "Yes, Lloyd, do that, that's an excellent idea, and see if you can track down some palatable wine."

"Right you are, sir." Lloyd rode off feeling quite cheerful, he hadn't seen that look on his Captain's face for a long while. If you had asked him to describe it, he would have failed, but he knew what it portended.

Michael found Sanchez and Strenuwitz in their office and was welcomed. "Captain Roberts, how was your trip, how was Wellington? Was he pleased with our little prize?"

"He was, Don Julian, very much. They were exactly what he is looking for. He asked me to give you his personal thanks."

"Did he? Good, and now we know just what he wants I do not think we need to send you as a messenger every time. It will be better to have you here to have a first look at anything we find."

"I think that's a very sound idea, Señor."

"Now will you dine with us tonight?"

"Forgive me, Don Julian. I have already engaged to dine with Señora Martinez."

"Ah, have you. Strenuwitz, should I be jealous?" He laughed with a twinkle in his eyes. "Very good Captain. Tomorrow perhaps?"

"Of course, Señor, it will be my pleasure."

"Then go and entertain the Señora, Captain!"

As Michael shaved he looked at himself in the mirror and held a conversation with himself in his head. He first considered Señora Martinez and what he knew of her, about her, her nature, which seemed promising, if a little distant. She was, however, not as distant as Catarina Cardoso, not in leagues that is. Catarina had seemed genuinely interested in him, if intelligence affairs had not intervened, who knew where things might have gone. That thought brought Elizabeth to mind. He was pretty sure that what she had learnt about him and his part in the intelligence war, the dirty war, had ensured that he could forget all about her, and would most likely never see her again. That was a shame, he had liked her, probably more than anyone since Elaine. He touched the scar on his face that was an ever present reminder of how he had met Elaine, Lady Travers. The dirty war had ended that, and was another reason why he would unhesitatingly account for Renard.

Things were different with Señora Martinez. True, he was on an intelligence gathering mission with Sanchez, but it had not yet impinged on their relationship, such as it was, which wasn't much. There was, he thought, the opportunity for a fresh start, and if it came to naught, he would soon be moving on. If it did come to anything, and he wasn't optimistic, then he would just have to see how thing developed. He did admit to himself, that he wasn't optimistic, but then again, faint heart never won fair lady, and Señora Martinez was undoubtedly an attractive woman.

He finished shaving, put on his best uniform, and went down to the dining room. In the hallway he came across Bradley and Silvia, apparently deep in conversation. At his approach Silvia blushed bright red and rushed off.

"I didn't know you spoke enough Spanish to converse with the maid?"

Bradley grinned. "Happen not, sir, but she knows a bit of English, learnt it from her mistress, so we manages well enough, sir. Anyways, begging your pardon, sir, I'd best go check the horses, sir."

"Yes, I think you had."

In the dining room he found Lloyd pulling the corks on a couple of bottles.

"Good evening, sir, one red, one white, I don't know what the lady's taste might be, sir, so I managed to get one of each. Don Julian's man says they're good and that the Don won't miss a couple of bottles, sir."

"Ah, just as well he's not coming to dinner as well then, eh?"

"Yes, sir. Hall and Silvia will wait on you, sir, he's a better hand at that than I am, sir. I shall just keep Mister Bradley company, sir, we are having a discussion about the best treatment for worms, sir."

"What? Do any..."

"No, no, sir, all our animals are well, sir."

"Good, well, carry on then Lloyd, and thank you for the wine."

"Ah, yes, sir, I did promise half a dollar a bottle, sir."

"What? Good Lord!"

"It was the best I could find, sir."

"Very well, I shall let you have it tomorrow."

At that moment the door opened and Señora Martinez entered. Lloyd sprang to attention and Michael turned to see a vision of beauty enter. Señora Martinez' hair was again artfully styled, but there was no mantilla and dark ringlets framed her fine features and somehow emphasised her eyes. Her dress was of emerald green silk, trimmed with ivory lace, around her neck a band of emeralds matching the long earrings that swung as she moved, flashing bright green as they caught the light from the candles on the table.

For her part, she saw a handsome, very handsome young man looking lithe in his long white pantaloons and his tight fitting jacket with its silver lace and buttons, a black silk neckcloth contrasting with the white flounce of his shirt that peeped out above his waistcoat. His scar was, strangely she thought, attractive rather than repelling, as might have been expected. It intrigued, piqued her curiosity.

They stood staring at each other for a moment, each making a rapid reappraisal of the other and the atmosphere in the room suddenly become charged with possibilities.

Lloyd coughed. "I shall just pour the wine, sir, and then send in Hall and Silvia."

"Yes, yes, do,"

"White or red, Señora?"

"White."

"Sir?"

"Red, Lloyd, thank you."

Lloyd poured the wine, Michael pulled out a chair and helped Señora Martinez to sit. Lloyd left the room. Outside Hall and Silvia were waiting.

"Just give them a moment, will you?" Lloyd winked and grinned delightedly.

In the dining room, Michael stammered a compliment to the Señora about her dress, and her jewels. She thanked him, fanning herself rapidly as she did so. She heard herself give way to her curiosity.

"Forgive me asking, Captain, but I have been wondering, how did you get that scar? Was it in battle against the French?"

It struck Michael that, in a manner of speaking, it was, but instead he regaled her with the story of the guest collapsing, Michael catching the man, and a broken glass slicing him open for his pains. He mentioned it was at an assembly for the Prince Regent.

"You know the Prince Regent?" She sounded impressed.

"No more than a very passing acquaintance, Señora, I know his brother, the Duke of York, much better." God forgive me for an exaggeration he thought, although in the strict sense it was true.

Hall and Silvia entered with the first of the dishes and their conversation was temporarily suspended. Both took the opportunity to sip a little wine and recover some equilibrium. Alone again, Señora Martinez asked about London. He described the theatres, the Tower of London and its famous menagerie. He casually mentioned meeting the Duke of York in Vauxhall Gardens. He didn't mention how it had come about and felt a twinge of guilt at the recollection of Elaine's company that night.

Michael asked her if she knew Madrid, but she had to admit she had never been. She did tell him about Salamanca and extolled its virtues as a fine city, with a university. She had been educated by a teacher from there. Her father had wanted to give his daughter every advantage that he could, and she admitted that her upbringing had been unusual, more like that of the brother she never had. She spoke a little of her farm, her determination to return one day and rebuild it as it had been before the French came.

Michael told her about his house in Lisbon, about growing up there, about the loss of his parents. The realisation of the losses each had suffered seemed to bring them a little closer. Then Michael asked about conditions in the village with Sanchez's men there.

A cloud came over her face. "It has been difficult at times. Don Julian is a good man, although I would not wish to cross him. I think he is a good friend, but a terrible enemy. Strenuwitz is also a good man, but I think he is a lost soul. I believe he would like nothing better than to go home. The others can be a nuisance, particularly the ones that see a young widow with property. She must, they think, be in need of a man, of a husband. Ha! I can assure you, Captain, that there isn't one of them who could hope to replace my late husband. In particular there is one who seems incapable of realising the truth of the situation. Although I think he wants my farm more than me. He tried to get himself billeted, is that the word?" Michael nodded. "Billeted on me. I had to be very firm with Don Julian. They are all peasants," she smiled at him, "whereas you are clearly a gentleman of taste." Then she realised what she had said and blushed.

"Señora, you are clearly a lady of quality, and I hope I may be of more service to you than any peasant."

A slightly embarrassed silence fell as they both wondered what to say next. It was Michael who seized the initiative.

"Perhaps, Señora, and, please, forgive me for repeating myself, but perhaps you would care to reconsider the offer of my protection against nuisances? For so long as I am here, at least. As a friend, of course. I understand your position and have no wish to cause you any embarrassment."

"As a friend, Señor?" She looked at him, thoughtfully, and saw only sincerity. "That would be pleasant, and reassuring. Sometimes, when Don Julian is away I have been quite concerned for, for myself. Thank you."

With that, apparently, settled, their conversation became more general. They talked about Michael's horses, and she explained that her horse had died some months ago and that she missed riding. Inevitably, Michael offered to ride out with her. The invitation was gratefully accepted. She had, she explained a side-saddle, perhaps it would fit one of Michael's horses? He undertook to get Bradley to look into the matter.

Out in the kitchen Lloyd was sitting comfortably in front of the fire, a glass of wine from another of Sanchez's bottles in his hand. Opposite, and looking equally comfortable sat Bradley. Lloyd looked up from as Hall and Silvia came in, carrying empty dishes and plates.

"How is it going then?" he asked.

Hall grinned at him. "I don't think they even noticed us going in and out. They're just sitting there talking quietly about this and that, but mostly just staring at each other."

Silvia lifted a kettle heavy with water and carried it towards the fire. Lloyd pulled his legs back, but Bradley leapt to his feet and took it from her. "Señorita, let me do that for you." He heaved the kettle onto the hook over the fire, and as he did so Lloyd and Hall exchanged smirks.

Silvia gave Bradley a shy smile, quietly thanked him and turned to help Señora Noriega with the other chores. Bradley sank back in his chair, watching her as she walked away. A convivial silence fell in the kitchen. Hall poured himself a glass of wine and came to stand by the fire. Lloyd glanced up at him.

"I should wait a while before you go in and ask about coffee. Give the Captain some time."

"Oi reckons as oi can do that, Corporal. Ere, Mister Bradley, 'as you'm told the Corporal 'bout tha' Miss Elizabeth?"

"Nay, happen as how I hasn't. 'T ain't none of our business."

Lloyd raised his eyebrows quizzically.

"Well, Corporal, as you ask, Miss Elizabeth were a young lady as the Captain met at Earl Harcourt's, or so I understand."

"Yes, that's right," Hall broke in, "at a fine dinner with Colonel Archer and his lady there. That's a right fine house of the Earl's."

"It is that." Lloyd answered.

"Anyways," Bradley went on, "nowt came of it. They went hunting together and to a ball or two, but that were all."

"She came to Falmouth to see 'im off," protested Hall!"

"Aye lad, that she did, but I did nae see owt but friendship."

"There's a shame," said Lloyd, "the Captain deserves some luck."

"Oh aye?" asked Badley.

"Yes, but don't expect me to tell you tales, no, I shan't do that to the Captain. He's a good man and, well, you both know as well as I do that he does some things no ordinary soldier has to, and us with him. And, chwarae teg, he looks after us as well."

Hall spoke up. "'E did ask oi if oi could keep moi mouth shut, keep a confidence loike."

"And you told him you could, and you have, or you'd not be with him now." Lloyd stated this as a simple fact. "I've ridden with him, fought with him, spent time with him, he's trusted me and I trust him." He paused as him mind went back the quay side in Oporto. "No, he's no love in his life just now, and I for one would not begrudge him a little happiness. Not after all he has lost in the past. And don't ask me, it's in the past and that's where it's staying. Now, Hall, fill up these glasses again, and then go and ask about coffee."

The coffee was finished and still they talked, but, eventually, Señora Martinez was unable to stifle a yawn. "Oh, forgive me, Señor," she raised her fan.

"No, there is nothing to forgive, I have been too demanding a guest and detained you far too long."

"Then," she replied, rising from the table and causing Michael to rush to help her with the chair, "I shall retire." They were standing close together. For a fleeting moment they looked into each others eyes. She held our her hand to him. He took it, squeezed gently. "Thank you for a most enjoyable evening," she said, quietly, "and now, goodnight."

The door closed behind her, and Michael sat back down. The candles had burnt low. He poured another glass of wine. That, he thought, had been a most enjoyable evening. He asked himself how he felt about the Señora, and was pleased with his conclusion.

Upstairs, Silvia was helping her mistress prepare for bed. She was standing behind her, brushing her long hair in front of the mirror on her dressing table. Almost hesitantly she said "The Captain's men were talking about him, in the kitchen."

"Oh?" Señora Martinez failed to keep her interest out of her voice.

Silvia continued brushing. "The Corporal says he has no woman in his life, he seems to think very highly of him, to trust him. I think they all do, a lot." She continued to brush while the Señora sat thinking. "I think there was a lady, but not now." She paused in her brushing. "I do not know what it is, but I think there are secrets in the Captain's life, he is no ordinary soldier, I think. I also think there is sadness in his life." She met her mistress' eyes in the mirror. "I think he is a good man, Señora."

Señora Martinez recalled that Sanchez had told her that he and Captain Roberts had spent time together. She thought she might, carefully, ask him about the Captain.

Chapter 11

The next morning Michael strode into the stables in buoyant mood. "Bradley!"

"Aye, sir"

"There should be a side-saddle around here somewhere. See if it will fit one of my horses. I am taking the Señora riding."

"Oh, aye, sir?"

"Yes, Bradley, oh aye!"

He returned to the house and found Silvia in the hall.

"Begging you pardon, Señor, Señora Martinez asks if you would care to take a walk with her, Señor?"

"Of course, I should be delighted. Shall we say in ten minutes?"

"Yes, Señor." Silvia bobbed a little curtsey and rushed off up the stairs.

It was a beautiful spring day, mild, with a gentle breeze and clear skies. Michael offered his arm to Señora Martinez and this time she took it. At the edge of the village there was a splendid view to the north, down a tree lined valley that gradually left the mountains behind and broadened out into gently undulating hills. They stood admiring the view.

"I don't know how many times I have seen this view, in all seasons, all weathers, and it still offers me something different every time."

"Yes, I know what you mean. It is like that where my grandfather lives." They turned to walk back and Michael found himself telling her all about his grandfather and his parish. She seemed rather amused that his grandfather was a priest.

Back at the house, one of Sanchez's lancers was waiting for him. He saluted and delivered his message. "Señor, Don Julian asks if you could join him."

"Yes, of course, I shall be along presently." The man walked off and Michael turned to Señora Martinez. "I fear duty calls, it is always the lot of the soldier."

She nodded, gravely. "Yes, it is, isn't it, you must go." As she watched Michael walk away she said, quietly, to herself, "Yes, I had forgotten that."

Michael was soon seated with Sanchez, coffee on the table between them. The topic of conversation surprised Michael.

"Captain, it is none of my business, but you are, in many ways, my guest and I have a responsibility for you. Lord Wellington speaks highly of you and I must see you come to no harm."

"I'm sorry, Don Julian, what do you mean?" He realised that Sanchez was embarrassed by something.

"It is Señora Martinez, Captain. It is, of course, none of my business," he repeated, "but I saw you walking with her, arm in arm, and I have to tell you that, if you are seeking, err, any sort of, err, particular friendship, please forgive me, but there is a man in the lancers who has expressed a strong determination to win her for himself. He is a very jealous man, he has threatened others, and I must caution you to be careful." He took a deep breath as Michael sat, silent and rather taken aback. "There, I have said it. Forgive me, but I felt it my duty to warn you."

"There is nothing to forgive, Don Julian. Señora Martinez has told me about, I assume, the same man. I have offered her my protection. As a friend."

"Then, Captain I have nothing more to say on the subject. French dispatches are another matter." There was relief in his voice. "I have sent out patrols to cover the main road and all the byways that we can." He shrugged, "we shall see what they bring in. I have also received information about a detachment of French infantry that has been to Alba de Tormes and is marching back to Salamanca in the morning. I am taking out one of my lancer regiments this evening. We will ride through the night and, hopefully, surprise them at dawn. Would you care to join us, with your men?"

"Of course, Don Julian."

"Then we shall leave at nightfall."

Don Julian was walking through the village early in the afternoon. He was heading back to his billet for some coffee and then some sleep before the coming ride through the night. He was a little surprised to meet Señora Martinez and even more surprised when she accepted his invitation to take coffee with him.

After initial pleasantries, Señora Martinez said "I understand that you are riding out tonight?"

It was no secret in the village and he replied, "Yes, Señora, but we should return before the end of tomorrow, God willing."

"And Captain Roberts is going with you. His men are busy preparing the horses."

"Indeed he is, Señora. He is well thought of by the Earl of Wellington, and I want him to take a favourable report with him when he goes back."

"How long do you think he might be billeted on me?"

Sanchez waved one hand vaguely. "Señora, that depends on many things, most of all on what Wellington decides to do. But I see little happening until the weather is better and the grass grows for the horses. Another month, perhaps." He watched her intently as he spoke, thinking of his earlier conversation with Michael, but she gave no reaction to that news.

"At least he is intelligent company, and an interesting man." Her tone was flat and Don Julian could read nothing in her words or expression. "I was intrigued by the story of your escape from Ciudad Rodrigo. Did you get to know the Captain well?"

"A little, Señora." He certainly wasn't about to tell her about the spy they had caught and hanged. "He was very helpful to my men, advising on the use of the sabre, which was a new weapon to them, and we taught him a little about the lance."

They sat and looked at each other for a moment. "Don Julian, will you tell me, honestly, what you think of the man who is under my roof and likely to be so for some time?"

"Señora, I believe you have nothing to fear from Captain Roberts. I believe he is an honest and trustworthy gentleman." He chuckled. "Were he not Señora, Wellington would not trust him as he does."

"And how does he?"

"Señora, it would be indiscreet of me to say anything, but he acts for Wellington on matters best kept secret. I can say no more, and that is too much. I am sure I can count on your discretion in keeping this confidential?"

Señora Martinez rose from her chair. "Don Julian, thank you for your reassurances and you may certainly count on me, and I on you, I trust?"

Sanchez rose and, with a little bow, said "Of course, Señora."

As darkness fell Sanchez rode away from the little village at the head of one of his two regiments, over four hundred lancers in four squadrons. On one side of him rode Strenuwitz, on the other side, Michael. Behind them rode Lloyd and Hall, followed by Fraile with an escort of a dozen lancers. Then came the rest of the regiment, led by their Lieutenant Colonel, organised like a British light cavalry regiment and riding three abreast.

They first marched west until they reached the banks of the Tormes. The water was bitterly cold as they splashed across a ford. Then they swung roughly north along the river. Sanchez explained the plan.

"We will follow the river until we are two leagues from Alba, then head across country for a point half a league from the town on the Salamanca road. There is a long climb up from the river, the French will be tired at the top, where there is excellent ground for cavalry to act. I will place half the regiment on one side of the road, and advance with them, the French will form to face them, and then the other half will come over the top of the hill and charge them from the rear. I expect they will surrender, or try to."

Just before dawn, as they were watering the horse in a stream that fed the Tormes and eating a little bread carried with them, it began to rain, gently at first, then harder, a stiff breeze blowing from the north west.

Sanchez laughed, "This is excellent, Captain, the rain will blow into their faces as they march, now they will be wet and miserable as well as tired."

Half an hour later the ambush was prepared. All of Sanchez's men were dismounted, waiting patiently by their horses. Michael and Sanchez stood waiting with them in the gap between two squadrons, Fraile and his little escort a few yards behind them. Away to the right Michael could see a small copse where he knew Strenuwitz was posted, with a clear view down the road to Alba de Tormes. He would signal when it was time to charge. The other two squadrons were slightly down hill of the road and under the command of the Lieutenant Colonel who commanded the regiment. He had little to do, save attract the attention of the French and then charge to the help of the others.

The day dawned and gradually it got lighter, the rain persisted. Sanchez tapped Michael on the arm, "Listen," he said.

Michael realised that he could just make out the beat of a single drum. Sanchez turned and waved and his men mounted, Michael, Lloyd and Hall with them. Michael stroked Johnny's withers as the horse fidgeted, wanting to move after the long wait. "Steady lad," Michael spoke gently. To his right Lloyd gently eased his sabre in its scabbard. Michael realised that the lancers would not need to draw swords. "Lloyd, Hall, draw swords." The three of them wrapped their sword knots around their wrists and drew their sabres.

Sanchez was staring intently away to the right. Suddenly shouts and the rapid beat of more drums came from over the rise in front of them. Still Sanchez stared to his right. Then he drew his sword, waved it once around his head and the two squadrons began to walk forwards. As they crested the rise, Michael saw a line of French infantry, no more than a hundred yards away, formed along the line of the road, in their usual three ranks, some eighty or ninety he thought, and they had their backs to them. From the top of the rise he caught a glimpse of the other two squadrons. Then Sanchez waved his sword again, put spurs to his horse and the whole line surged forward. Michael touched Johnny lightly on his sides and the horse needed no more urging. He leapt forward, straight from walk into a gallop, stretching out, tearing down the slope towards the French. Michael felt his heart start to pound felt the excitement course through his veins, felt the icy calm that came on him in combat. They were riding straight at the centre of the line where there seemed to be a slight gap, between two companies, he thought.

The Spanish lancers came down without a single shout or trumpet call, the sound of their hooves deadened on the rain softened ground and drowned out by the drum beats. Michael thought they were less than twenty five yards away when the first Frenchman glanced over his shoulder. He shouted, grabbed the man next to him. In the middle of the little gap Michael saw an officer turn and look straight at him, his face a picture of shock and fear.

Then they were on them. Johnny crashed through the gap, sending the officer flying, Michael turned him, as hard and fast as he dare on the wet grass, and went back, he saw Lloyd cut down one man, Hall thrust into the face of another man trying to bring his musket to bear. Everywhere lancers were spearing infantrymen. There were sporadic shots, then more as the French turned. Michael closed with the officer who was struggling to his feet. He made to cut at Michael, who parried and sliced into the man's shoulder as he went past.

Michael was vaguely aware of the other two squadrons arriving to lend their weight to the one sided combat. In a few more moments it was all over. As had been the case when Michael had charged with Sanchez before there were no prisoners.

The ambush had worked perfectly, but the lancers had lost four men killed, another half dozen or so wounded, two seriously. Michael looked around and saw Lloyd and Hall nearby, swords ready, looking around. They were unharmed. So was Sanchez who, Michael saw, was grinning with pleasure at his success. He was shouting out orders, organising the lancers to get them on the move in case of any French cavalry. Strenuwitz rode up to Michael.

"That was well done, eh, Captain?"

"It was, but no prisoners?"

"Come, Captain, you know very well what they would do to us, even though we are part of your army."

"Yes, I suppose so, but still..."

"Yes, I know, this is a nasty war. Sometimes, Captain, sometimes I wish nothing more than to be back home in my mountains. One day, perhaps." He shook his head and looked at Michael who suddenly saw what Señora Martinez had meant.

"I most sincerely wish it for you, Major."

Strenuwitz nodded appreciatively. "Thank you, Captain."

They got back to the village in the late afternoon. One of the wounded men had died on the way and once the initial exuberance of the success had worn off the lancers were subdued and rode back quietly. The lancers formed in a field, Sanchez addressed them, thanking them, announcing that their comrades would be buried in the morning, and then dismissing them. He spoke quietly to Michael once they had reached the house Sanchez used.

"I think the men would appreciate it if you came to the funeral tomorrow."

"Of course, Don Julian."

"Thank you. There will be no dinner tonight, can you fend for yourself? Yes, of course you can, forgive me. The funeral will be at ten o'clock. Perhaps you could meet me at my quarters a quarter hour before?"

"Yes, certainly."

"Then I shall bid you good day."

Michael led the way to Señora Martinez's house and into the stables. There they dismounted and Badley appeared to greet them. He looked over the horses.

"Bye, that Billy's looking fair done in!"

They gathered to look at Billy, his head drooping. Hall defended his horse, "He'll be alright, sir, just needs a bit o' rest and some good forage, sir."

Lloyd spoke up, "It's alright, lad, we know he's a good horse, but what we've been doing is hard on any horse, even the likes of Johnny and Rodrigo, they're both needing a rest."

"Lloyd is quite right, Hall. He can have a couple of days rest, but I think we need to do something about him. This is not really work for a remount."

"Come on, lad, cheer up," Bradley, patted Hall on the arm, "we'll not be shooting him just yet."

Hall smiled at the jest.

"Well, see what you can do for all of them," said Michael, he removed his tarleton and sword and belt, handing them to Hall. "Give these a clean, Hall, the rain has got to them, I'm going in and I'll see what the cook can do for us for some dinner."

The three men thanked Michael and he left them to it, walking in through the back door of the house. In the hall he was surprised to see Silvia listening at the drawing room door.

Michael heard Señora Martinez's voice, loud and insistent, and a man's answering voice, hectoring, threatening. "Silvia, what's going on?"

"It's that lancer, Señor, the one that won't leave the Señora alone, he knows you are away with Don Julian and he pushed his way in, Señor."

Michael was at the door in three strides, throwing it open wide and bursting into the room. Señora Martinez was standing with her back to the wall, one hand clutched against her chest, the other arm outstretched as if to fend off the man who stood in front of her. He turned at the sound of Michael's entrance.

Michael advanced on him, shouting, "What the Hell is going on here?" His anger had flared at the sight of the confrontation and while he shouted he was icy calm. The thought flashed briefly through his mind, that's twice today.

"It's none of your damned business," came the response, "this is between the Señora and myself, get out, Englishman."

Over his shoulder he could see Señora Martinez, eyes streaming tears, her chest heaving, her expression frightened, but hoping. "I think it is my business and I'm damned if I'm going to be spoken to like that by a peasant. "He picked his words quite deliberately, he wanted to provoke this man into something stupid. It worked.

The man shouted back, "You bloody English bastard" and his right hand went to his belt, coming back up with a knife. Michael was expecting it, and a swift kick sent it spinning across the room. He followed the kick, stepping forward and his fist smashed into the man's jaw, dropping him to the floor. The man saw his knife, scrabbled for it, grabbed for it and turned, to find the point of Michael's knife just in front of his eyes. He dropped his knife and froze.

Michael spoke very quietly. "Get out of here before I cut your throat. Don't come back or, I swear, I will kill you." The look in his eyes left no doubt that he meant every word. The man started to rise but

Michael's foot pushed him back down. "No, crawl, you bastard, crawl out like the vermin you are."

Michael realised that Lloyd was in the doorway, "Lloyd, see this peasant out, please. No need to be gentle." He spoke to Lloyd in English, but his meaning was clear from his tone.

Lloyd stepped forward and grabbed the man by the collar of his jacket, half dragging him from the room. Behind him the concerned face of Silvia was revealed. "Silvia, brandy, two glasses, if you don't have any, ask Hall, he has some somewhere." She nodded and scurried off. Michael shut the door and turned just in time to catch Señora Martinez as she threw herself into his arms, sobbing. He hugged her close, stroking the back of her head, feeling the smoothness of her hair, her perfume filling his nose, making him only too aware of his own war and travel stained condition.

"Shh, now, it's alright, he's gone, and he won't be back." He gently eased her away and looked at her tearful face. "Come on now, let's get you sat down, and, anyway, I must smell awfully of horse."

She gave a little, half hysterical chuckle. "You smell better than that peasant."

He got her into a comfortable chair just as the door opened and Silvia came in with a bottle and two glasses. "On the table, please, Silvia. Can you organise some dinner in a while?"

"Yes, Señor, I'll get Señora Noriega to work." She busied herself away towards the kitchen.

He saw Lloyd hovering outside the door. "Any problems, Lloyd?"

"No, sir, went as quiet as a little lamb, sir."

"Good. Let Hall and Bradley know what's happened, they will need to keep an eye open for our friend. And I know I said we would rest the horses, but I want to ride tomorrow, say midday, after the funeral, I want Johnny and another with the side saddle. Has Bradley tried it?"

"On Thor, sir."

"Good. Johnny and Thor then. Just a quiet little walk around, tell Bradley."

"Yes, sir."

"That's all, oh, unless you can find another couple of bottles of that wine?"

"I think I might manage that, sir."

"Good, good. And thank you, Emyr."

Lloyd nodded and smiled and closed the door.

Michael poured two glasses of brandy and took them to where Señora Martinez was sitting, quieter now. "Here you are, now, sip it slowly."

She sipped and sniffed, then coughed. "Señor, forgive me, I am sorry..."

"Señora, you have nothing to apologise for, I am pleased to have been of service."

She smiled and took another sip. "Then let me thank you." She smiled, a little shyly. "I am afraid that I am barely presentable for dinner."

"We can soon see to that, but first, finish your brandy."

Slowly she did so, and a little colour came back to her cheeks, a little sparkle to her eyes, a little straightness of her back. When she had finished Michael opened the door and called for Silvia.

"Silvia, take your mistress and help her to prepare for dinner. I'm sure Señora Noriega can manage on her own for a while."

Señora Martinez stood up and left the room with her maid. Michael gave them a few minutes and then bounded into the kitchen where Lloyd, Hall and Bradley were watching the pots on the fire. "Hall, you stay here, help Señora Noriega if she needs it, you too Bradley. Lloyd, sorry, but I must ask you to be my batman again for a brief period. I need hot water, quickly." He managed to wash, shave and change in record time and get back to the drawing room. Then he drew breath and calmed himself. He realised that he had been taut, like a bowstring even if he had been absolutely clear headed.

He had hardly had time to settle himself when the door opened and Señora Martinez entered, a woman transformed. He bowed, "Señora, you look wonderful, may I take you in to dinner?"

She gave a little curtsy, "Of course, Captain."

In the dining room Lloyd was just pulling the corks from two bottles, one white, one red. "Good evening, Señora, Captain. I managed the same arrangement, sir."

"Thank you Lloyd, tell Silvia and Hall they can serve dinner in five minutes."

"Yes, sir."

Afterwards, Michael would have been hard pressed to remember what they had for dinner, his whole attention was on the Señora. They talked, he said he was taking her riding the following day, he told her about Thor and what he was like. She told him of a pleasant ride through the woods behind the village, not too far, not too strenuous. She admired the wine, he confessed as to its origins and she laughed, a clear, proper laugh, her eyes bright and teeth flashing.

Then the dinner was over, but there was still wine left. Hall and Silvia cleared the table. Michael dismissed Hall. Señora Martinez said, "That will be all tonight, Silvia, thank you for everything." Silvia bobbed a little curtsy and left the room without a word.

Eventually the wine was gone and Señora Martinez stood, Michael following suit. She stepped close to him. "I wonder, may I call you Miguel, in private, of course?"

"I should be honoured, and..." he hesitated.

"And you shall call me Victoria, in private."

Michael closed the little distance between them. "Victoria...?"

"Yes, Miguel, please." Victoria took Michael's hand. "Bring the candelabra," she said, and together they walked out of the dining room and climbed the stairs to Victoria's bedroom.

Later, as they lay together by the light of the low burnt candles, her head on his chest, she spoke quietly to him. "Miguel, I want no more from you than this. I expect nothing more. Once this war is over, perhaps sooner, I will go back to my farm and start to rebuild it. You will follow your duty, as soldiers must, and after the war you will go home, to England, or perhaps to Lisbon, and that will be alright, but just now, I need you. Do you understand?"

"Yes, I do, perfectly." And he truly believed that he did.

The day dawned clear and bright, the rain had passed, but a cool breeze still blew from the north. Michael slipped away from Victoria's bed at the first cock crow and left her sleeping. He had just time to drop his uniform on the floor and climb into bed when he heard rather slow and heavy footsteps coming along the corridor. Hall usually moved quite silently. Oh, God, he thought, they know. There was a pause, then a loud knock on the door.

"Come in, Hall."

He breakfasted alone, in his best uniform for the funeral. Of Silvia and Victoria there was no sign, which he hoped was not a bad sign. He supposed he would find out when it was time to go riding. Out in the stables he found Hall cleaning his tack and Lloyd and Bradley giving Thor and Johnny a thorough grooming. Lloyd and Hall saluted him, straight faced, but Bradley brazenly grinned at him. Michael returned the salutes.

"Is all well here?" he asked no one in particular.

It was Lloyd who answered. "Yes, indeed, Captain. A little light exercise won't hurt them at all."

"Good. I can get myself ready for the funeral, Hall, you can carry on here."

"Begging your pardon, sir." Lloyd spoke up.

"Yes, Lloyd?"

"I was wondering if I might attend the funeral with you, sir, show my respects to the dead, sir."

"Oh, yes, of course. That's good of you. We shall leave," he consulted his watch, "in half an hour."

Michael returned to the house and dropped into a chair in the sitting room. He let his head fall back and closed his eyes. He was running over the events of the previous day, recalling the fight with the French, the fight with the lancer, he realised he didn't even know his name. Then he recalled the events of the evening. He wondered if everything was going to be alright. He heard the door open and opened his eyes to see Victoria there. She was dressed completely in black, in mourning, a veil over her face. Michael leapt to his feet, his heart hammering with anxiety.

"Good morning, Miguel," she said and Michael felt a great relief, everything was going to be alright. "I thought that I would come to the funeral with you, if that is acceptable?" She lifted her veil and smiled.

Michael crossed the room to her and took her hands. "Victoria, I will be honoured."

There was a cough from the hall and Michael saw Lloyd standing there, immaculately turned out. "I brought your sabre and tarleton for you, sir."

They stepped out of the house, Victoria had dropped her veil and she took Michael's arm. Together they walked to Sanchez's, Lloyd a few paces behind. Both men were carefully watching for any sign of yesterday's trouble. They need not have worried, there was no sign of the man at all.

The funeral of the five lancers was a solemn affair. Although the Latin service and mass was lost on Lloyd, Michael was more aware, and it reminded him of Senhora Santiago's funeral, a mere few months ago. Afterwards a number of lancers, comrades of the fallen men, came up to Michael and thanked him, Lloyd and Victoria for their attendance. Sanchez invited Michael and Victoria to his billet for some refreshments while Lloyd was practically carried off by two lancer NCOs.

Michael called out to Lloyd as he went. "An hour, Lloyd, then back to the billet."

"Yes, sir." Lloyd called back, over his shoulder.

At Sanchez's there was coffee and small cakes and light conversation with Sanchez's officers. Victoria was the centre of polite attention. As soon as they could, Michael and Victoria made their excuse and left. Back at her house Victoria went to change into her riding habit and Michael went to check that all was ready in the stables. Lloyd was also back and the horses were ready.

"How is Thor with that saddle?" Michael asked.

Badley chuckled. "Oh, he's reyt grand, sir. Ah took him for a little trial me sen while tha were gone. T' Señora should have nay problems, sir."

"Splendid, thank you."

"Begging your pardon, sir," Lloyd said, "I was talking to some of Don Julian's NCOs sir, and I took the liberty to enquire about the fellow that gave you that trouble yesterday, sir." He scratched the back of head. "They don't like him, sir, don't like him at all. Reckon he's a nasty piece of work, bit of a bully apparently. Comes of a decent family but has ideas above his station."

"I see, any sign of him."

"Not that I could see, sir."

"Good." Michael saw Victoria approaching in a dark blue riding habit and hat with a veil over her face. "Let's say no more. Bring the horses out and we'll be off."

Half an hour later they had left the village behind and were riding quietly through a fine forest, fresh, spring growth was everywhere. Victoria was having no difficulty with Thor and it was clear to Michael that she was a good horsewoman. Horses and riding became the main topic of their conversation and Michael told her about Johnny and hunting in Cornwall, and the horse fair where he had bought Robbie and hired Bradley. For her part she told him about her father's farm, the horses they rode to manage the cattle, learning to use the lance they employed on the cattle to herd them.

The conversation was relaxed, from time to time one or the other would stretch out to touch the other. Michael was feeling comfortable, better than he had for a long time. He was in the middle of some anecdote or other, looking at Victoria smiling and nodding, when he saw her stiffen, and clutch his arm.

"Miguel, look!"

They had ridden out into a clearing in the wood, perhaps fifty yards long and half as wide. They both reined in. At the other side of the clearing was a horseman, a lancer, it was the man who had pursued

Victoria. Without a word he dropped his lance to the level and spurred his horse straight towards them.

Michael snapped out, "Quick, into the trees, now." He had no doubt the man intended to kill him, but he also knew the lance's limitations. Victoria grasped what he meant, spun Thor to the right and pushed him between the trees. Michael drew his sabre, no time for the sword knot, waited a moment until the man had halved the distance between them, then turned Johnny sharply left and he too pushed in amongst the trees.

A few yards in and he turned Johnny around a big chestnut, putting the tree between him and where he had ridden in. As he had expected, had hoped, the man turned after him. The wood was quite open, undergrowth and young trees kept down by grazing pigs, but it was enough to limit the nine foot or so long lance. Michael turned Johnny again and rode quickly further in, weaving and turning as he went. As he went he manged to get the sword knot around his wrist, which made him feel better. He glanced behind. The man was about ten yards behind, his horse, a powerful looking chestnut, was forging head as he tried to close the gap.

Ahead Michael saw a nice big, broad oak tree, its branches low, but not so low he couldn't ride under them. It would do nicely. He played softly down the reins and Johnny's speed dropped slightly. A glance behind showed him the rider was now only a few yards behind, almost close enough for a thrust. Michael rode close to the tree and as he came level with it he pulled Johnny up, turned him on his haunches to the right and pushed the horse as hard as he could around the tree, as close as he could, ducking, laying almost flat along Johnny's neck. He almost left it too late. As they turned he felt a searing pain across his back as the man's lance thrust scored across him. Then he was around the tree and behind the man as he tried to pull up and follow. He saw Michael coming and tried to spin his lance for another thrust, but it snagged on the branches of the oak tree. Michael was coming in from behind as the man pulled the lance free. He twisted almost completely round in the saddle and thrust desperately at Michael, but he was already moving Johnny left. He parried the lance easily and, coming up on his opponents left hand side, he cut once, into the man's neck, almost severing his head.

The body swayed for a moment, and then crashed to forest floor.

Michael led the chestnut into the village, leading it along on his right, the body over the saddle. Victoria rode on his left hand. She had, he realised, lifted the veil from her face and she sat upright, proudly, openly riding beside him. The message was clear. By the time they reached Sanchez's billet a silent crowd of lancers was following them. Someone ran ahead and Sanchez came out as they reached the house.

Sanchez took in the situation with a quick look. "Was it a fair fight?" he asked.

Michael shrugged, "It was lance against sabre."

A voice came from the crowd, it was Fraile. "He is wounded, Don Julian, in the back."

Don Julian walked around, glanced at the dead man, his head hanging loosely, and looked at Michael's back. "Lieutenant Fraile, see to the body." Fraile came forward, beside Michael, who handed him the reins of the chestnut. Fraile led the horse away. Sanchez addressed the assembled lancers. "I believe this was a fair fight, you all know what Rubio was like," so that was his name, thought Michael, "and that he had ambitions regarding Señora Martinez. I believe he got what he deserved. Now, go, about your duties."

Sanchez came to Michael's side. "Go and get that wound seen to. Then you and the Señora will dine with me tonight, I insist. There will be no difficulties. I shall send the horse around later."

Michael was beginning to feel a bit light headed. "The horse, Don Julian"

"Of course, to the victor, the spoils. Now, go, before you fall off your horse and spoil everything."

Chapter 12

Michael and Victoria rode slowly into the stable yard of her house, Lloyd was sitting on an upturned bucket with a mug in his hand, Hall polishing a pair of boots and Bradley leaning on the nearby door post.

Victoria called out to them, "Quickly, your Captain is wounded!"

Bradley went to Johnny's head while Lloyd rushed to Michael's side, reaching up to help him down.

"Dammit, Lloyd, I can manage," Michael snapped, and then grimaced as he moved to dismount. "My apologies, Lloyd," he managed a tight lipped smile, "it really isn't bad."

As he turned his back to Lloyd and slid down to the ground, Lloyd could see the slice in Michael's jacket and shirt, both stained with drying blood. "Uffern gwaedlyd!" Lloyd cursed. "What's happened, sir?"

Victoria answered, "One of the lancers attacked him. Your Captain killed him." She jumped down from Thor and thrust the reins at Hall. "Miguel, I need to see to that wound. Get inside and into the kitchen."

At the use of Michael's first name Lloyd, Hall and Bradley exchanged glances.

Michael was soon sitting in the kitchen, arms and head resting on the table, his jacket and shirt removed with help from Lloyd, and Señora Noriega had a kettle of water on the fire. Victoria gently washed the dried blood away from the cut across Michael's shoulder blade. She examined it closely. "Good, it's not deep, it will not require stitching up." She placed a pad of linen over the cut and bound it in place with strips of linen.

Once she had finished she stood back and said "There, that should do it."

Michael cautiously straightened himself up and flexed his shoulders. He winced a little. "Thank you, Victoria, thank you very much." He smiled at her, a smile that was warmly returned. He looked at his jacket lying on the floor. "Damn, that's my best jacket."

Victoria stopped picked it up and examined the bloody damage. "I think Silvia and I can do something with that, and in time for dinner with Don Julian tonight."

"Thank you."

"You do realise why Don Julian invited you to dinner tonight?"

"Er, no, is there a special reason?"

"Of course there is. He is telling everyone that you are in the right, that he believes you about that man, that you are his friend. His men will accept that."

"Oh, I see."

"Yes, and now I shall go and change and you should put a fresh shirt on."

An hour later, Michael, in a fresh shirt and his old jacket, was out in the stables talking over the condition of Billy when Fraile appeared leading the chestnut ridden by Rubio. He greeted Michael, "Hello, Captain, I trust your wound is not serious?"

"No, Lieutenant, it is not, just a bit sore."

"Good, I am pleased to hear that, and here is your horse."

"Thank you, Fraile, I have to say that I am surprised to receive him."

Fraile shrugged. "Who else should have him, Señor? He was Rubio's own horse. He attacked you, wounded you, he would have killed you. It seems fair that you should have the horse." He laughed. "Be careful, Captain, if you stay too long with us you might end up with a herd, first Rodrigo, now this one..."

"Oh, no, Rodrigo was one thing, and, anyway, Rodrigo is Lloyd's. No, I have no wish to gain anymore horses, particularly not in that manner."

Fraile laughed, "So, what will you call him? I've no idea what Rubio called him."

Michael thought for a moment, then said "I have no idea, it will have to wait."

Victoria was as good as her word and Michael's jacket was returned to him, cleaned and with a barely visible repair in good time for him to get ready for dinner. They walked, arm in arm, to Sanchez's, through the quickly falling night. They passed by a few of the lancers, but Michael detected no ill will from any of them.

Sanchez was effusive in his welcome for Michael and Victoria. Also present were Strenuwitz and Fraile. They all asked about his wound and were relieved to hear that it was not a deep wound and that he should be fit to ride out in a few days and fully recovered in two weeks or so. Under pressure from Sanchez he was forced to describe how he had bested Rubio.

Asked for her version, Victoria was forced to say that she had seen nothing after Michael rode in amongst the trees. She emphasised her gratitude to Michael, reminding them of Rubio's persistence and telling them about his assault on her and her rescue by Michael. This was news to Sanchez who announced he would have sabred the man himself had he known. Thereafter, at Victoria's urging, they moved on to other, more palatable topics, but only after Sanchez declared that he would not take Michael out again for a week.

It was late when the party broke up, and Michael and Victoria walked back arm in arm again. Victoria tapped lightly on the door and it was opened by Silvia, accompanied by Hall.

"Good evening, Señora." Silvia greeted her mistress.

"Evening, sir," said Hall, "Lloyd and Bradley have turned in, sir. Just me and Miss Silvia here to see to anything, sir"

Michael found that there were things he wanted to say, but with Hall and Silvia's presence he restricted himself to "Thank you for everything, today, Señora."

"Sleep well, Captain" was the response. "Tomorrow I will change your bandage, but be careful until the cut has properly closed up." She smiled. "There has been more than enough excitement for one day, I think." With that she waved Silvia ahead of her with a candle and followed her up the stairs.

Michael said to Hall, "You had better help me off with my jacket and shirt and then you can turn in as well." As they climbed the stairs he thought that, all in all, Victoria was probably quite right about enough excitement.

The next week passed slowly as Michael waited for his wound to heal. He watched Lloyd put the new horse through its paces. "He moves reyt well." Bradley observed as he stood with Michael. "Happen as he'll do very nicely, sir."

"You and Lloyd have been over him, and you found no problems?" Michael asked.

"Nothing as we could find, sir. We reckon he's about eight year old. He's a handy size and sharp, but, as you can see, he's willing enough."

"Sharp?" Michael laughed. "He certainly came after me and Johnny quick enough. Almost too quick."

"Aye, sir." Bradley and Michael watched as Lloyd put the horse into a nice collected canter. Then Bradley went on. "The Corporal and I were thinking, sir."

"Oh, yes?"

"Yes, sir, well, it's Hall's Billy, sir. He struggles on a long hard day. We thought that, if you gets on with this new un, sir, then Hall might ride Thor, sir. He has ridden him and gets on well wi'im."

"That's a good idea, and at least Thor is a black, like most remounts, wouldn't be quite so obvious as a chestnut." He thought for a moment. "Let's see how I take to him," nodding at the chestnut, "and if it works Hall can ride Thor until we rejoin the army. He will have to go back on Billy then, most of the time, at least."

After the first night following his wounding, Michael joined Victoria in her bed every night. Somehow, given the circumstances under which their affair had begun, it seemed to be completely natural, acceptable, and went unremarked on. That it did continue was probably due to a conversation Michael and Victoria had late one night. They were lying close together.

"Miguel?"

"Yes?"

"What will you do if you give me a child?"

"What!?" Michael was startled. "Well, err, I..." he stammered.

She laughed at his reaction. "Now, Miguel, calm yourself, I have no intention of getting with child, there are, err, well, never mind, but it is a possibility."

"I, err, I err, I..." It was, he realised, a very fair question. He also realised that he felt strongly enough about Victoria to be entirely truthful in his response. "If that should happen I would marry you."

She kissed him lightly. "Thank you, Miguel."

At the end of May a bundle of dispatches, official documents, reached Sanchez from Wellington's headquarters. Among them was a note of recent changes in personnel, including in the Sixteenth. Sanchez showed the document to Michael. Archer had retired. Pelly replaced him as Lieutenant Colonel and would, presumably, be coming out from England to take command. Lygon stepped up to replace him as a Major. Buchanan got the captaincy vacant due to Lygon's promotion. Michael felt both sadden and relieved by Archer's retirement. He was still a fairly young man, but his health would not allow him an active service career. Michael wished him well.

Sanchez also took the opportunity to invite Michael to ride with him on another visit to the road to Madrid.

The weather was fair, the night out not so cold. Michael was accompanied by Lloyd and Hall. Lloyd was, as usual, riding Rodrigo, Hall was on Thor and Michael was taking out the chestnut for the first time. Fraile had assured him the horse was used to this sort of work, he had carried Rubio with the lancers since he had joined a year ago, but Michael was keen to find out for himself what he was like.

They settled down to watch a different part of the road, where it snaked between hills through a dense woodland. Sanchez had ridden out with a hundred men, half of whom he sent out to scour the countryside and by-ways. They stayed quiet when a battalion of infantry marched along from the direction of Madrid. Later the same day, however, one of the patrols came in with a captive. They had come across the man, on foot, making his way through the woods and trying to stay hidden as much as possible. It had done him no good. Brought before Sanchez he protested that he was creeping along because he was scared of the French and that he was a true patriot. When Sanchez asked him what he was doing and where he was going he claimed to be going to Salamanca where he had a sister who was getting married in a few days time. He had come, he said, from a small village two days walk towards Madrid.

Sanchez listened to all this carefully, nodding encouragingly. Then he ordered, "Search him."

Michael had seen this before and wasn't surprised when the man ended up naked, his clothes being minutely examined. They found the dispatches on tiny pieces of thin paper sewn into the collar of his jacket. Sanchez handed them to Michael to examine. They were all in code and Michael recognised the simpler cipher.

He handed them back to Sanchez. "Yes, these are French, the sooner they get to Wellington the better."

"Excellent." Sanchez turned to one of his sergeants standing nearby. "Choose four men, get these to Wellington as fast as you can, take fresh horses from the village, don't stop."

The Sergeant saluted, took the dispatches and strode off calling the names of the men he chose. Sanchez, gesticulated vaguely at the naked man. "This one we will hang by the road side as a warning."

The man dropped to his knees, hands clasped to his chest. "No, please, no. I am just a poor man. They said they would kill my family if I didn't carry these papers. I don't even know what they are. Please, spare me!"

Sanchez looked down to the road. "There is a tall chestnut tree there," he pointed, "hang him from that, then we will move a little closer to Madrid."

In the middle of the following morning the day was beginning to warm up. Michael lay under a tree, eyes closed, listening to the hum of the occasional insect and the quiet chatter of the lancers. They were a hundred yards or so into a wood overlooking the road that lay at the bottom of a long slope. Sanchez had pickets out in both directions and would get ample warning of anything coming along from either direction. The horses were all saddled and bridled, standing quietly, tails swishing, some cropping a little grass. It was peaceful.

Michael became aware of approaching hoof beats, a horse coming fast. He propped himself up on his elbows to watch one of the pickets arrive. The lancer spoke excitedly to Sanchez who listened carefully, nodded and waved to his men to mount. Michael mounted up and walked his horse across to Sanchez who grinned at him, not a nice grin, but one full of malice.

"Captain Roberts, there is a small party of French cavalry, dragoons, coming from the direction of Salamanca. They will be here shortly, only a dozen or so, well, they will get no further." He wheeled his horse away to give more instructions.

Lloyd and Hall rode up. "Let's go and have a look," said Michael. He hadn't liked the look on Sanchez's face, he remembered the time they had attacked a convoy near Ciudad Rodrigo. He hadn't liked it, but he had accepted it. He could accept Spanish traitors getting summary justice, God knew, he had meted out enough of that himself. But this was different, these were soldiers, like himself, like Lloyd, like Hall.

They reached the edge of the wood, hidden in the shadows. A little down the road the French dragoons were just coming into sight. He guessed Sanchez would wait until they were opposite this spot and then his men would swoop from in front and behind. Fifty lancers would make short work of a dozen dragoons. For some reason he thought of Renard in Madrid, Renard who wanted to kill him, who Michael wanted to kill. An idea came to him, a madcap idea.

He put spurs to the chestnut and started out of the trees and down the slope. "Follow me!" he shouted.

Behind him he heard shouts from the Spanish pickets. He pushed the horse into a flat gallop, straight towards the dragoons. From his sleeve he pulled a handkerchief and began to wave it madly above his head. He had no idea if Lloyd and Hall were following him, if not it was too late to worry. Ahead of him the French had halted, then they formed a line across the road, drawing their long, straight swords as they did so. A young officer sat just in front of them and Michael hauled his horse to a standstill a few yards in front of him, gratified to see Lloyd and Hall pull up next to him, relieved that they hadn't drawn their sabres.

Breathing heavily, Michael called out to the officer. "Monsieur, you are about to be attacked by a hundred Spanish lancers and they do not take prisoners. Surrender to me, now, and I will protect you."

The young officer looked around in confusion, to his right a veteran sergeant looked around and saw Sanchez's lancers issuing from the wood. He shouted, the officer looked, he saw lancers in front, saw lancers behind. He shouted back to Michael, "Monsieur, do you give me your word of honour?"

"Monsieur, I swear I shall do all I can to protect you and your men."

The officer looked at the approaching lancers, Sanchez leading them, he looked at his sergeant who nodded. Then he slipped the sword knot off his wrist, reversed his sabre and offered it to Michael, shouting to his men to sheath theirs. Michael rode forward and took it.

"Thank you, Monsieur." Turning he shouted, "Lloyd, Hall get around the back, stop those lancers." He turned to face the oncoming Sanchez.

Sanchez halted his men some twenty five yards away and advanced alone towards Michael. "What the Hell do you think you are doing Captain Roberts?"

"Taking the surrender of these men, they are my prisoners and under my protection."

"What, are you mad, have you been out in the sun for too long? These are French soldiers, Captain, I do not take French prisoners!"

"No, Don Julian, but I do, and as my prisoners they are under the protection of the British army and the Earl of Wellington."

Don Julian turned puce with rage and for a moment Michael thought he might order his lancers to attack.

"Damn you, Captain, I shall see you, you... I shall speak to Wellington myself!" He took a breath. "Very well, Captain, but they are your entire responsibility, any attempt by any of them to escape and I will have them all killed, do you understand me?"

"Completely, Don Julian." Michael turned his horse to the young officer. "Tell me, quickly, what are doing here?"

"I am carrying dispatches from Marmont to Jourdan."

"Then give them to me, now." The officer hesitated for a moment. "Now, quickly, before Don Julian changes his mind."

The officer put his hand in his coat and pulled out a small package, handing it to Michael.

"Thank you," said Michael. He turned and threw them to Sanchez. "Dispatches, and just what Wellington wants."

Sanchez grunted and ordered his men to return to the wood. Michael heaved a sigh of relief. Now for the second part of his idea.

"Monsieur, what is your name?"

"Lieutenant Lapointe, Fifteenth Dragoons."

"I am Captain Roberts. I want you to make sure that you remember my name." Lapointe looked puzzled. "I assume you are a man of honour?"

"Captain, you do not need to ask, my family has..."

"Very good!" Michael interrupted. "Then will you give me your parole that you will not engage against British, Portuguese or Spanish troops until you have been exchanged?"

"What?" Lapointe exclaimed in surprise.

"Now listen." Michael started to explain. "I am an officer on the staff of the Earl of Wellington. Give me your word and I will write a note saying as much and giving you free passage to Madrid. Hopefully you won't need it if you stay on the main road. I shall be with Don Julian and there are no other forces out here. When you get to Madrid there's a man I want you to find and give a message for me." Lapointe nodded. "Do I have your word, your parole?" asked Michael.

"You have my solemn word, Monsieur."

"Thank you. The man in Madrid is called Renard, he is the head of French intelligence services in Spain." Lapointe looked completely surprised and thoroughly confused. "All I ask is that you go to him, use my name, you will have no difficulty getting an interview." Lapointe nodded again. "Then, when you see him, tell him that I am going to kill him."

Lapointe's confusion was now complete. Michael let that all sink in while he opened his sabretache and took out his notebook and pencil. Resting the sabretache on the front of his saddle as a desk, he wrote a carefully worded pass, improvised, but making use of Wellington's name and clearly signed by himself.

"Here you are, my name, rank and regiment are on it, in case you forget." He smiled encouragingly. "Now, I'll give you a few minutes to explain to your Sergeant. Tell him I will make sure he and all your men are well treated. I have a man I trust that I can send along with an escort to the British army."

In a very short time everything was settled. Michael thought it best to see the Lieutenant on his way himself and they rode a little way down the road to Madrid. As they went Michael pointed out the lancers shadowing them to the Sergeant, who acknowledged the fact with a grim faced nod.

A mile or two on the little band halted and Michael bid farewell and good luck to Lapointe who, with a nervous glance at the lancers set off at a trot. The Sergeant rode up next to him.

"What now, Monsieur?"

Michael gave him what he hoped was an encouraging smile. "Now, Sergeant, we get you safely into the arms of the British army."

In the end it was all easier than Michael had expected. Sanchez soon calmed down and even expressed admiration for Michael's brass faced nerve. The entire force returned to their little village, an escort to Fuenteguinaldo was arranged and Sanchez agreed to Michael's request that it be commanded by Fraile and that Lloyd should go along as well. Until the dragoons and their escort left Michael made sure that he, Lloyd and Hall were around where they were being kept. Then he had to promise Sanchez that their horses would be brought back once they had been delivered. Sanchez made a comment about Michael capturing his own herd and that was the moment that he began to feel confident it was all going to work out.

Michael wrote a lengthy report for Wellington, which he entrusted to Lloyd. Fraile assured him that he would see the French safely delivered. And then they were gone.

Michael returned to his billet and went to check on the horses before anything else. Bradley was, as always, in the stables.

"Hello, sir. Hast tha thought of a name for t' chestnut, sir?

"No. Yes, we will just call him Castano."

"What's that, sir?"

"Spanish for chestnut. It's what we've been calling him, so we might as well carry on."

Hall was grooming Billy and spoke up from behind the horse, "You mean like the Spanish General, sir, Castanos?"

"What? Oh, well perhaps not that then. But the Portuguese Castanha is different enough, we can use that."

Chuckles came from all three men and then Michael bid them goodnight.

Inside, Victoria was waiting and they dined together before retiring for the night. Of course, she wanted to hear all about what had happened. The story had swept around the village as soon as the lancers had returned. What no one knew was why Michael had sent the French officer on his way. Victoria wanted to know.

He tried to be vague, but she pressed him. In the end he told her, "There's a man in Madrid, a Frenchman, I wanted to get a message to him."

"A Frenchman? What message could you want to send a Frenchman?" She thought for a moment and remembered something Sanchez had told her. "Is this something to do with the secret matters you are involved with for Wellington?"

"What? Who told you about that?"

"Don Julian. So, is it?"

"Yes, but, please, don't ask more about it."

"Of course not, a bit of mystery about a man can be quite appealing." She laughed and kissed him.

Lloyd and Fraile were gone five days. When they returned Lloyd reported to Michael. "Duw, that was a hard ride, sir, but, sir, the Prime Minister's been killed, sir, shot down in Westminster!"

"What! Damn that's bad"

"Aye, sir, all the talk at headquarters was about who would be the new Prime Minister and how that might affect the war here, sir."

"Is it known who did it? Was it a French agent?"

"No, sir, by all accounts it was some merchant who was ruined and blamed the government. They hanged him."

"Oh, I see." Michael paused for a moment. "And how about everything else?"

"It all passed off alright, sir. I think the Frenchies were quite pleased to get properly fed, sir. I gave Lord Wellington the report, personally, and he thanked me! Seemed quite pleased the French were taken and not just cut down. And then we just came back, sir. Brought the horses back as well, Lieutenant Fraile was relieved about that. And I just saw Bradley as I came in, told me about Castanha. I like that, sir."

"Thank you, Lloyd, you've done well. Castanha did well these last few days, tough and sharp, just what I like, and it will give us another horse to help keep us all in the saddle, particularly Hall. Having so many seems a bit much sometimes, but it would only need one or two to go lame on these mountain tracks and it would a different story."

"Yes, sir, Rodrigo's a little knocked up as it is, but a day or two's rest should see him right again, sir."

"Then let's hope we get that."

"Err, there is one thing, sir." Lloyd spoke hesitantly.

"Oh? What's that?"

"Lord Wellington did ask about what happened to any couriers Don Julian took. I, err, had to tell him they were all hanged, sir. I don't think he liked it, but he didn't say anything, sir."

"Thank you, but I don't see how Don Julian could do otherwise."

"No, sir."

Later, sitting alone in the drawing room before dinner, Michael thought about the couriers, summarily hanged as traitors. He recalled a story he had heard. During the siege of Badajoz, a Spaniard carrying a message from the besieged Governor to Marshal Soult in Seville, had ridden into the British camp and offered to sell the message for the same amount he was being paid to carry it. Instead of adopting Sanchez's approach, Wellington had paid him! The message was handed over, copied and the man sent on his way with the promise of further pay if he delivered any more messages he was given to carry. He wondered if he might try the same approach at some time. Then Victoria came in and they went together to dine.

Michael's wound was almost completely healed and causing him no difficulties when orders came in from Fuenteguinaldo. Wellington had started the long awaited advance towards Salamanca and he wanted Sanchez to join him and operate around Salamanca, an area Sanchez and his men knew very well.

When he heard the news from Sanchez he walked back to Victoria's house to set his people to packing and to break the news to Victoria. He found her in the kitchen talking to Señora Noriega and asked her to come into the drawing room with him. Looking slightly puzzled, she did so.

Michael closed the door and said, "Victoria, I'm sorry, but we are leaving tomorrow."

It took a moment for his words to sink in, then Victoria came to him and he held her close. After a moment she looked up at him, her face tear streaked. "We knew this would happen, Miguel. Where are you going?"

"It seems Wellington is advancing on Salamanca."

"Oh!" Her face lightened at that. "Then perhaps I will be able to go to my farm?"

"Yes, you might, if Wellington takes Salamanca and beats Marmont's army. It would be safe for you again."

She forced a little smile. "That is good, Miguel, and, perhaps, I shall come to Salamanca and see you there?"

"That would be very good, if it's possible." He smiled at her and kissed her. "Otherwise I shall miss you very much."

"And I you. And Silvia your Señor Bradley."

"What?"

Victoria laughed at him. "Oh, Miguel, you did not know? Then you must be the only person in the house who doesn't." She became serious again. "When do you leave?"

"At first light tomorrow."

"Then we must make tonight special in case we never see each other again."

.   .   .

In Madrid, Renard was at his desk when there was a nervous tap at his door.

"Come in, come in," he snapped. Faucher appeared. "What is it? Come on, man, don't dither."

"I, err, beg your pardon, Monsieur, but we have heard from the man who went to Lisbon to look for Loiro."

"Yes?"

"He could find no trace of him, Monsieur, none at all."

"Merde!" Renard tapped his fingers on his desk for a moment. He was irritated, but not surprised by the news. "The business of the British officer, Roberts. Have you found anyone to send after him yet?"

"Err..."

"Faucher, you've had six weeks, can you do it or do I need to send you to a new posting, up north, perhaps?"

"No, no, sir. I think I might have found a man, sir , I am expecting to speak to him again in a day or two, sir."

"Think, Faucher, think?" Renard was suddenly screaming. "I don't want you to think, you useless lump of excrement! I want Roberts dead, do you understand? Dead! Find someone before I send you! Now, get out!"

Chapter 13

It was a long day's ride to Salamanca. Michael was riding with Sanchez at the head of the long column, nearly a thousand lancers, followed by another thousand or so infantry and the two guns. First they stuck west, fording the Tormes where they had crossed before the attack on the French infantry. Then they turned north, directly for Salamanca, riding easily across the gently undulating countryside. Towards the end of the afternoon the advance guard reported they had run into pickets of the Eleventh Light Dragoons. Michael could well imagine the nervousness of the pickets when they saw the column approaching. Sanchez thought likewise.

"Captain Roberts, would you be so kind as to go forward and speak to the English pickets? I would hate there to be any misunderstanding."

Michael cantered forward and a mile ahead found the lancer's advance guard halted and looking across a low valley at a troop of the Eleventh formed opposite them, some half a mile away. With a wave to the lancer's officer, he cantered on and rode up to the light dragoons. Their officer greeted him.

"Captain Roberts, ain't it? Damn glad to see you, thought they might be French lancers."

Michael laughed. "No, it's Don Julian Sanchez and his little army. On our way to join Wellington at Salamanca. You might want to send a warning ahead, it's a fair size force."

Night was falling as Michael and Sanchez rode up to Wellington's headquarters in Salamanca. They were met by Colonel Lord Somerset.

"Good evening, Don Julian, Roberts. Lord Wellington will be with you shortly. He is just with our host, the Marquis Seralbo." He chuckled. "Must be attentive to the man who has made available this rather splendid palacio." In the distance a cannon roared. "Ah, that's the French garrison. They have fortified three convents, damn nuisance, stronger than we expected, means we can't use the bridge. Most of the army is north of the city on the high ground. There's just one division here to take the forts." An orderly appeared and nodded. "Ah, the Earl will see you now. This way, gentlemen."

He led them along a dark corridor and into what appeared, under normal circumstances to be a dining room. The table was covered with papers that Wellington was poring over by the light of a single candelabra. He looked up as they came in.

"Don Julian, glad to see you, Señor, and my congratulations on your work, the dispatches you have taken have proved most useful."

"Thank you, my Lord."

"Marmont and his army are away to the north of us, and what I would like, Don Julian, is for you to get around 'em, harry them, and the more dispatches you can take, the better. I am particularly anxious that a good watch be kept on the road to Madrid."

"Of course, my Lord."

"I am afraid that I must ask you to divide your force." He gave Sanchez a little smile. "You know how it is, but I should like you to leave your infantry to bolster de Espana's division, and one of your lancer regiments as well. I am sure you can do all that is required with just one of your regiments, Don Julian."

Sanchez gave a tight little smile. "I am sure I can, my Lord, and I understand how it is."

"If there's anything you need, you can ask De Lancey, he will have your written orders. I'd like you to leave as soon as possible tomorrow."

"Certainly, my Lord, a few hours to collect some rations and so on and we should be ready."

"And you, Captain Roberts."

"Yes, my Lord?"

"You are to stay with Don Julian for the moment."

"Yes, my Lord."

"However, I want you here an hour before dawn, there is some information for you from Scovell."

"Yes, my Lord."

Michael and Sanchez left together and the Spaniard advised Michael, "We should be ready two hours after dawn." Then he gave a little chuckle. "Looking after two thousand men is a little harder than what I had in Ciudad Rodrigo. Everything takes longer. It will be a pleasure to leave someone else to do that and ride with just my best men."

Michael was surprised to find Tomkinson at Cotton's headquarters and greeted him, "Hello, what are you doing here?"

Tomkinson grinned as they shook hands, "Got my captaincy in the Regiment and I've arranged to exchange with Lord Clinton, but the confirmation has yet to arrive and until it does I am acting as an extra ADC for Sir Stapleton."

"Congratulations!"

"But no troop for you, eh? I gather you are a sort of special ADC? Gallivantin' all over with Don Julian?"

"Yes, well, it's interesting."

Tomkinson looked at him. "Hmm, well, it seems to suit you more than Regimental duties. Can't say it would appeal to me."

A good hour before dawn Michael left Lloyd, Hall and Bradley getting everything ready for their departure and took the short walk to Wellington's headquarters. He was taken to the same dining room, and was surprised to find, in addition to Wellington and Scovell, a priest.

Wellington turned as he entered. "Ah, Roberts, there you are. Scovell has something you should know about."

Michael wondered what it was all about and Scovell informed him succinctly. "It's about the batch of dispatches that was brought in last. One of them concerns you."

"Me!"

"Yes, it was from Madrid, from Renard." He paused as Michael looked shocked.

"What did it say?"

"It was a request for information on your whereabouts. It suggested," Scovell gave a little apologetic cough, "that the request had the authority of Napoleon himself behind it."

"What!"

"Err, yes, I am afraid so. The, err, request suggested that you are a particularly dangerous enemy of France."

Wellington had remained silent, watching Michael, now he spoke. "Thank you, Scovell. I think you can leave us now."

With a relieved, "Yes, my Lord," Scovell slipped out.

"I think," Wellington began, "That this rather reinforces the advice given by Mister Musgrave."

"My Lord." Michael was startled by Wellington's frankness and threw a glance in the direction of the priest who sat, silent in a dark corner of the candlelit room.

Wellington's response was another surprise. "Do not concern yourself, Captain. But now I want to know about the courier who was carrying those dispatches. I would have you understand that I approve of your actions in getting those men to surrender, but I also understand that you let the courier, an officer, go. Why?"

"I did get his parole, my Lord."

Wellington's voice took on an irritated tone. "Yes, Roberts, I don't doubt that you did, but, for God's sake, why?"

"I wanted to send a message, my Lord."

"Yes?"

"To, err, to Renard, my Lord. I asked the officer to take it for me."

"And what was the nature of this message?"

"I asked him to tell Renard that I was going to kill him."

"Now why did you do that?"

"I am not sure, my Lord. It seemed to me that we have spent a lot of time worrying about him and what he is doing and that it was about time that he had something to worry about. I am sorry, my Lord, if that was wrong."

To Michael's surprise the priest began to chuckle, and then, in a broad Irish accent, said "Oh, now, that is priceless my Lord, priceless."

Wellington grunted, "Yes, well, I suppose it does no harm, might get the man looking over his shoulder a bit, distract him, eh?"

"We can but hope so, my Lord," the priest replied.

"I think an introduction is order," Wellington addressed Michael. "This is Father Curtis, of the Irish College here in Salamanca, and a supplier of a considerable amount of intelligence on the French. Something that you'll be good enough to keep to yourself."

Curtis spoke, "Although I am a man of God, I must confess," he crossed himself, "that it would give me great pleasure to hear of the demise of Monsieur Renard, God forgive me. He has caused me a lot of trouble in the short time he has been in Madrid. Little more than a month and I have lost contact with a number of correspondents and I know at least two of them are dead. All thanks to this Renard. I have learnt, however, that he holds you personally responsible for French intelligence failures in Portugal. He wants you dead, Captain."

"There we have it, Roberts. Renard is after your head, and you his." Wellington shook his. "However, until you have the opportunity to disappoint him, the best thing you can do is continue to annoy him. Make the dispatches a priority, Captain Roberts, a priority."

"Yes, my Lord. My Lord, if I may?"

"Yes, what is it?"

"My Lord, since I took the parole of that officer, I have been thinking about the civilian couriers we might take."

"Yes?"

"I understand that at Ciudad Rodrigo there was one who came to you, was paid, his dispatch copied, and the man sent on his way, with the promise of further reward for further dispatches?"

"Yes, what of it?"

"Don Julian summarily hangs the ones he catches, my Lord, but it occurs to me that it may be possible to persuade these couriers to serve us."

Wellington asked "And how do you propose to do that? We never heard again from the courier at Rodrigo. If you copy the dispatches and send them on their way there is nothing preventing these couriers just delivering their messages and simply carrying on in French service."

"I do not propose to copy the messages, my Lord, but to seize them and send the courier on their way without them, but with an offer of rewards if they provide us with any information in the future. I believe that they will not be prepared to trust to French mercy by revealing what happened. They will simply not arrive and disappear, like many couriers. Their only hope of further reward would be to work for us."

Wellington looked thoughtful. "What do you think of that idea, Father?"

Curtis thought for a moment. "I don't see that it can do any harm, my Lord. It has possibilities."

"I suppose it has," mused Wellington." But payment only by results, d'ye understand, Roberts? We've little enough hard cash as it is."

"Yes, my Lord, thank you." Michael chose not remind the Earl of the money he had from the paymaster.

The day was beginning to get hot when Michael, again on Johnny and with Lloyd on Rodrigo, joined Sanchez. Michael rode beside him as he led his lancers out of Salamanca, along the north bank of the Tormes until they forded the river at Santa Marta and headed east, away from the city and the army. Hall was back with Bradley and the baggage, Hall leading the two baggage ponies and Bradley leading Michael's three extra horses. The Tormes looped around to the south and they crossed again, heading steadily east. The landscape was open and rolling, interspersed with occasional stretches of woodland.

Sanchez explained to Michael where they were going. "With Wellington in Salamanca, the road most likely to be used by any courier going to Madrid passes through Arevalo. We will watch the country any courier must cross to get to that road. We will establish ourselves in a little village on a ridge that runs more or less north south across the path of any courier, it's about fourteen leagues. We will send out patrols and there is a church tower from which you can see many leagues. Of course, any troop movements will go the same way, so we will need to be watchful."

Sanchez seemed to be in a cheerful mood as the column of lancers walked steadily on across the plains of Castille. He looked like a man at ease with himself and the world. He was even singing quietly to himself. Michael decided to strike up a conversation and see if he could take advantage of Sanchez's cheerfulness.

"It's different from summer in England, Don Julian."

Sanchez glanced at him. "I can believe that. A cold and very wet country by all accounts."

Michael laughed. "Not always, but not as hot as it gets on these plains in mid summer."

Don Julian shrugged. "We are used to it, Captain."

"And we do have some excellent horse fairs." Michael hoped that would catch Sanchez's interest, it did.

"Is that so? How big?"

"I went to one where over fifteen thousand horses were traded in two weeks. It's where I got my bay horse."

"Ah, he is a fine animal, but I see you still favour your black." He gave a little wave at Johnny.

"Yes, I do. I would rather ride him in a fight than any other. If you remember I was on him when I fought Rubio."

"Hmm. That was unfortunate event. How is your back?"

"It is quite healed, and, as you say, it was unfortunate." He paused. "But then it is always unfortunate when a man dies unnecessarily."

Sanchez grunted noncommittally. "Do you have someone on your mind?"

"Yes, I do,"

"Who?"

"I don't know." Sanchez looked askance at him and Michael went on. "I had an interesting conversation with Lord Wellington this morning."

"About an unnecessary death?"

"Yes."

"Very well, Captain, just tell me what it is you are dancing around so delicately."

Michael drew a deep breath. "It's about any couriers that you might capture."

"Ha! Traitors, they deserve to be hanged. I do not consider their deaths unnecessary, they serve as a warning."

"Yes, indeed, Don Julian, but what if they could be turned against the French, used to our advantage?"

Sanchez was silent for a few yards as they walked on. "And just how would you do that and what might it achieve?"

"Do you remember when we first met, when Sir Stapleton visited you?"

"Yes, what has that to do with this?"

"We talked of personal reasons for fighting the French, the loss of our families because of them."

Sanchez's face hardened. "Yes, I remember."

"A little while ago, in Lisbon, my babá, my niñera, who was a second mother to me, was murdered."

"I am sorry to hear that Captain."

"Thank you, but, you see, she was murdered by an agent of the French trying to kill me."

"What?"

"The man is now dead, but the man who sent him is in Madrid, a Frenchman. And I want to kill him."

"Of course, I understand this."

"But I shall need help, and I would like to have an agent of my own in Madrid."

Understanding flooded Sanchez's face. "Just how do you expect to manage that?"

"I put the idea to Lord Wellington that it might be possible to persuade one of the Spanish couriers for the French to work for us. He thought it was worth trying."

"Did he now? And just how would you persuade such a man?"

"First, Don Julian, you say you are going to hang him. I intercede and offer him his life and freedom, with the offer of future reward if he works for us. We will have taken anything he carries, and if he goes to the French they will not believe him, they will probably hang him for us. It is well known that couriers who are caught are not released and sent on their way. He might just disappear, then again he might be useful."

Sanchez stroked his chin. "That is truly devious, Captain." There was a silence. "And you say Lord Wellington approved?"

"He did."

"Then I shall give you one man, Captain, one man of your choice, the rest can hang." He looked thoughtful for a moment. "I shall ask my men to try to bring in anyone alive, but if they make a fight of it, I promise nothing."

In the early afternoon a long low ridge started to rise out of the plain. Sanchez began to send off detachments of a dozen lancers each to take positions along its length. A couple of hours later they arrived at the ridge top village and Sanchez sent out further detachments to the north. Then they settled down to wait.

On the first day, Michael amused himself for an hour or two by taking himself up to the top of the church tower and scanning the rolling landscape through his telescope. He could see some of the patrols Sanchez had sent out across the countryside towards Salamanca. He watched as they disappeared over gentle hills, distorted by the heat haze. Eventually it became almost unbearably hot and he sought refuge in the house he was sharing with Sanchez and his senior officers. Stretching out on his bed he tried to sleep. As the day finally began to cool, fresh patrols were sent out to relieve those watching along the ridge. Michael roused himself and wandered out of the billet. The horses were stabled under open sided sheds, allowing in what breeze there was. Bradley, as ever, was with them. Tails flicked at flies and the horses chomped happily at the fodder made available by the local people. So far this and the neighbouring settlements had not been occupied by the French and life had continued almost normally.

Michael found Lloyd and Hall sitting under a wide spreading tree with half a dozen lancers, Hall endeavouring to the amusement of all, including himself, to improve his Spanish. This regiment, of the two Sanchez now had, contained many of the men who had taken part in the break out from Ciudad Rodrigo, and they accepted Lloyd for his part in that. Hall was with him and that was enough for them. He watched for a while from a distance and then became aware that some one had come to stand beside him, he looked and saw Fraile.

"Hello, Captain." He nodded to the group under the tree. "It makes you wonder why men cannot get along better, eh?"

Michael nodded his agreement, then asked, "What do your men think about me killing Rubio?"

"It is forgotten, Señor. It was a fair fight, he was a good man with a lance, but not so good in other ways. He is not missed."

Michael nodded, appreciatively.

"They also admire you for your success with Señora Martinez where so many others failed."

"My what?" Michael exclaimed.

Fraile chuckled. "Come, Señor, it is no secret. She is an attractive woman. If I was not married..." He chuckled again, "I am sure I would have failed like the rest."

Late in the afternoon a patrol came in from the north west, riding hard. Their NCO reported to Sanchez who listened carefully to what the man was saying and then assembled his officers, Michael with them.

"There is a body of French chasseurs, a small troop, fifty, perhaps sixty, about four leagues away. They appear to be looking for forage and cattle. They have a few poor beasts with them already. They are coming along the road towards us, but making slow progress because of the cattle. There is no great rush, we will ambush them tomorrow as they march." He turned to address Michael. "I have an idea that you might be able to help us, Captain," and he gave an evil smile, "after all, we don't want any to escape."

Dawn found Michael lying under a scrubby tree, tarleton on the ground next to him, his eyes closed, listening to the sound of crickets and the occasional stamp of a hoof or clink of saddlery from the horses. The tree was almost at the top of a ridge, from which could be seen miles of rolling plains, covered with grass waving gently in the light breeze, looking like a golden sea, rippling in the heat of a Spanish summer.

'Dust, sir'. The words came from Lloyd, where he lay at the top of the slope, watching the landscape for any signs of movement.

With a groan, Michael rolled over and crawled up next to Lloyd and squinted in the direction indicated.

Several miles away a small cloud of dust rose from the road they were watching. He extended his telescope, covering the lens from the sun to avoid any tell-tale reflection, and focussed on the slowly moving cloud.

"Yes, that's them. Let's go." He and Lloyd wriggled back below the crest of the ridge, put on their Tarletons and strode down to where the Hall was waiting with the horses, Johnny, Rodrigo and Thor for Hall. The three men mounted quickly.

"Right, now, casually, until they see us, and then run for it, but not too fast." He grimaced. "I just hope Don Julian is ready."

With Michael in the middle, they walked their horse slowly up the slope and over the crest, towards the oncoming French.

"They've got flankers out, sir," Hall said.

"Well spotted, Hall."

"Eyes like a bloody hawk, he has," muttered Lloyd.

They walked slowly on, and then they were seen. Two pairs of flanking riders started towards them, cantering their horses across the rolling grass. Half a dozen more suddenly came forward for the main body.

"Right, that's got their attention. Threes about, canter march!"

The three men put their horses into a steady canter, one that could eat up the miles. Half a mile on, Michael looked back. To his satisfaction he saw that the flankers had joined the others from the main body and the whole group was coming on after them, fast.

They kept up the pace. Two hundred yards off to the side of the road was a large wood, where Sanchez was supposed to be with the bulk of his men. There was no sign of them. Michael hoped, fervently, that that was a good thing. Another half mile ahead the road climbed a gentle slope to disappear over yet another ridge.

Michael took another look behind. The group of chasseurs had spread out a little, but the closest were now only a couple of hundred yards behind. As he looked he saw a puff of white smoke followed a moment later by the sound of the shot. He looked at Lloyd and Hall cantering along easily beside him.

"Well, that's a waste of powder and shot." He looked up the road ahead. "Another hundred yards and we will give them their heads."

The hundred yards was covered in seconds and Michael shouted, "Now, gallop!" He touched Johnny's sides and felt the horse surge ahead into a flat out gallop. Rodrigo and Thor stayed with him and they thundered up the road to the crest of the ridge and over. Two hundred yards beyond the crest a hundred lancers were waiting. As they galloped on, the line of lancers started to move forward, towards the crest.

"Halt, threes about!" Michael bellowed.

They pulled up the panting, sweating horses and faced about the way they had come. They were just in time to see the chasseurs breast the ridge and then desperately pull up their horses and turn about.

"Walk, march!" ordered Michael.

The lancers swept past them, now cantering steadily up the slope and over. By the time the three dragoons reached the crest after them it was pretty much all over. The main body of the troop of chasseurs had hastened after their comrades and as they passed the wood, the lancers had charged them. There were no prisoners.

Hall swore at the sight. "Yes, lad," Lloyd observed, "it's not pretty, but then you haven't seen what the French do, yet." Hall started to say something. "No, don't ask me, not now," Lloyd said.

Early evening found everyone back in the little village, the patrols being relieved as before. Then came what Michael had been hoping for. Three lancers from one of the northernmost patrols that had not been involved in the fight, rode in leading a man on a mule, his hands bound behind him, his stirrups crossed in front of him to prevent any attempt at escape. The man was led up to where Sanchez was waiting, alerted to the arrival by his sentries. The sergeant with the small group pushed the man hard and he fell to the ground, lying winded.

"We found these on him, Don Julian."

The Sergeant offered some miniscule scraps of paper, which Don Julian took and passed to Michael. He looked quickly over them. They were definitely French dispatches, part ciphered, some not. One appeared to be from the French commander, Marshal Marmont, addressed to Marshal Jourdan in Madrid. He looked at the man who had struggled to a sitting position, blood pouring from a cut on his face. He was cursing the Sergeant. Michael caught Sanchez's eye and nodded.

Sanchez walked over to the man and with his foot pushed him onto his back. "So, what are you doing with French dispatches?"

The man tried to struggle up again. "Taking them to Madrid, what the Hell do you think?"

"You don't deny it?"

"That would be a bit bloody pointless, wouldn't it?"

This was not the expected response. Sanchez looked at Michael and raised his eyebrows in question. Michael gave a little shrug and a brief nod. Sanchez looked down on the man.

"What is your name?"

"What's it to you, General?"

"You know who I am?"

"Don Julian Sanchez I suppose. What is it they call you? El Charro! Bah!"

Michal winced as Sanchez's response to the use of his nickname, meaning horseman, or cattle herder, was to kick the man in his side.

"How much were you paid?" Sanchez demanded.

"Not bloody enough!" The man coughed, spat blood and struggled back to a sitting position. Then he noticed Michael. "Hey, who the hell are you? Are you English? Are you going to let this, this charro treat me like this?" He grinned, "It's not much fun, you know?"

Sanchez shouted to his men standing around. "Get a rope, he can hang from that tree."

A couple of men ran off and for a moment the man's face fell. Then he seemed to brace himself up. "At least give me a drink of something? A nice red wine, perhaps?"

Michael decided it was time to intervene.

"Don Julian, would you be so good as to permit to talk to this man before you hang him? He might have some useful information."

Sanchez looked at the man as if he would like to cut his throat, then he turned his back on him. Facing Michael he winked, and said, "You can have him until dawn, it's getting too dark for a decent hanging, and I suppose we should find a priest as well." He walked past Michael into his billet, and as he passed he said, very quietly, "Good luck," With Sanchez's departure his men started to drift away.

Michael said, "Hall, secure that mule. Put it with our horses."

The sergeant handed the reins to Hall and rode away with his men, leaving Hall to lead the mule away. Michael and the man stared at each other.

"Lloyd?"

"Yes, sir?"

"I think we should just take this traitor to a quiet spot and cut his throat." Michael watched carefully, but there was not the slightest flicker of understanding.

"Right you are, sir." Lloyd's face was expressionless.

"It seems he doesn't speak English. So, lets take him somewhere quiet where we can have a little talk to him."

"Behind the stables, sir? There's a dung heap, but a bit of open ground that's not overlooked."

"That sounds ideal. Bring him along." Michael watched as Lloyd hauled the man to his feet and then he said to him, "We are going to have a little talk, behave and it might just benefit you."

The man looked confused, but came along quietly enough. Hall was at the stables, about to strip the saddle and bridle off the mule.

"Leave that for the moment, Hall. Go and get two chairs, a bottle of wine and a couple of glasses." Hall bustled off. "Lloyd, cut him free."

Lloyd produced his knife and the man gulped as he opened it and locked the blade. Lloyd stepped behind him and sliced through the ropes. He looked at Michael, confused, but grateful, a little hopeful.

"Thank you, Señor." He rubbed his wrists as he spoke. Looking around the secluded area he relaxed a little, particularly when Lloyd put his knife away. His confusion increased when Hall appeared with a bottle and two glasses, followed by one of Sanchez's servants with two chairs. Michael pointed where he wanted the chairs and the man hurried off as soon as he put them down.

"Señor, please, sit down." Michael took a seat on one, pointing to other. "Hall," he continued in English, "open that bottle and give our friend a glass, and one for me."

Nervously the man sat and accepted the offered glass. He didn't drink until Michael did, which made Michael smile, getting a little shrug of the shoulders in return.

"Now, Señor," Michael began, "Don Julian will undoubtedly hang you in the morning, unless you accept my offer."

"Your offer, Señor?"

"Yes. I want you to go on your way to Madrid, obviously without the dispatches you were carrying. I would urge you not to go empty handed to the French, I don't think they would believe your story and they will hang you if Don Julian doesn't."

The man pulled a face, and said "That is very true, Señor, but why should you do this?"

"Because I want a man in Madrid, someone to work for me."

"Señor?"

Michael didn't respond, instead he asked "Why were you carrying those dispatches?"

The man's shoulders sagged slightly. "Because I wanted to go home, Señor, I was in Valladolid, to visit my sister and her family. Then the French forbade travel. I heard they were looking for people to carry messages for them to Madrid, they would pay well, when the messages were delivered. In Madrid."

"What is your work in Madrid?" Michael asked.

"I was a clerk in a waggoner's business, Señor, but the French seized all the horses and the wagons. So I thought I might as well visit my sister. I should have stayed in Madrid."

"Without a job?"

"I manage Señor, I write letters for people, and read them letters they receive."

"Then you can go back to that, and do something for me at the same time."

"Señor?"

"There's a man in Madrid, a Frenchman, an important man called Renard. I want you to find out where he lives, where he goes, who he meets, everything that you can. When the British army comes to Madrid, you can find me and I will pay for what you tell me. I will pay generously if tell me what I want to know about Renard."

"The British army is coming to Madrid?"

"Sooner or later, Perhaps this year, perhaps next, it doesn't matter when. Look, what is your name?"

The man took a moment to reply. "Inigo Montero, Señor."

"And I am Captain Roberts of the Sixteenth Light Dragoons. A name I would advise you not to mention, it is not popular in certain parts of the French army."

The two men raised their glasses to each other in acknowledgement of the introductions.

"Look, Señor Montero, it's a simple proposal, if you don't accept it you will hang in the morning. Accept it and I will see you safely on your way. Of course, I realise you could just return to Madrid and forget all about this, but I don't think you will. I am prepared to believe that you will do this in return for your life. I think will honour our agreement, if we make one. What do you say, Inigo Montero?"

As he finished speaking he extended his hand to Montero who looked at it for the briefest of moments and then grasped it firmly and they shook hands on the agreement.

Michael turned to Lloyd and Hall who had been silent spectators. "Lloyd, Hall, take our friend and get yourselves some dinner. Then get the horses ready, we are going for a ride, I want to leave at midnight, it should be quiet by then."

Chapter 14

Michael found Sanchez at dinner, and joined him at his invitation.

"So, Captain," Sanchez asked, "do you have your man?"

"Yes, I do, Don Julian. We will leave at midnight and escort him to the Madrid road. Perhaps you could warn your pickets and have them let us pass unchallenged?"

Sanchez waved a knife vaguely, "Of course." He shook his head. "It is a strange thing to do, I hope it works for you." He drank. "He is certainly a man of spirit, it would have been a shame to hang him. Perhaps he will also turn out to be a man of honour and keep his side of your bargain."

The summer night was warm and the rolling plain was lit by a full moon that was occasionally obscured by clouds passing in a light breeze. They mounted without speaking and rode slowly out of the village to the east. They heard no one, saw no one. The lack of sentries seemed not to strike Montero as odd. Once clear of the village Michael told Hall to ride ahead and pick the way. He added, "And make sure there are none of Don Julian's pickets to get in the way." He let Hall get well ahead and then spoke quietly to Montero.

"I have no doubt that you will be glad to get back to Madrid?"

"I shall be very glad, Señor, if I do."

"We will do what we can, see you safely to the road and clear of Don Julian's Lancers."

"Thank you, Señor."

They rode on silently, the moon casting their shadows on the grassland.

Michael spoke first. "Let me tell you something of Monsieur Renard." He glanced sideways at Montero. "I think it is only fair to tell you that he is not only important, but extremely dangerous." Michael rode on, silently, waiting for a response.

"Señor?"

"Yes?"

"How is it that he is a dangerous man?"

"He is in charge of French secret agents in Spain and Portugal. He has been sent to Madrid by Napoleon personally. He hasn't been there long, but he has already had loyal Spaniards killed for helping us, the British. He has also tried to have me killed."

Montero started slightly at that and asked, "Why you Señor?"

"There are several reasons, Señor, but mostly because I have destroyed his spy networks in Lisbon. He considers me to be dangerous" Michael shrugged. "I seem to have a gift for tracking down traitors."

"Señor, I am not a traitor."

"You were carrying messages for the French."

"That is true, but all I wanted was to get back to Madrid, and this way is better." He gave a snort of amusement. "It's certainly better than hanging from that tree."

"Yes, but you had better stay away from the French, they will hang you for losing the messages. Fortunately the French in Madrid won't know who you are, it would be best to become just another courier who disappeared on the road to Madrid."

"Yes, Señor, I think I shall just slip quietly back and take up my old life again, saying nothing to anyone."

"And Renard?"

"Señor, you saved my life, I think I can do what you ask, but unless you come to Madrid I don't see how I can give you any information."

"As I said, one day the British army will arrive in Madrid, when that happens, find me."

"Yes, Señor, I give you my word."

"Thank you."

They rode on in silence through the night for several hours until they found Hall waiting for them at the top of a gentle rise. He pointed down the slope to where a lighter coloured line ran across the countryside. "There you are, sir, that's the road."

"Well done, Hall." Michael turned to Montero. "There you are, Señor, the road to Madrid"

Montero looked down the slope for a moment before he replied. "Thank you, Señor, I wasn't sure you meant what you said, but now I see that you did."

"And I hope, Señor, that you will be good to your word."

Montero looked at Michael, nodded, and started his mule off, down the slope. As Michael watched him go, Lloyd rode up alongside him.

"Begging your pardon, sir, but do you think this will work?"

"I don't know, but if we ever do get to Madrid we will find out. Hall, are you sure that is the road to Madrid?"

"Yes, sir, I asked those pickets, sir."

"What pickets?"

Hall pointed away to the left and Michael could just make out two horsemen sitting on a low rise.

Michael chuckled. "Well done, Hall, now, can you lead us back?"

"Yes, sir, Don Julian's pickets will be expecting us. I did have to ask a few to hide on the way out here, sir."

Michael laughed. "Well done, now, let's get back."

After a few hours sleep and some breakfast, Michael went to find Sanchez.

"Ah, Captain! Good morning, coffee? And do you think you have been successful with your new friend?"

"Good morning, Don Julian, yes, please, coffee would be welcome, as for Señor Montero we will only know if he is a friend if we get to Madrid."

"Then let us hope that we find out soon. I think you had better take the dispatches to Wellington, then you can tell him what you have done and I can go back to hanging traitors."

The grim look on Sanchez' face left Michael in no doubt that Montero was a very fortunate man.

On the ride to Salamanca Michael chose to ride Robbie. Lloyd was, as ever, on Rodrigo, but leading Johnny. Hall, on Billy, was leading the two baggage ponies while Bradley, on Jasper, led Thor and Castanha. Michael realised that he was going to have to get some more help or get rid of a horse, this last being something he was reluctant to do. He had been lucky so far, only losing one horse in four years and he wanted to make sure that, at the very least, he and Lloyd were well mounted and ready for any eventuality. He would talk to Bradley when he got the chance. He decided he would rather have more help with the horses than replace White with another valet. Frankly, he told himself, he didn't need one, Hall was a perfectly good batman.

It was early evening, the day finally cooling a little, when they got into Salamanca. Michael left his party at Cotton's headquarters with Captain White complaining at the sudden appearance and the strain on the billets. Michael thought he would rather do anything else than be a quartermaster, there was never enough adequate housing. At Wellington's headquarters, in the Palacio San Boal, he found Scovell in a small room, with his decoding work spread around on a table and every other flat surface in the room. He looked up as Michael knocked on the half open door.

"Hello, Roberts, got anything for me?"

"Yes, sir, took these yesterday. I think at least one is Marmont to Jourdan."

"Is it, by God, let's have a look?" Scovell examined the tiny scraps of paper carefully. "Yes, you are quite right. In the new cipher as well, damn it. Still, we make progress, slowly, but progress none the less."

"Will you let The Peer know I brought them, that I'm back?"

"What? Oh, yes, of course, certainly. He's out somewhere, no idea where."

"Thank you, sir. I shall be at Sir Stapleton's if I'm needed."

Cotton's billet was deserted save for a few servants and a harassed Captain White who informed Michael that the best he could do was to put him in with von der Decken again.

"That's quite alright with me," Michael said.

"I just hope von der Decken feels the same," was the worried reply, "and dinner will be in an hour and a half."

Over dinner everyone listened attentively as Michael described Sanchez's ambush of the French chasseurs. They were particularly interested to learn of the poor condition of the French horses. Cotton was particularly pleased, and shared the information that had come in that the French had tried to boost their cavalry numbers by taking the infantry officers' horses away from them. All in all there was an air of confidence about any meeting with the French cavalry.

After dinner Michael went out to the stables, he wanted to have a word with Bradley. He knew Hall was inside, sorting out Michael's kit and he wasn't surprised to find Lloyd in the stables with Bradley.

Lloyd saluted and Bradley touched the brim of his hat.

Michael returned the salutes and spoke. "I'm glad I've found you both, I want a word about looking after the horses."

Bradley suddenly looked concerned. "Hope there's nowt wrong, sir?"

"No, no, well, not unless you reckon on there being too many?"

"Beg pardon, sir," Bradley replied, "I don't catch tha' meaning?"

"It's simple, if Lloyd here and Hall are both with me and we are on the move, you can't manage Jasper, the two ponies and my three spare horses on your own."

"Well, no, sir, tha's reyt there."

"Even without the addition of Castanha it was getting difficult, was it not?"

"Aye, happen thee's right, sir."

Lloyd broke in. "Begging your pardon, sir, and Mister White didn't really help much, sir. Not a horseman at all, sir." He shook his head sadly. "I suppose we might manage with just one pony, sir, but if anything were to happen to it..., and I don't suppose you want to get rid of one of your horses, sir, not the riding we are doing. And Billy isn't fit for that sort of work, sir. Look how often Hall has ridden Thor, sir."

Bradley looked thoughtful. "I've seen some as have got young lads t'elp 'em, sir. If'n we had a lad as could ride ah reckon as we could manage, sir."

"I think that's a good idea," Michael said, "see if you can find someone. I think I can offer two dollars a week and food, but I think that when we are on the move Hall had better stay with you and the baggage."

"Aye, right you are, sir. I'll start wi' askin' t'groom here."

The bombardment of the fortified convents still held by the French continued through the night and then, at day break the following morning, the firing on the convents intensified. By then Michael was already out with Cotton and his staff. The French army was in position some six miles from Wellington's army, which was drawn up on the Heights of San Cristobal to the north of the city. There had been sporadic manoeuvring and skirmishing, but neither side was prepared to attack. Cotton spent the morning watching the French for signs of movement and visiting all his brigades. Then, at about midday, the sound of the bombardment of the convents suddenly stopped. There was silence save for birdsong. The convents had surrendered.

It was dark by the time Cotton, Michael with him, returned to his quarters in Salamanca. In the stables he found Bradley with a young Spanish boy who looked to be about fourteen.

"This is Marcello Linares, sir, he would like to be a groom for you, sir. He," Bradley gave a little embarrassed cough, "err, he's Silvia's nephew, sir."

"What? Señora Martinez's maid Silvia?"

"Aye, sir."

"Tell me Bradley!"

"Ah, well, sir, I asked t'groom 'ere abaht any likely lads, sir, but he said as he couldn't help, sir. So I thought I might just take a bit of a walk and see if I came across anyone, sir. Well, sir, I did, Silvia, I mean Señorita Linares."

Michael heard a chuckle and turned to see Lloyd in the gloom behind Rodrigo, assiduously grooming the horse.

"So Señora Martinez is here, in Salamanca?"

"Aye, sir, that's right." Bradley shifted a little uncomfortably. "Anyways, I told Señorita Linares what I was about and she said she knew someone as might do and this is 'im, sir." Bradley finished in a rush. He added, "He does know horses, sir, grew up on the Señora's farm, sir, but his mother died years ago and his father, the Señorita's brother, was killed by the French, sir."

Michael looked at the boy who was watching him with big brown eyes, a worried expression on his face as Michael and Bradley were clearly talking about him, but he couldn't understand what was being said. "What's your name?" Michael asked him in Spanish.

"Marcello Linares, Señor."

"Has Senor Bradley told you what your duties would be, what it is like marching with the army?"

"Oh, yes, Señor!"

"And that the pay is two dollars a week?"

"Yes, Señor."

"Lloyd!"

"Yes, sir?"

"What do you think of the lad?"

"He does know horses, sir, says he can ride, but we haven't tried him out. We do know where he comes from, sir. Sort of a recommendation, like."

"Very well. Try him out on Jasper tomorrow. If he can manage him he has a job." Michael spoke to Marcello in Spanish and repeated what he had just said. The boy's face lit up.

"Thank you, Señor!"

"Now, tell me, what is Señora Martinez doing in Salamanca?"

"She came once she heard the French had left, Señor. She has a house here and wanted to see how it was. I just came along with my aunt."

"And where have you been living?"

"With an old widow woman who lives near the Señora's farm. The French left her alone, I kept out of the way. I know the land well."

"And how is the Señora's house?"

"Not too bad, Señor, I think a French general had it, but anything valuable has gone."

"Very well, thank you, Marcello." He switched back to English. "I shall be dining with Sir Stapleton shortly, I shall leave you to look after the boy."

Dinner was a brief affair, everyone was tired after a long day in the saddle under a blazing hot sun and another early start was planned. It wasn't long before Michael was lying on his bed listening to von der Decken snoring. So, he thought, Victoria is in Salamanca. He was all too aware of how they had left things, tomorrow he would call, if duty allowed. At the least he could send Marcello with a note. He drifted off to sleep.

Once again he was up and out before dawn, accompanying Cotton as he rode along the army's position with Wellington. They found that the French had gone. The rest of the day was taken with organising the army to follow, but Wellington gave a dinner that evening for his senior officers and the city organised a ball for the officers of the army still in Salamanca. Michael sent Marcello with a note for Victoria, inviting her to accompany him to the ball. He came running back with a reply, he was to call for her at seven o'clock, Marcello would show him the way.

In the late afternoon Michael was summoned to the Palacio San Boal and taken in to see Wellington. He found the Peer in the dining room, his staff busy around him.

Wellington spoke to him briefly. "Roberts, I have heard from Don Julian, he tells me you did good work with him and might even now have a man of your own in Madrid. We shall see, Don Julian was sceptical. That, however is not why I sent for you. For the moment I want you to continue with Sir Stapleton, he is in need of more staff, and I think Don Julian knows his game. That is all, good day to you, Roberts."

As arranged, Marcello led Michael through Salamanca to Victoria's house, a fine building just to the north of the main plaza, and away from the destruction around the convents. Michael had managed to find time to change into his dress uniform with its tight, white pantaloons, black hessian boots, his best jacket and barrel sash. The bearskin crest on his tarleton was freshly brushed, he suspected one of the horse brushes had been used. Marcello knocked on the door and then said he had better get back to the horses and left Michael standing out side the house. A moment later, Silvia opened the door, showed him into a small sitting room and left him there. It was bare of any furniture.

A few minutes passed, slowly, then the door opened and Victoria came in. She was wearing the emerald green silk dress he had seen before, complete with the necklace of emeralds matching the long earrings. She closed the door behind her.

"Victoria, you look wonderful."

"Ha, you have seen this before, but it is the only decent dress I have left."

They both took a step towards each other, a little tentatively, then they were in each others arms and kissing.

The ball was an enjoyable diversion from the hardships of campaigning and Michael thoroughly enjoyed it. Victoria was an accomplished dancer, and Michael had to share her with other officers. He watched her, thoughtfully, as she danced with von der Decken and even Sir Stapleton, who had come along after Wellington's dinner. She was an extremely attractive young woman, they enjoyed each others company, and yet. She was, he realised, from a completely different world. She had a farm, a large one that had been prosperous, if all her property was an indication. She was Spanish through and through, tied to Castile and the Salamanca region. Tomorrow, he knew, the army would march before dawn, and in all probability he would never pass this way again.

Like a fugitive recollection of a dream, a picture of Catarina came into his mind, followed by Elizabeth. The realisation came upon him that until the war was over he was unlikely to be able to pursue any woman with any sense of fairness, fairness to her. A soldiers lot was nothing if not uncertain.

He watched across the dance floor, and then Victoria's eyes caught his, and he saw a look that was serious, thoughtful, much as he must look, he thought.

The ball finished just after midnight and Michael walked Victoria home, arm in arm, through the streets alive with preparations for the morning departure. Neither spoke, both were deep in thought. At the door to her house, Victoria turned to face Michael.

"Miguel...," she began.

"No, it's alright, Victoria. Let's just say goodnight and goodbye here." He gave a forced little laugh, "After all, I have to be on the march in a few hours."

"Oh, Miguel. Please, be careful."

"And you, Victoria. I hope you can rebuild your farm, I am sure you can."

Victoria leant into him, her head on his chest, his arms went lightly around her shoulders. "There isn't really anything for us, together, is there?" Her voice barely a whisper.

"No, and better to know it now, when we have to part anyway."

She looked up at him and their lips met, then they moved just a little apart, Michael took her hands in his. "You are right," she said, "but thank you for everything, for your protection when I needed it, for your friendship, for your love." She kissed him again, quickly, lightly, and then she was gone, the door closing behind her.

Dawn found Michael, Lloyd at his side, riding across the rolling plains north of Salamanca. Just ahead was Cotton with Colonel Elley, the rest of the staff following on in no particular order. The army was advancing after the French in three columns spread across the landscape. Cotton was right up with the advanced guard, behind them marched the Light Division and Pack's Portuguese Brigade, ahead of them was Alten's light cavalry brigade, pushing patrols further ahead after the retreating French.

Several times they got glimpses of the French rear guard just disappearing on its march. Then on the fourth day the advanced guard got close enough to open fire on the French with artillery. Wellington restrained Cotton from pushing forward, concerned that Marmont was about to turn and fight. They didn't, instead the French withdrew completely across the wide Duero river, barricading the bridges.

Cavalry headquarters was established in the town of Rueda, along with both Anson's and Alten's brigades. Anson had only rejoined from England a couple of days before. A rather half hearted attempt to force a crossing of the Duero came to nothing and Michael saw nothing of it, only hearing the distant firing. Wellington and the army headquarters moved into Rueda and Cotton, along with Anson's brigade, moved three miles to the village of La Seca to make room.

News arrived that war had broken out between Britain and the young United States of America. There was concern that this would stop the shipments of American flour that fed the British and Portuguese army. There was nothing anyone could do about that, but a failure of supplies would result in ignominious retreat into Portugal, and possibly back to Britain.

Then came cheering news, Tomkinson's exchange with Lord Clinton was confirmed and he took command of B Troop, which formed part of the centre squadron under Captain Buchanan. Michael felt a twinge of envy for a moment. Then he considered that command of a troop was a fine thing, but he had other work to do that he seemed gifted to succeed in.

It took some arranging and a lot of goodwill on the part of the rest of the brigade, but a week later there was a dinner of all the officers of the Sixteenth and Michael was able to catch up with friends both old and new. Cotton, as a Lieutenant Colonel of the Regiment, was present, and they indulged in the local white wine. Major Hay was nursing his broken arm, Captain Murray relishing the opportunity to command the Regiment in Hay's place if it came to action. Cotton informed them that Lieutenant Colonel Pelly would be coming out from England to take command. It was an occasion of considerable conviviality and late when Cotton and Michael walked together back to headquarters.

As they neared their billet, a commotion came from a nearby building where the staff's horses were stabled.

"Damn it," Cotton swore, "sounds like someone has too much wine. Go and see will you, Roberts. You can be lenient, God knows they deserve it, if I get involved I shall end up having somebody flogged. I'll wait here, finish this cigar."

Michael walked towards the noise, and then broke into a run as he recognised the voices, it was Hall and that bloody Butler. He burst into the stable, dimly lit by a single lantern, and found Hall backed up against a wall with Butler prodding him in the chest. Butler was slurring and swaying slightly, swearing at Hall and calling him all the names under the sun and adding a few choice comments about Michael. Michael realised that his arrival was timely. Butler hadn't noticed, but Hall's right hand was down by his side, with his knife in it.

Michael bellowed in his best parade ground voice. "Butler, what the hell do you think you are doing?"

Butler jerked round and Hall took the opportunity to slip away sideways. Michael glanced at him and saw the knife had vanished. Butler peered blearily at Michael and failed to salute, but then so did Hall. "Oh, begging your pardon, Captain Roberts, sir." His voice was dripping with contempt and sarcasm. "I was just 'avin' a little chat with my friend, Hall, here." He waved an arm vaguely towards Hall.

"Hall!"

"Yes, sir?"

"Get out of here."

"Yes, sir." Hall slipped quickly away and out of the stables.

"Butler, you're drunk. You're a bloody disgrace to the Regiment."

Butler swayed and said, "I'm a disgrace, Captain no troop Roberts? Always off galivanting around the countryside with your Spanish friends, leaving the real fighting to the rest of us. I rather think you are the disgrace, sir."

"I'll have your stripes for that, Corporal."

"Really, sir?" He leered at Micchael. "And just 'ow are you goin' to prove anything, Captain high and mighty special friend of the Peer Roberts. You've no bloody witness. Christ, I could fillet you like a fish and no one would know."

Butler lurched forward and Michael's hand crept towards where his knife was concealed. Then a voice, full of authority, came from the darkness of the doorway.

"I imagine that I will make a suitable witness, Butler." Cotton stepped into the lamplight. He spoke over his shoulder. "Hall, go and find a sergeant and a couple of men."

A Regimental Court Martial was convened the next day, and with Cotton as the main witness it did not take long. Butler was reduced to the ranks and for threatening violence to an officer was sentenced to be flogged, a thousand lashes was the number given by the court. The sentence was to be carried the following day, but was postponed when orders came to move. First they returned to Rueda while Wellington moved to Alejos. A further delay to the flogging was caused by the French manoeuvring to take the offensive by forcing the crossing of the Duero.

At the same time considerable confusion was caused in the ranks of the Sixteenth by the arrival of four Lieutenants from England along with ninety horses and a reinforcement of dragoons. There were more pressing matters than Butler's flogging as Wellington, out manoeuvred by the reinforced French, ordered a retreat. Cotton, Michael, the Sixteenth and the rest of Anson's brigade found themselves arrayed along the high ground south of the village of Castrejon along with the rest of the army's rearguard. Cotton was in command of the rearguard. Butler almost forgotten, was back in the ranks, shunned by his fellow dragoons. The baggage was ordered to the rear, Bradley, Hall and Marcello heading off with all the other baggage and spare horses to the line of the Guarena where Wellington planned to halt the French. Johnny had worked hard and Michael chose to ride Thor.

Chapter 15

Long before daylight Cotton was riding along the position, he had been reinforced and now had two light cavalry brigades and two infantry divisions drawn up along the high ground south of Castrejon. At the first hint of daylight, he began sending out patrols to look for any sign of a French advance. Michael and Lloyd were sent towards the centre of the position, where a road snaked down into the valley and across the shallow stream from the direction of the French. As the sun rose it revealed that the valley bottom was full of thick mist. Somewhere down in that mist were the pickets of the Sixteenth, lining the banks of the stream, straining to detect any sounds that might indicate the approach of French cavalry. Michael and Lloyd were to pass through them, ride up and out of the valley and then go a few miles beyond.

They paused for a moment, peering down at the mist and listening intently. Lloyd removed his carbine from his saddle and clipped it to his shoulder belt, carrying it in his right hand, ready for use. Michael checked his pistol, but left it in its holster.

"I would be happier if we could see the pickets," Michael observed. "I hope they know which way they are looking." He took one last, long look, nothing stirred. "Right then, walk, march."

They slowly picked their way down the valley side towards the bank of mist, riding a few yards apart, Michael slightly ahead. The vague, dark shapes of trees began to emerge from the mist. Then there was a flash that lit the mist in the trees, followed by a crack and Thor staggered under Michael. A vague shape of a horseman was briefly revealed and Lloyd snapped off a return shot.

"Iesu mawr," Lloyd swore, "he was wearing a tarleton!" He began to reload.

"I saw," snapped Michael as he dropped to the ground off Thor, who stood, shaking, blood streaming from his shoulder. "Damn, damn, damn, it's bad." There was another, distant shot. "What the hell's going on?" Michael and Lloyd looked towards the mist that was a blank, off-white wall, hiding everything.

Suddenly a riderless horse galloped out the mist followed by two dragons in pursuit. Lloyd watched them carefully, his carbine ready and cocked. The riderless horse slowed and one of the dragoons was able to size its reins and bring it to a halt. The other spotted Michael and Lloyd and saluted.

Michael returned the salute and shouted, "What's going on, whose horse is that?"

"Butler's, sir" came the surprising reply. "He was out on our flank and we heard him fire a shot, thought he must have seen a Frenchie, sir. Then we heard him go hell for leather that way." He pointed in the direction from which the French were expected. "It sounded like he crossed the river, sir. Couldn't see anything in the mist though. We heard him shouting something, sounded like French, sir. Then there was another shot and a few moments later his horse came galloping back without him, sir."

At that moment there was fusillade of shots and soon after the picket of the Sixteenth came galloping out of the mist. In charge was Troop Sergeant Major

Whitmore who galloped to where Michael stood at Thor's head.

"A whole troop of chasseurs coming, sir!" He saw Thor. "Bloody hell, begging your pardon, sir."

"Sergeant Major, form your picket facing the French."

"Yes, sir." He started shouting orders, getting the dozen or so men into a single rank.

Michael turned to Lloyd, "Take Thor, try to get him to Bradley, or a Vet'n'ry. Do what you can." He called out to the dragoon with Butler's horse. "Thornton, I'll take him!"

Within seconds Lloyd was on his way and Michael, on the unfamiliar horse, was sitting in front of the picket, sabres drawn, watching the mist that was slowly dissipating as the sun rose. Two French chasseurs appeared briefly out of the mist and then turned back in. Michael waited as long as he dared.

"Picket! Threes about, march, trot match"

The little command set off up the slope out of the valley. They soon caught up with Lloyd and Michael halted them and faced about. A quarter mile away a troop of French chasseurs emerged from the mist and stood looking at them. Why don't they charge he wondered?

Then Whitmore shouted, "Behind us, sir!"

Michael twisted in his saddle and saw Buchanan's squadron sitting a few hundred yards behind them. He sighed with relief. "Threes, right about, march, walk march."

Michael led the picket back, past Buchanan's squadron, who gave him a friendly wave. Lloyd had vanished from sight and Michael led the picket back towards the main body of the brigade waiting a mile further back. Off to one side he caught sight of Cotton and his staff.

"Whitmore, you can take the picket back from here, I am going to rejoin Sir Stapleton."

"Very good, sir." They exchanged salutes and Michael cantered across to Cotton.

"Found the French, I see. And a new horse?"

"Yes, sir, mine has been shot and Lloyd is taking him to the rear."

At that moment, before Cotton could ask any questions, Wellington rode up with his staff, accompanied by Beresford and his staff.

"Sir Stapleton, good day to you. I have brought up Le Marchant and Bock and placed them on your left. The French seem to have an idea of trying to turn your left flank with infantry."

"Thank you, my Lord."

Michael rode quietly to the rear. He saw Major Warre and walked his horse across to him. They exchanged salutes and Warre, looking at Michael's remount observed. "Looks like warm work, Roberts?"

"Yes, sir, my charger was badly wounded in the shoulder."

"We had a bit of a time of it as well, over on the left. Got charged by some French cavalry. It was a bit sticky until the Eleventh came up." He looked to the front. "Our chiefs seem to have decided what they are doing. Good luck, Roberts."

"And you, sir."

Wellington and his entourage rode off in the direction of retreat, heading for the new position along the Guarena river, Warre along with them.

The rest of the morning was taken up by a careful withdrawal over some ten miles of rolling countryside, one regiment at a time falling back and then turning to face the French and cover the others as they fell back in their turn. The heavy cavalry brigades of Le Marchant and Bock manoeuvred threateningly and slowed the advance of the French infantry to a crawl. Several times the French got artillery into long range action, but casualties were light. Michael was kept busy, riding backwards and forwards helping Cotton to coordinate the movements, his work load increased when von der Decken was wounded, hit by a carbine shot in his thigh.

At the Guarena the force was able to pause for a moment and slake the thirst of men and horses, then they marched up the steep slopes to take their places in the line that was formed along the valley. The French made a desperate attempt to turn the left of the position, but were thrown back after a short but sharp engagement. Things went quiet after that, the two armies looking at each other across the intervening valley. Michael got permission from Cotton to go and look for a fresh horse. Butler's had done well, but it was exhausted.

He rode quietly to the rear looking for any sign of the headquarters' baggage. He found the headquarters established in the small village of Canizal, a few miles from the Guarena. As he approached he saw Lloyd standing at the outskirts with Rodrigo and Robbie. He could see as he approached that Robbie had all the tack that had been on Thor. He exchanged salutes with Lloyd who looked grim faced.

"How's Thor?"

"Sorry, sir, but he dropped dead just as we got to the Guarena, sir."

"Damn." Michael climbed down from Butler's horse. "But you got everything off him?"

"Yes, sir, and then rode up here and found Bradley with the baggage, sir. I thought I'd bring you Robbie, sir, Johnny would still be better for a bit of a rest and as it looks like there might be a fight tomorrow, sir, I thought you'd want him fresh for that, sir.

"Yes, thank you, Lloyd." He passed the reins of Butler's horse to Lloyd and took Robbie's from him. The horse stuck his head out and nuzzled his arm, blowing at him though his nostrils. Michael stroked his head. "Hello, lad, glad to see me, are you? Well, I'm glad to see you." He turned to Lloyd, "Any idea where the Regiment is?"

"Oh, yes, sir," Lloyd looked a little more cheerful. "Just the other side of this village sir."

"Then let's go and return this poor animal."

Michael mounted Robbie and the feel of the big, bay horse under him lightened his mood a little as they rode around the village.

"Begging your pardon, sir."

"Yes?"

"Do you reckon as it was Butler took that shot, sir?"

Michael rode on, silent for a moment, running over the events of the morning in his mind. "I think it might well have been. He would no doubt blame me for the flogging he was due. Saw a chance and took it. I suspect he had already decided to desert, to avoid the flogging." He rode on silently for a few yards. "No doubt Sergeant Major Whitmore will have reported him as missing and I think it might be as well to leave it at that. It was misty, no one could see much, no point in speculating, so let's not say anything about pot shots in the mist."

"Right you are, sir, but I hope the Frenchies killed the bastard, begging your pardon, sir."

"Yes, Thor was a good horse."

"Oh, aye, sir, but better the horse than you, sir."

The day was well on, but still burning hot, when they found the Sixteenth, formed in line, dismounted, the men resting as well as they could. Riding across the rear they found the Adjutant, Lieutenant Barra, sitting in the shade of his horse and talking to Regimental Sergeant Major Williams. The two men clambered to their feet as Michael and Lloyd approached. Michael dropped off Robbie and exchanged salutes with Barra.

"I've brought you Butler's horse. I'm afraid I've worked him rather hard."

Williams stepped forward to relieve Lloyd of the horse and Barra asked, "Any idea what happened? I've heard from Whitmore, he didn't see anything."

"No, I heard shouting, heard shots, then the horse appeared. It was damned misty down in the valley bottom." Michael glanced at Williams who was looking over the horse with Lloyd who had dismounted from Rodrigo to join him. "I can't help but wonder if he was trying to desert, escape his flogging."

Barra nodded thoughtfully. "The same occurred to me. I wonder if he's dead or alive?"

"The way that horse galloped back..."

"Yes, I see what you mean." Barra shrugged. "I doubt if we will ever know. But thank you for bringing the horse, sir, a night's rest and we can get another man mounted." He called across to Williams, "How is he, Sar'nt Major?"

"Right enough, sir, he'll do."

Michael and Lloyd rode off in search of Cotton, who they found with Wellington, in the centre of the position, carefully watching the French. For their part, the French simply drew up opposite and did nothing.

It was a long night, or it seemed so. The army slept in its positions, the cavalry did what they could to feed and water the horses. The Guarena was too close to the French, small streams were dry, the nearest available water course was up to two to three miles behind the position. An hour after dark Wellington and Cotton, accompanied by their staffs, rode back to Canizal to get what food, water and sleep they could.

Michael sought out Bradley, Marcello and Hall amongst the baggage.

Bradley touched his hat to Michael and said, "'Tis a crying shame 'bout Thor, sir, he were a fine animal. But happen that's as what occurs in war, sir."

"Yes, it is," was all Michael could manage by way of a reply. He went on, "How's Johnny?"

"Right as rain, sir, will you be wanting to change horses, sir?"

"No, not yet, Robbie's not done much today. I'll stay on him for the morrow and then switch to Johnny, assuming I get the chance."

"Aye, well, sir, we shall have to see as what we can do 'bout that then. Ah reckon it will depend on whether or not they send us off to t' rear."

The baggage stayed. Michael managed a few hours sleep, but before dawn was on Robbie, trotting along with the staff towards the French. They drew up on the heights as the army stood to all around them. The rising sun revealed the French army exactly where it had been when the sun had gone down. Everyone waited, poised to take action. Nothing happened.

An hour after dawn, when it became apparent nothing was going to happen, the infantry sat down in rank and file, the cavalry dismounted and tried to sit in the shade of their horses, who stood, listless, swishing ineffectively at the flies with their cropped tails. There was little water to be had. Michael heard his stomach growling and tried not to lick his parched lips. A fly busied itself around his face and he tried to swat it away. There were tens of thousands of men, but little noise save for the constant hum and buzz of insects, the occasional shouted order or the stamp of a hoof. The tension among the staff was palpable. Wellington and Cotton rode together along the front, and back again. Halting, briefly to look at something through a telescope before closing it with a snap and riding on. Where they went, the staff went. Now and then one of them would be dispatched on some errand, trotting off through the shimmering heat haze. They passed by Anson's brigade and Michael was surprised to see Tomkinson sitting in front of Captain McIntosh's squadron instead of being with his own troop. He manged to swing by close enough for a quick word.

"Where's McIntosh?"

"Fever got him, fainted and fell off his horse a couple of hours ago." Tomkinson replied. "Promotion in the field, eh?" He grinned and Michael gave a little chuckle as he rode away.

The midday heat came and went as the sun slowly began to get lower in the sky. Then drums began to beat and the French army seemed to heave itself up and start to move. Not towards them, not to attack, but towards the British right, towards the southwest and Salamanca. Wellington barked a few words, staff officers began to gallop away, Cotton shouted to Michael, "Roberts, go to Anson, tell him to move right, get out ahead of us, them, watch the flank, front, damn it, get him moving that way!" He pointed off to the right.

Michael put spur to Robbie and shot off towards where Anson's brigade was sitting, Lloyd with him. They arrived to find the brigade already mounted and ready to move.

"General Anson, sir, Sir Stapleton wishes you to move to the right, to cover the head of the army as it moves."

Within minutes the British, Portuguese and Spanish army was marching parallel to the French. At some point toward nightfall British artillery got into position to fire and succeeded in setting fire to a vast expanse of the ripening corn that covered the land around. Then the marching stopped as the sun went down. From his place with Cotton's staff, Michael could see the flames, driven by the wind, ripping across a mile or more of the corn fields. He was reminded of the fires on the hill top at Talavera and thought about being wounded and watching fire approach, unable to move. He shuddered, patted Robbie on the neck and made some remark to Captain Campbell who happened to be riding nearest to him, anything to divert his thoughts.

At nightfall the march of the two armies ended for the day and they bivouacked in their lines of battle for another night. Michael found the baggage, which had been marching at the rear, protected by a Portuguese cavalry brigade. Hall was able to provide cold rations and water for Michael and Lloyd and Michael asked Bradley about Johnny.

"If you don't mind, sir, I would say Castanha is the fitter at the moment. Another quiet day or two and ah reckons Johnny will be a fit as ever again."

"Very well, I'll ride Castanha, change the tack over now, there won't be time in the morning, we will be sleeping out again tonight. Lloyd, how is Rodrigo?"

"He's just fine, sir, diolch. He's a tough one, never seems to tire."

"Good, but make sure you say if he's not fit at all. You can always ride another of mine, you know," he laughed, "except Johnny, of course."

"Right you are, sir," Lloyd answered with a smile.

An hour before dawn the army stood to, ready for battle and waited for the sun to reveal what the French were doing. The French continued their march and the British, with their Portuguese and Spanish allies, followed suit. The valley of the Guarena was left behind as the river divided into its various tributaries, inconsequential brooks with gently rolling hills in between, vacant save for patrolling cavalry scouts. Late in the morning the French changed direction slightly and the two armies found themselves beginning to converge, each in plain view of the other. It was an incredible sight, Michael gazed at the entire French army, some forty-five to fifty thousand men marching along, no more than a mile away. From time to time the French artillery opened fire, but with little effect until they were passing a small village. There the French artillery got on some heights and opened fire, causing a few casualties amongst the infantry. In response the marching infantry simply veered away out of range.

Cotton was riding with the light cavalry, at the front of the line of march with his staff. In the late afternoon Wellington joined him and after a short conversation the line of march changed, swinging away from the French towards high ground they knew well, it was where Marmont had formed his army a month before. They were getting closer to Salamanca and by the end of the day the head of the French army had reached the river Tormes.

There followed yet another night bivouacking out, but from the high ground Michael could see the camp fires of the French army, stretching out over some six miles of countryside, from the river back to where the main body of the French lay, a mere five miles or less away from where Michael stood. It was a striking sight. In the dark Michael decided not to try to find the baggage, but to stay on Castanha for another day. It had been an easy day for the horses.

He and Lloyd slept out at their horses' heads, managing a few fitful hours, their reins in their hands, the horses asleep on their feet, or trying to graze.

Once again the army stood to before dawn, but this time they stayed, unmoving, watching the French cross the Tormes. For the infantry this brought a welcome period of further rest, but the cavalry were pushed forward across the river to form a screen opposing the French. Cotton, as usual, was up at the front of this advance with his staff. As soon as it became clear that the whole French army was crossing over, the rest of Wellington's army followed, using fords just outside Salamanca itself.

The day finished, as the previous three had, with the two armies facing each other across the Spanish countryside. The British cavalry screen was close to the French, in places less than a mile apart. Headquarters had been established in the tiny village of La Pinilla and Michael and Lloyd were in the makeshift stables with Bradley looking over the horses by the light of a single lantern. There were a lot of horses, all those of the staffs of Wellington and

Cotton were crammed into stalls and pens and even the odd small room, but at least they were under cover. Hall was in the largest house with the rest of the servants and batmen trying to put some sort of dinner together.

"They all seem to be in reasonable condition," Michael observed. "Aye, sir, happen as they are. Fresh grass has helped a lot."

"Yes, and is there any reason why I shouldn't ride Johnny tomorrow?"

"No, sir, he's as fit as a fiddle, sir."

"How is Marcello doing?"

"Grand, sir, he knows what he's about and has a way with the ponies. Leaves me more time for the horses, sir."

"Good. Where is he?"

"Just gone to get summat to eat, he should be back soon."

The dark of the night was split by a brilliant flash of light followed almost immediately by a crashing peal of thunder. The horses started, pulling at their tethers, tossing heads, whinnying in fear and panic, crashing into walls and panels in their surprise, kicking out blindly. In seconds there were grooms, batmen and officers everywhere, grabbing at horses, trying to calm them. Marcello appeared, breathless and went straight to the two ponies who were rolling their eyes and bucking against their tethers. Michael, Lloyd and Bradley were trying to calm the horses when the rain started to hammer down on the roof. Another bolt of lightening rent the black sky and the thunder rolled around. There was a yell from somewhere as someone was trodden on. Hall was suddenly with them, soaking wet, and going to Billy.

The intensity of the storm lessened slightly and the next peal of thunder was further away. Gradually they got the horses calmed, but it was after midnight before the storm passed and the horses were settled enough to allow some food to be hastily eaten and a few hours of sleep to be grabbed.

.   .   .

There was no storm in Madrid that day. Renard was, as usual at his desk, when there was a knock at his door and Faucher came in, looking pleased with himself. Renard looked up as the young clerk approached.

"I beg your pardon, Monsieur, but I have a man ready to go after Captain Roberts."

Renard lay down his pen, looked up at the ceiling and sighed. "That, Faucher, is the best news I have had in a long time. Tell me more."

"Well, Monsieur, he is a Spanish muleteer, Monsieur..."

Chapter 16

Michael was woken by Hall shaking his shoulder. "Come along now, sir, I've a cup of coffee and a lump of bread for you, sir, best I could find, sir."

Michael opened his eyes to see the rafters of the outhouse he and three other officers were sleeping in, wrapped in their cloaks, heads resting on valises. It was dark and the only light came from two lanterns. There was a general stirring as everyone was roused by their servants, blinking, yawning and stretching stiff and aching limbs. Michael propped himself up on one arm and took the mug of coffee from Hall. It was lukewarm and bitter, very bitter. Michael coughed and swallowed.

"Sorry, sir, it's all there is."

Michael grunted and handed the coffee back so he could rise to his feet. Upright he said, "Thank you, Hall, anything is welcome. Did you mention some bread?" He ran a hand over his chin and scratched. Five days now without a shave, he dreaded to think how he looked.

Half an hour later he was sitting on Johnny, Lloyd at his side, amongst the officers and orderlies of Wellington's and Cotton's staffs. It was, he reckoned, an hour or so before dawn. A door opened and Cotton strode out, as immaculately dressed and turned out as ever. Clean shaven as well. Michael had no idea how he managed it. Cotton swung up into the saddle of his horse and addressed his staff.

"Come along, gentlemen, let us go and see the pickets and see if there is any life in Monsieur."

They rode eastward, past the infantry divisions where men busied themselves about small fires, trying to get something warm to eat and drink even as their officers were calling them to fall in. They found Alten's light cavalry brigade, formed up and ready in support of the advanced infantry pickets. The sky was just beginning to lighten, promising a hot day under a cloudless sky, when the first shots were heard. It became clear that French light infantry was skirmishing with British light infantry up on the high ground ahead of them.

Once he was satisfied that everything was under control, Cotton led the way due north where Bock was with his brigade of German heavy dragoons. He spoke briefly with Bock and then turned to ride back south. They passed Alten's again and Cotton halted when he found Wellington on high ground in the centre of the British position. Both groups of staff waited below the skyline, out of sight, while Wellington and Cotton observed the French from amongst the infantry on the position.

Michael looked away to the north in the direction of Salamanca, but despite its proximity it was hidden by the folds of the ground. He hoped that Victoria had left for somewhere safe. He felt a passing twinge of regret.

The sun got higher, the day got hotter, then Colonel Elley rode down from where he had been in attendance on Cotton. He looked over the assembled staff and his eye lit upon Michael.

"Roberts!"

"Yes, sir?"

"There's something going on with Alten's brigade, go and see what it is."

"Yes, sir."

Michael and Lloyd trotted away on to open ground and then cantered on steadily. It wasn't much over a mile to the ground where Alten's brigade stood. As they approached Michael caught sight of squadron of Bock's brigade closed up behind them. To Michael's surprise he found Colonel Arentschildt sitting on his horse where he had expected to find General Alten. He rode up and saluted.

"Sir Stapleton's compliments, Colonel, he sent me to see if all is well?"

Arentschildt's thick German accent was clear. "Ach, the General is wounded in the knee." He grinned mirthlessly at Michael. "So the brigade is mine." He pointed to the distance. "Some difficulty with some dragoons we had, but Le Marchant sent a squadron and the French away they went. You can tell Sir Stapleton all is well."

Michael and Lloyd returned to find Cotton talking with Colonel Elley down off the high ground. He saw Michael approach and returned his salute. "All well, with Alten?"

"General Alten has been wounded, sir, Arentschildt has the brigade and says that everything is in hand, sir."

"Good, but you are going to have to go back. Tell Arentschildt that he is to move his brigade to the extreme right of our position. It seems the French are up to their usual game, I want the light cavalry at the front, or the right, whichever. Off you go."

"Yes, sir."

As they retraced their steps again, Michael and Lloyd could see, away to their left, the bulk of the infantry, three divisions, marching steadily south. Despite the night's rain they were beginning to raise the dust. Michael gave Arentschildt his orders and turned back again. He was beginning to think it was going to be another long day of fruitless marching, matching the French step for step.

Michael was in earshot when Cotton, along with Beresford, dissuaded Wellington from launching an attack on one of the two hills that dominated the landscape. Each army held one of them, the Arapiles. Instead they continued to watch and match the French moves.

At first it seemed that Michael's thinking was correct. One by one, the divisions of infantry moved along, as did the French. Both sides pulled after them the forces they had left across the Tormes. Michael had been kept busy, riding the countryside, shifting cavalry brigades south and west. In the case of Anson's they had left one regiment, the Twelfth, in the north, covering the flank and rear of the army along with Bock's German Dragoons. Then, everything changed.

Wellington had dismounted, his servants had found him, and he was taking an early dinner in the yard of a farm overlooking the open, bare landscape between the armies. He was sitting on the ground, leaning back against a horse trough looking completely unconcerned, concentrating on his plate, spreading mustard on a slice of cold meat. Cotton and Beresford, who was limping from a slight wound to his leg inflicted during the retreat to the Guarena, were also there. Standing and sitting idly around were the staffs of the three generals, eating if they had anything. It was a quiet scene, convivial, and only disturbed by the continuing exchange of artillery mounted on the two Arapiles. Michael was talking to Warre who was commiserating with him on the loss of Thor. Across the farmyard he could see Lord Fitzroy Somerset leaning on a wall, watching the French. He saw Somerset turn and say something to Wellington, who dropped his plate, leapt to his feet, joined Somerset at the wall and scanned the opposition with his telescope. The sudden movement brought all activity and conversation to a halt as everyone's attention became fixed on Wellington. Michael realised that he was holding his breath, and let it out slowly.

Wellington snapped his telescope closed and turned. "That will do, bring my horse!"

Suddenly all was hustle and bustle with officers calling for their horses, orderlies milling around with those horses, everyone getting mounted as quickly as possible. Michael saw Wellington speak briefly to Cotton and then he rode away towards the rear. Cotton also rode rearwards, in a slightly different direction, Michael and the rest of the staff hurrying to follow him. They rode for a mile or so, only Cotton knowing what was going on, until they found Anson's brigade, or rather two thirds of it, the Eleventh and the Sixteenth Light Dragoons, behind a small village, the men dismounted and resting. Michael was close enough to hear the last of what Cotton said to Anson.

"... so you will come up behind Le Marchant's brigade and support his attack, but you need to hurry, he's a good half mile ahead already. Follow on after me."

Even as Anson started shouting orders, Cotton turned his horse and trotted off towards the south east. As they went he turned in his saddle and called out to his staff. "We are attacking, the French have over extended. Le Marchant will take his brigade in between Pakenham's and Leith's divisions who are advancing. Anson's will support him."

They cleared the village and the high ground to the west of it and Le Marchant's brigade came into view, or rather the dust cloud that hid it. Cotton led the way around its left flank and, as they got ahead of the dust, Michael got his first clear view of what was happening. Le Marchant's brigade was advancing at a steady walk with six squadrons in line in front, another two in support behind. It was a mass of nearly a thousand men, big men, dragoons and dragoon guards, on big horses, fresh horses. There was an overwhelming impression of force, of irresistible force.

Away to the right was another dust cloud marking the position of an infantry division that, so far as Michael could tell, was throwing itself across the line of the French advance and attacking the leading French division. To the left another division was throwing up a cloud of dust as it too closed on the French. Michael saw Cotton pointing to the front, speaking to Le Marchant, and he realised that Le Marchant's brigade would be riding into the gap between the two infantry actions now developing in front of them.

Cotton led his staff back, behind the heavy cavalry and halted, waiting for Anson's to catch up. The clouds of dust hung in the still air, combining with ever increasing clouds of smoke from the infantry combats. It became impossible to see exactly what was happening as the heavy cavalry disappeared into the distance.

Anson led up his brigade, each of the two regiments with two squadrons in front and one behind. Without hesitation, Cotton led the way forward, towards the huge clouds of dust and smoke, following the direction taken by Le Marchant's brigade. They walked steadily forwards, covering a mile or more before they started to see evidence of the fight that had taken place. First came a scattering of redcoated bodies, then more in blue, amongst them small parties of French, prisoners guarded by British infantry.

Cotton gradually changed direction, starting to swing to his left on a wide curve, Anson and the brigade wheeling with him. As they walked on the ground began to rise, dead and wounded infantry of both sides became frequent. Then they started to come across scores of dead and wounded French with sabre wounds and the occasional redcoated casualty from Le Marchant's brigade. More parties of French prisoners appeared, hundreds of them, many with sword cuts. It became clear that Le Marchant's brigade had torn through the French infantry, completing the job started by the infantry by destroying two divisions of French infantry.

They reached the top of the long ridge that had been the French position and Cotton ordered a halt. Below the dust still swirled, but there was less smoke as the fighting diminished. In the distance Michael could see the two British divisions, Leith's and Pakenham's, in line, side by side, still advancing. To their right he could make out cavalry, it looked like Alten's and D'Urban's light brigades. Anson had ridden up and was sitting on his horse next to Cotton. They took in the view before them. Michael heard Cotton speak to Anson.

"It rather looks as if it is all over, but your brigade is the only intact cavalry reserve that we have. We shall stay here for the moment and then follow up slowly."

In the distance the French were beginning to disappear into the woods behind their positions. A few groups of redcoated dragoons were slowly gathering together into squadrons. A horseman broke away from one group and slowly rode up to where they sat, watching. It was a dragoon officer, hatless, face streaked with blood, he and his horse clearly exhausted. He saluted Cotton.

"I have to report, sir, that General Le Marchant is dead." He paused as if he could not believe what he was saying. "The brigade has broken two divisions of French infantry, sir. Colonel Lord Somerset is rallying the brigade, but begs to inform you that it can take no further action."

"Very good, please convey to Colonel Lord Somerset my thanks and inform he may act as he sees fit."

The officer saluted and rode his weary horse back towards his brigade. It was only an hour or so since Le Marchant had led his brigade forward.

The French army was now in full retreat. Unseen by Cotton and Michael and the others, another attack had driven in the French centre. One division was endeavouring to cover the retreat of the whole French army. Cotton turned to Anson.

"Time for you to go and relieve Arentschildt and D'Urban, I think. Get on the right flank and keep up pressure on the French, but don't get engaged any more than you have to. It will be dark before too long. Good luck."

Anson led his brigade forward, riding east and casting long shadows as the sun began to sink. Michael watched on as a fierce engagement was fought out between the French rearguard, desperately holding their ground, and a British and Portuguese division equally desperate to drive them off. The crash of musketry reached them and great billows of smoke rose into the evening sky. The final straw seemed to be the sudden appearance of Anson's brigade on the left flank of the French line. It simply crumbled away as the men fled into the woods behind them under cover of the encroaching night.

As the day darkened, Cotton gave orders to his staff. "Gentlemen, get you out and recall all the cavalry, I want them all back by Las Torres. Roberts, you go and find Anson, tell him I want a squadron of the Sixteenth for picket duty, bring them here. Off you go, gentlemen."

Michael urged Johnny into a trot and set off into the gloom. He had a fair idea of where he would find Anson and his brigade, but he was glad to have Lloyd with him, as they rode into the confusion of the battlefield. Everywhere around them were groups of French prisoners, and thousands more French were pouring through the woods in a confused mass, heading for the Tormes and the safety of the far bank.

He found Anson and the brigade sitting outside the woods, reluctant to go any further in the evening gloom.

"General Anson, sir!"

"Roberts! Have you got orders for me?"

"Yes, sir. Sir Stapleton wants all the cavalry to return to Las Torres, sir, but he has asked for a squadron of the Sixteenth for picket duty, sir."

"Very good." He turned in his saddle and called out to the nearest squadron commander. "Captain Tomkinson!"

"Yes, sir?"

"You are required for picket duty tonight! Captain Roberts will guide you." He turned back to Michael. "Frankly, I'm damned glad not to be riding into the woods in the dark. I shall leave Tomkinson with you. Carry on."

Michael rode over to Tomkinson who greeted him with "Damn it, I was hoping to get some sleep tonight. Where are we going?"

"To Sir Stapleton, I think he wants to put the pickets out himself."

When they returned to where Cotton waited they found him alone, save for his orderly. "Evening, Tomkinson. Roberts, I've sent everyone else to Las Torres to organise matters there, but you and your orderly will come with me while I post the pickets. I am concerned about leaving the ford at Huerta unguarded."

It was a march of ten miles or so and it was getting on for midnight by the time Tomkinson and his pickets were posted and Sir Stapleton, his orderly, Michael and Lloyd turned their horses to ride wearily to Las Torres. They were tired and rode quietly along through the darkness. The challenge was a surprise, it was called out in Portuguese. Cotton managed a startled "What?" and then two shots rang out. Cotton reeled in his saddle and cried out in pain, his orderly gasped and fell from his horse.

Michael shouted, "Hold your fire, it's General Cotton, you have shot him"

Confused shouting followed and then a Portuguese officer appeared, shouting, "Who are you?"

"Michael shouted back, "It's General Cotton and his staff, you have shot the General."

The officer came cautiously forward, saw Cotton and his party and swore. Within a few moments he had men helping up the orderly who had been struck high in the shoulder. Michael put Johnny alongside Cotton who stayed in his saddle, "Sir, where are you hit?"

Though gritted teeth Cotton managed "In my left arm," and then swore, loudly and long.

Michael addressed the officer, "Where is your surgeon?"

"In Calvarrasa, sir."

"Get me a guide."

"Yes, sir."

"Lloyd!"

"Sir?"

"Can you find your way to Las Torres? Find the Earl of Wellington, he needs to know what has happened."

With a brief "Yes, sir," Lloyd rode into the night at a brisk trot.

It was a slow ride to Calvarrasa, with Cotton cursing and swearing all the way. His orderly was in a bad way, bleeding profusely and it had only been with difficulty that he had been hoisted back on to his horse and then supported by a Portuguese infantryman on each side. At the village Cotton was helped from his horse and laid in a straw filled trough in a semi-derelict barn, the only thing resembling a bed left in the village. His orderly was laid on the floor nearby. The Portuguese regiment's surgeon attended, but was little help beyond bandaging the wounds.

He had hardly finished when there was the clatter of hooves outside and then Wellington himself burst into the room. "Cotton, my dear fellow, how are you? Roberts, what the devil is going on?"

"My Lord," Michael answered, "Sir Stapleton had posted a picket on the ford at Huerta, on the way back he was shot by a Portuguese sentry, he was rather quick to fire and, perhaps, we were a little slow to respond to the challenge. Sir Stapleton's orderly is also wounded, my Lord, and the surgeon here is not much use."

"Damn it, you know Beresford has been wounded as well? Leith and Cole too. I shall send a competent surgeon as soon as possible, stay with him, Roberts." Wellington stalked out of the building shouting for someone to go and find a British surgeon.

Lloyd slipped in after Wellington had left. "Begging your pardon, sir, I've got all the horses billeted, sir."

"Thank you, Lloyd."

Cotton, through gritted teeth added, "Good man, thank you."

Eventually the surgeon of the Fourteenth Light Dragoons arrived and after examining Cotton's wound recommended amputation. Cotton point blank refused. "Roberts, get this bloody sawbones away from me. Get me McGrigor!"

It was a sleepless night. Michael took the opportunity to scribble a brief letter to his Grandfather. He would soon hear about the battle and Michael did not want him worrying about how he was. He added that Lloyd and Hall were also well. The Fourteenth's surgeon hovered around, Cotton periodically allowing him to change his bandages. The Portuguese supplied food and wine to Michael and Lloyd, and Cotton managed to sip a little wine. Just after dawn Colonel Elley arrived and with him Doctor McGrigor, the army's senior medical man. McGrigor concluded that amputation was not necessary and arrangements were made for Cotton to be conveyed to Salamanca for his recovery. Elley also brought news for Michael.

"Roberts, General Bock has assumed command of the cavalry, but Wellington wants you to join his staff at once. He is managing the pursuit of the French, so you will need to ride hard after him."

"Yes, sir. Do you know which road he has taken?"

"He crossed the Tormes at Alba, I think he was taking the main road to Peñaranda."

"Thank you, sir."

Michael wished Cotton well and went out to find Lloyd and the horses. Soon they were mounted and heading across the battlefield towards the bridge at Alba de Tormes. Their route took them across the area of the heaviest fighting and Michael was once again reminded of Talavera, but this, if anything, was worse. Hundreds of bodies lay scattered, some almost in straight lines where there had been fierce firefights, flies were buzzing in huge clouds and vultures circled high in the sky. Groups of British, Portuguese and Spanish infantry were scouring the ground, looking for the wounded. With them was a host of women, camp followers looking for loved ones or simply out to pillage the dead, ruthlessly stripping them naked. The sun was rising, promising another hot day and already there was a sweet, metallic smell in the air. Large parties of prisoners trudged disconsolately towards Salamanca, guarded for the most part by Spanish infantry, who poked and prodded at their charges with bayonets.

On the way to the bridge they passed by where they had ambushed the French infantry with Sanchez before dropping down the long hill to the river. Reaching the Tormes they took the opportunity to water the horses, careful not to let them drink too much too quickly. All around them was the abandoned debris of the fleeing French army, wagons, carts, dead horses and more bodies. Dismounting, they filled their canteens and wineskins with water and drank their fill themselves.

Riding across the battlefield both men had remained silent, but now Michael spoke. "I have no intention of pushing the horses hard, it's going to be too hot. God knows when we might meet up with Bradley and Hall again. I would think they are still with the cavalry headquarters baggage wherever they are."

Lloyd gave a grim little chuckle. "Halfway to Ciudad Rodrigo, I shouldn't wonder, sir."

"More than likely," Michael smiled. "Come on, we had better get going. Easily, but not too slowly."

Up on the road the Light Division was marching across the long bridge to Alba, and they managed to slip in between two battalions and walk the horses steadily on. An infantry captain came up next to Michael and spoke to him.

"Good morning, Sixteenth, ain't you? Anson's? Heard they were well ahead of us."

"Sixteenth, yes, but attached to Wellington's staff, wherever he is," Michael replied.

The Captain waved a hand vaguely across the river. "Out there, somewhere. Leading the cavalry apparently. I heard General Cotton was wounded?"

"Yes, shot by a Portuguese sentry in the dark."

"That's damn bad luck."

They reached the far side of the bridge and the road opened wide enough for Michael and Lloyd to trot on and they soon left the infantry behind. An hour later they were approaching the village of Garcia Hernandez when they met a small detachment of German heavy dragoons escorting hundreds of French infantry.

Michael called out to a young officer who seemed to be in charge. "What's happened?"

The young man grinned. "We broke two squares! Four battalions, took them all prisoner."

Michael gaped in astonishment as the officer rode away. Lloyd muttered, "Iesu mawr!"

A long column of prisoners was coming along, so they put their horse across country and rode on after Wellington. They finally caught up with Wellington and Anson's brigade bivouacking on the bank of a small river. Wellington was sitting on the dry ground surrounded by his staff. Miraculously, his servants had somehow kept up and he was dining on cold rations. Leaving Lloyd to look for fodder and water for the horses, Michael slowly walked over. De Lancey caught sight of him and spoke quietly to Wellington, who looked up and then got up, meeting Michael as he approached. Michael saluted.

"Roberts, glad to see you, a word, then you must have something to eat."

"My Lord?"

"Tell me, how is Sir Stapleton?"

"Mister McGrigor says he will not lose his arm, my Lord, he was being taken into Salamanca when Colonel Elley told me to join you, my Lord."

"Good, good news indeed. General Bock has command of the cavalry now, and while Sir Stapleton is well aware of your activities, Bock is not, and the fewer that know the better. That is why I have brought you onto my staff." He paused. "And there is every likelihood I shall be needing your particular skills very soon."

.   .   .

In Madrid it was very, very hot. Renard wiped his brow and looked at the man standing before him, in the traditional garb of a muleteer and smelling like a mule as well.

"Faucher."

"Yes Monsieur?"

Renard spoke in French. "Have you explained to this, err, gentleman, exactly what is required before he earns his money?" The man met Renard's gaze with a look of incomprehension.

"Yes, Monsieur."

"And do you think he is capable of the task?"

"He came with recommendations from some very unsavoury characters, Monsieur."

"And how do we know that their opinions can be trusted?"

"I asked the Chief of Police, Monsieur. He had no doubts, Monsieur."

The man had watched the exchange, his eyes flicking from to the other, but with not a hint of understanding.

"He has a description of Roberts?"

"Yes, Monsieur, particularly the scar."

"Very good, Faucher, send him on his way. Well done."

"Thank you, Monsieur."

Faucher ushered his man out and Renard walked across to the open window. The slightest of breezes brought a little, very little relief from the heat. He smiled to himself. He considered himself a good judge of character and the muleteer was a murderous villain if ever there was one. He decided that it would be about four weeks before Roberts was dead. A cold, mirthless chuckle escaped his lips.

Chapter 17

The pursuit of the French from Salamanca ended when they abandoned the city of Valladolid on the river Pisuerga. Wellington and his army were greeted by ecstatic citizens and the great and the good immediately organised a ball in honour of the Earl of Wellington, Marquess of Torres Vedras and Duke of Ciudad Rodrigo. As Michael listened to Wellington being announced at the ball, he thought that it was little wonder he was referred to by his staff as the Peer. It was a grand affair despite the speed at which it had been staged. Michael leant against the wall at the side of the ballroom, candles flickering in the failing, early evening light that made its way in through a few windows high in the far wall. Like many present, he was still in his day to day uniform, scruffy and travel stained. The baggage was still some way off, he'd heard it might arrive later that night. He would be glad as it would allow him to change horses. He'd been riding Johnny for the best part of a week now, and while the horse was managing, the long days and many miles covered were having their effect and he was loosing condition and weight. He could not imagine that there was any immediate prospect of action so he would be glad to rest Johnny and ride, probably Robbie, who was comfortable and had stamina.

The ladies of Valladolid had certainly put their all into their appearance tonight. They whirled and danced excitedly with any officer they could seize. Michael was persuaded to dance by several of them despite his appearance, he hadn't even shaved for three days, but he was not alone in that. One or two, or even three, he conceded, were very attractive women, some with husbands, some without although a host of older ladies, chaperones was gathered around the floor, watching everything carefully. They had nothing to worry about as far as he was concerned, he thought. He was tired and felt no inclination to seek out fresh company.

He was startled when an orderly appeared at his side. "Begging your pardon, sir, but the Earl would like a word, sir, when this is over, sir."

"Very good, thank you."

Wellington was standing amongst a group of senior officers of the Light and First Divisions who had been leading the advance of the army. Around them was a positive cordon of ladies of all ages, hoping to catch the eye of the man of the hour. It was, in fact, more than two hours before Michael saw Wellington making his excuses and heading for the door, his closest staff with him. He hurriedly followed. All the staff was billeted together in one of the largest houses in the city centre. In the hall of the house the group broke up, each heading for bed. De Lancey caught his arm.

"This way, Roberts," he said, and led Michael into a sitting room where Wellington was waiting alone.

"Roberts, come in. Thank you, De Lancey, that will be all."

The door closed behind De Lancey and Wellington said, "I need you to go to Salamanca, quickly, you must leave at first light."

Michael was taken aback, but answered, "Yes, my Lord."

"Ostensibly you are enquiring on my behalf after the health of Marshal Beresford and Sir Stapleton. When they might be able to return to active service, that sort of thing. However, what I need you to do is seek out Father Curtis. Tell him that I am considering a march on Madrid." Michael was visibly surprised and Wellington's lips tightened in a grim smile at Michael's reaction. "Yes, Captain, and if I do decide upon that particular course of action I shall need you to use all your undoubted skills and clear out any spies left there, ferret 'em out. I don't want them reporting what I do next. Father Curtis will be able to provide you with useful information to help you."

"Yes, my Lord."

"You had better take that orderly of yours, it's a spare horse for you if anything goes wrong."

"Yes, my Lord."

"You have three days, you will find me at Cuellar by then. Is that all clear?"

"Yes, my Lord."

"Then I shall bid you goodnight, Captain Roberts. If you see one of my servants, send 'em in."

"Yes, my Lord, goodnight, my Lord."

Michael and Lloyd left Valladolid an hour before dawn after a very short night's sleep. It was some eighty miles to Salamanca, he hoped to manage it in fourteen or fifteen hours. The road was reasonable, the only difficult bit was the climb up and then down into the Guarena valley, but at least they did that in daylight. They rode slowly into Salamanca just as the sun was leaving the sky and made their way to the

Palacio San Boal where both Cotton and Beresford were being cared for. He quickly learnt that Cotton was expected to recover in two months or so, but that Beresford, while in no danger, might take as long as six months before he was fit for duty, it was uncertain. His ostensible duty done, Michael checked on Lloyd and the horses, found all was well, found somewhere to lay his head and fell into a long sleep.

After breakfast the next morning, Michael left Lloyd tending to the two horses. They were tired and would need rest and attention before making the return trip tomorrow. It hadn't occurred to him to ask Wellington how he was to find Father Curtis, and he didn't like to ask too many people, given the nature of his task. He thought the university would be as good a place to start as any. He knew he was a Professor of astronomy and natural history at the university and had held the post of Rector of the Irish College. Wandering up to the university he asked for directions to the library. He thought he might pose as someone with an interest in astronomy and find Curtis that way. He was in luck. Curtis was working in the library and an attendant pointed him out as the man he needed to speak to.

Curtis was sitting at a desk with a large, ancient looking book in front of him. As Michael approached, Curtis looked up and surprise flashed fleetingly across his face.

"Father Curtis?" he asked, in Spanish.

"Yes, my son?"

"I have an interest in astronomy and I was hoping you can help me?"

Curtis leant back in his chair and looked Michael up and down before answering. "We cannot speak here, my son, it is a library." He rose slowly from his chair. "Follow me and I will see how I might help you."

Curtis led the way through halls and corridors and up wide staircases until he finally showed Michael into a small study. There were papers and books everywhere. Curtis cleared a chair for Michael and waved him to sit while he took his chair behind a large desk. With bookcases, two chairs and the desk there was not a lot of room, and it was hot and stuffy.

"Now, Captain Roberts, isn't it?"

"Yes, Father."

"You do realise, of course," Curtis had switched to English and his Irish brogue became obvious, "that if I hadn't met you in Wellington's company, heard your conversation, that we would now be discussing the phases of the moon?"

Michael smiled and Curtis asked him, "So why has Wellington sent you to see me? That is, I assume you have come from him?"

"Yes, Father, I have. He is considering an advance on Madrid." Curtis suddenly looked as if he understood. "If he takes Madrid he wants me to clear out any French spies. He would like his subsequent moves to be a secret from the French for as long as possible. He thought you would be able to give me information to help with that."

"Oh, he did, did he? Well, not as much help as I might have a month or two ago. Renard has been rather effective in finding out my correspondents. As I said, at least two are dead. The others, understandably,

316

have gone silent. I have heard nothing for some time now." He looked intently at Michael. "I have had no further news about his, err, vendetta against you, Captain. It may be that by now he has sent someone after you."

Michael was shocked. "Do you think that is a serious threat?"

"I think that Monsieur Renard is a man not to be taken lightly. I think you would be well advised to take the threat seriously, so long as Renard lives. I believe that where you are concerned he is not entirely rational. I say this simply to put you on your guard. Particularly if you do find yourself in Madrid."

"Thank you, Father, but it's not as if he hasn't tried before."

"Is that so? But he only has to succeed once." He paused to let that sink in. "Now, more practical help, help in Madrid should you get there. To be frank, there is not a lot I can suggest. My correspondents had their informants who I do not know. As I said, they have all gone silent and two are dead. There is, however, one who might be in a position to help you."

"Yes, Father?"

"But you will need to be very, very circumspect in how you approach her"

"Her?"

"Yes, a lady of position in Madrid society, a guest of and hostess to generals, even the court of Joseph. Any approach must be under the cover of social occasions, of which there will, no doubt be many, if Wellington enters Madrid."

"Of course, I understand."

"Her name is Señora Ortega. When you meet her, as I said she is well known and I imagine you will have no difficulty meeting her somewhere, say that a mutual friend with an interest in astronomy sends greetings, a Señor Orion. Then do as she tells you. And that Captain, is as much as I can do. I know, it seems precious little, but you may not have to do much to neutralise the French agents in Madrid. Take out the key people and the organisation will cease to function. It is the organisers you want, not the poor agents out in the streets and the rich ones in the salons."

Michael nodded appreciatively at that advice.

"And now, let me guide you out of this labyrinth."

Curtis stopped a little short of the exit from the university building. "If you don't mind, I shall leave you here." He held out his hand and they shook. "Good luck, Captain."

Michael walked slowly through the streets of Salamanca, deep in thought. He was both discouraged and encouraged by his meeting with Curtis. He had come away with a single name, but the suggestion of just needing to take out a few of the right people gave him grounds for optimism. The idea of being a hunted man, however, was disturbing. It was one thing to take one's chance on the battlefield, but to be specifically targeted was something else entirely. He could only see one answer, kill Renard.

He paused in a small square, right would take him back the Palacio, left would take him to Victoria's house. After the barest hesitation he turned right and left her behind him.

The ride to Cuellar was long and tiring. The road was not as good, it was unfamiliar and the horses were not fully recovered from the ride to Salamanca. It was several hours after dark that they rode in, passing uneventfully through the lines of vedettes, pickets and sentries until they reached Wellington's headquarters. Wellington, they learnt, had only arrived that day and the army was still gathering around the town. Leaving Lloyd to deal with the horses, Michael went to report to Wellington.

Wellington was busy with De Lancey and several of his Divisional commanders. Wellington glanced up and saw him. "All well, Roberts?"

"Yes, my Lord."

"Good, that will be all."

Michael found Hall looking for him. "I heard as you were back, Captain, your billet is this way, sir. I've saved you a little supper, sir, and I'll bring you some tea shortly."

"Tea?"

"Oh, aye, sir, all the best things in these headquarters, sir."

"Excellent, and see if you can find something for Lloyd as well. He'll be with the horses, wherever they are."

Half an hour later, Michael was asleep.

They had two days of rest at Cuellar, while the army gathered around and waited for orders. Michael received a very welcome letter from Senhor Furtado. He read it and bellowed out, "Hall, fetch Lloyd, lively now, and bring a bottle of something good and glasses!"

Hall appeared a few minutes later with a bottle of brandy, two glasses and Lloyd. "Sorry, sir, it's only half a bottle, it's the best I could do, sir."

Michael beamed. "Never mind. My congratulations, Lloyd, you have a daughter! Hall, pour a couple of glasses, find one for yourself as well."

Lloyd stood gaping, then a huge grin appeared on his face. "Diolch yn fawr, Captain, sir, diolch yn fawr."

Michael handed him a glass of brandy. "Right, a toast, to, what's her name, Lloyd"

"I don't know, sir, we didn't discuss names, sir."

"Very well. A toast, to Miss Lloyd!"

They emptied the glasses, leaving Hall spluttering. Michael handed his glass to Hall. "Go and have a glass with Bradley."

The two men left and Michael sat down to consider the rest of the letter, which was not bad news, but needed some consideration. Furtado told him that Senhora Pinheiro had married and left, Frederico going with her. That was damned inconvenient, particularly with Mrs Lloyd in the house. He would have to get some help in. Furtado had also received a further communication from Senhorita Cardoso pushing to buy the quinta. He sat back and closed his eyes. Catarina! That was, was, he wasn't sure what it was. An opportunity, perhaps lost for good or ill, and he didn't know which. If he ever saw her again he might find out. Suddenly he felt lonely, in need of company. Not the company of comrades, nor of a simple lover, but the company of a lover and companion, a true love. He envied Lloyd. He thought of his room in Lisbon, of the big portmanteau and the oilskin wrapped package with its portrait and letter. He smiled at the memories the thought evoked and felt a little better.

That evening came the orders that they were advancing on Madrid. Michael felt a thrill of excitement, of anticipation at what was to come for him. He told Hall to be ready to march before dawn and went down to the stables to tell the others. He called Lloyd aside.

"Lloyd, when we get to Madrid I am going to be hunting spies again and I shall need you with me."

Lloyds eyes lit up. "Duw, there's good, sir, better than some duties, and I hear that Madrid is a mighty fine city, sir."

"Yes, well, we shall see. There's another thing that I want to discuss with you."

"Oh, aye, sir?"

"Yes, well, I have to tell you that Senhora Pinheiro has left, got married, Frederico has gone as well. Just as well I sent White."

"Oh!"

"Yes, it's a damned nuisance, though I wish her well. So, I was wondering if Maggie, Mrs Lloyd, would care to take on the job of housekeeper?"

"Duw, diolch yn fawr, sir, that would be very good, sir, very good indeed." He stopped himself. "If she is happy with the proposal, that is, sir."

Michael laughed. "Of course, Lloyd. I shall write to Senhor Furtado to discuss it with her and we shall see. I can tell him to employ some help for Mrs Lloyd as well, whatever she feels she needs. May I pass on your approval of the idea?"

"What? Yes, of course, sir. Diolch yn fawr."

Michael wrote accordingly to Furtado, also telling him to refuse Senhorita Cardoso for the moment, telling her the owner hoped to be able to visit the quinta during the coming winter and would make a decision after that.

.   .   .

When the news of Wellington's advance on Madrid was confirmed there was a great rush by the French to evacuate the city. In the midst of the chaos Renard found time to speak with his best agent in Madrid.

"Father," Renard welcomed his visitor, "I am sorry that it has come to this."

"Thank you, Monsieur, it is indeed a sad day, but, God willing, you will return."

"Let us hope so. But there is something I need to tell you before we leave." He paused for a second. "There is a British officer, a very dangerous man who is likely to come into Madrid with the British." The priest raised his eyebrows quizzically. "I say dangerous with some certainty. He has been very successful in eliminating our agents in Lisbon. I have no doubt that he will be set to the same work here."

"Do you know who this man is?"

"Fortunately, yes. He is a Captain Michael Roberts, a cavalry officer, a light dragoon, serving on the staff."

"There are many such men, they all look alike in their uniforms, much as we priests do."

"Yes, Father, but this one has a scar, on his cheek, from here to here." Renard ran his finger down his left cheek.

"What would you have me do?"

"I think it would be advisable for you to leave Madrid for the time being, at least until this man leaves himself. We cannot risk your capture, Father, you are too useful to us." The priest nodded in agreement. "I also think you should warn your people, and if it could be arranged for some accident to befall him..." Renard left his sentence unfinished.

.   .   .

A few days later Wellington entered Madrid. The French had evacuated the city with minor resistance and fled southeast, leaving a small garrison holding the citadel and arsenal of the Retiro, a fortified area on heights to the east of the city. The welcome received by Wellington and the army was one of enthusiasm and elation. For five miles out of the city the road was lined with crowds bearing flowers, bread, wine, grapes, lemonade and every conceivable treat. Michael grinned and laughed as drinks were pressed on him and young and not so young women grabbed at his arms, tried to fling their arms around his neck and pull him down for a kiss. Wellington was almost pulled from his horse by the cheering crowds.

Somehow they found their way to the Royal Palace and began to take up residence.

While the staff set about establishing headquarters and infantry secured the area and surrounded the Retiro, Michael and Lloyd went exploring in the Palace. There were plenty of rooms that showed clear signs of long term residency, now being occupied by delighted staff officers and their servants. Huge salons and dining rooms were again pressed into service for conference rooms and offices. Michael and Lloyd went higher.

Under the roof they found more evidence of offices and quarters for the French occupiers. They walked all around the upper floor, but nothing obvious grabbed their attention. There were not even chalked names on doors to indicate who the occupants might have been. After a fruitless hour and more, they returned to the hustle and bustle of the lower floors. Order had been established, quarters allocated and sentries posted. Michael saw Colonel De Lancey, who called out to him.

"Roberts, there you are, come and get your allocated quarters. A room for you and one for your people." He turned and called out to an orderly. "Here, show Captain Roberts his rooms." He consulted a list. "Yes, yes," he looked up, "and the same orderly will show you where the stables are, all the baggage is being brought in there."

Another hour of chaos and confusion followed. The quarters were splendid, the windows had glass in them, and there were beds! Admittedly without mattresses or bedding, but even so! It was unaccustomed luxury. The staff all dined together in a magnificent room, high ceilinged, and fortunately in no need of artificial light as the sun streamed in through tall windows. A long table dominated the room, but they all had to bring their own chairs, the French had pillaged the palace thoroughly before leaving. As night eventually fell, servants came in with lanterns of all descriptions and the air filled with the smell of cigars. It was after midnight before Michael fell into his very welcome bed.

Breakfast was a more subdued affair. Coffee and bread rolls were consumed in relative silence. A short stroll took Michael to the stables, which were far better than a lot of billets he had known. He returned the salutes of the grooms and batmen and found Lloyd, Hall, Bradley and Marcello hard at work on his animals. He was assured all was well with all the horses, that Bradley and Marcello had very good quarters over the stables and that there was nothing he was required for. He decided a walk would be in order, to clear his head. He could start thinking about his task. He hadn't seen Wellington yet, but had a feeling that when he did he would be expected to have made some progress. He admitted to himself that he had no idea where to start beyond, hopefully, making contact with Señora Ortega at some point.

Michael strolled around the city seeking inspiration. A short walk brought him to the Plaza Mayor. Further to the east he could hear sporadic gunfire coming from the Retiro. He leant against a pillar of the colonnade that ran around the square. He watched as bemused private soldiers wandered across the square, gawping at the sights, some of them appeared to be already the worse for drink.

Suddenly a voice from just behind him said "Who is the most beautiful woman in Madrid?"

Michael spun around in amazement. "Antonio!"

"Hello, Miguel," A grinning Antonio answered him.

"What the devil are you doing here?"

"Now that, Miguel, is an interesting story, one that requires a little lubrication. Come on, this way."

An utterly bemused Michael allowed his friend to take his arm and lead the way out of the square, around a few corners and into a small taverna. At that early hour it was empty and they took a table towards the rear, Antonio calling for coffee for them both.

Michael recovered from his surprise. "Antonio, what are you doing in Madrid."

"Now Miguel, please don't ask why I am here, that would just be an embarrassment to both of us. However, what I am doing, just now, will be of interest to you, I think."

"And just what is that?"

"Oh, Miguel, I am so sorry," his grin widened, "I am being paid to kill you!"

"What?"

"Yes, by your Monsieur Renard, no less."

"Antonio, please, just explain."

"Ah, well, you see, I just happen to be here, visiting some old friends, and one of them came out with a wonderful story. Apparently there was some French clerk asking around for someone who would like to earn a lot of money for dealing with some British officer. Said he particularly wanted a muleteer. It made me think about your problems, so I asked where this clerk might be found, made a joke of not enough profit from my trip. Anyway, I found him and asked him what it was all about." Antonio shrugged. "It was ridiculous, really. The man would have been knifed and left lying in an alley if he wasn't so amusing and generous with his money, night after night. Of course, I asked him about it, assured him I was a muleteer, just wearing my best clothes for a señorita. He told me that his chief, a very important Frenchman called Monsieur Renard, was being caused considerable difficulty by some English officer and he would be very pleased to pay to have him killed."

"How much?" Michael broke in.

"I don't think I should tell you."

"Why not?"

"If you think it is too little you will be disappointed, if it is a lot you will get big headed!"

"No! Come on, how much?"

"Alright, two hundred and fifty dollars."

"Oh!" Michael wasn't sure what to make of the amount.

"It doesn't matter. I suspect it would never have been paid."

"But you said you would do it?"

"I did, eventually, I made him work hard to get me. Anyway, this clerk took me to see Renard. That was interesting, I dressed up like a muleteer, smelt like one too. Made out I don't speak any French, my

Spanish was good enough to fool them." He sipped his coffee. "Renard gave me the once over, asked if this clerk thought I was capable of the job. Little bastard said he was sure because he'd checked me out with some unsavoury people, which I know is a lie. If he had, I would have been told. Then Renard told this fellow to send me off to kill you. And that's all there is to it. Oh, and Renard knows you have a scar. His clerk gave me quite a good description."

Michael sat, stunned by Antonio's story. After a few minutes had passed in silence, Antonio spoke.

"So, Miguel, my friend," his face was expressionless, "I reckon that you owe me two hundred and fifty dollars."

Michael stared at him, "What?"

Antonio burst out laughing. "Oh, Miguel, your face!"

Michael had little choice but to laugh as well. Then a thought struck him, it was Antonio's remark about his face that sparked it. "How does Renard know about my scar?" He touched it lightly, unconsciously.

"Somebody must have told him, given him a description of you."

"Yes, but who?"

Antonio shrugged as if it were no matter, but it was irritating Michael and he sat thinking about it.

"Come on, Miguel, you have been seen by enough French agents."

Michael looked at his friend. "And how many lived to tell Renard?"

"Well, there was, err, ah, yes, I see what you mean."

"Yes, it bears thinking about." He sipped his coffee. "Of course! I know!"

"Who?"

"Lieutenant Lapointe, it must have been him!" Michael told him about sending him with a message for Renard.

Antonio was sceptical, "I hope you don't come to regret that, Michael."

"Well, anyway, he must have told Renard when he delivered my message. I should have liked to have seen that." He took another sip of coffee. "Do you remember where Renard's office was?"

"Yes, of course, I do."

"In the Palacio?"

"Yes."

"Then you can show me where it is, come on."

On the way they collected Lloyd who was as surprised to see Antonio as Michael had been. The office was one of the rooms up under the place roof. Next to it Antonio pointed out another room that was where the clerks had worked. Together they went carefully through both rooms, looking for anything left behind. As they did, Antonio told Lloyd about his meeting with Renard. He was as taken aback as Michael had been and swore, fluently, in Portuguese. They found nothing, and sat, disconsolately, on the floor. Then Michael explained to Antonio his task in Madrid.

"Look," he said, "these people you know here, do you think they might know anything about people who might be French agents?"

"I doubt it, and I don't think it would be wise to go asking them questions, they keep to themselves and are only interested in business."

"Business?" Michael asked.

"Yes, making money, and they don't care how."

"Will you help me?"

"Of course. Do you think you can remember where that taverna is we were just in?"

"Yes."

"Leave a message there for me. Just say you need to see Antonio from Lisbon. I assume you are living here?" Michael nodded. "Then I can find you. And if I do learn anything, I will let you know."

They left Renard's office and Michael let Lloyd escort Antonio out while he went to where Wellington and his staff were at work. De Lancey, looking harassed as ever, saw him and said, "The Peer was asking after you," he pointed towards a door, "best go and see him, just knock and go in."

Wellington and a few of his staff were sitting around drinking tea. "Roberts!" exclaimed Wellington, "Good hunting?"

"Not yet my Lord, but I have identified Renard's offices here and searched them. They were quite empty. I have also recruited some local help."

"Good, but press on Roberts, press on. Now, General de España has been appointed Governor of Madrid. It has been deemed expeditious to keep the Chief of Police in post. I gather he was not keen in his pursuit of the enemies of France, but, unfortunately, Monsieur Renard was rather more effective. The Chief of Police does not like Renard, not at all. I think you might find him helpful, but do not rely on him. So, press on Captain, press on."

"Yes, my Lord," and Michael left the room.

Chapter 18

The following morning the French garrison in the Retiro surrendered. Michael went to watch them march out and into captivity, some two thousand men. In addition it was discovered that there were roughly five hundred wounded who were unable to be moved. It was getting on in the afternoon by the time the little drama was concluded and Michael returned to the Palacio to dress for a ball being given that night. He was rather hoping there might be a Señora Ortega there.

Michael was early arriving at the ball. He wanted to take no chances of missing Señora Ortega and took up position near the entrance, where he could hear the arrivals being announced. A small orchestra was playing. Gradually the ballroom and the refreshment rooms began to fill, people began to dance. Wellington arrived and brought the ball to a halt as the civilians present applauded him. The orchestra played what sounded vaguely like God Save the King. Wellington waved graciously and began to circulate around the room. The music started again.

Then the master of ceremonies announced "Señora Ortega!"

The woman paused for a second in the entrance and then swept into the room. Michael put her as in her thirties. Handsome rather than pretty. Her black hair was beautifully styled and interwoven with chains of pearls, matched by the pearls at her throat and hanging from her ears. Her dress was a deep, rich burgundy colour, the silk shimmering. Long, white gloves reached above her elbows and she carried an ivory fan. Michael was impressed. He watched as she was immediately surrounded by both men and women and, very shortly, was presented to Wellington. He smiled graciously at her and then took her out on to the floor for a dance.

Eventually, for she was a popular person in the ball, Michael managed to get close to her and took advantage of the confusion between two dances to say to her, "Señora Ortega, I believe we have a mutual acquaintance with an interest in astronomy, Señor Orion."

Michael was impressed as she gave no indication that Michael's words meant anything. She was busily fanning her face and without looking she said to Michael, "Come and see me tomorrow morning, at eleven, alone." Then she was gone, whisked away for the next dance.

Michael watched for a while, and saw her give him a long look of appraisal. He smiled to himself, and went to bed.

Michael had no difficulty finding out where Señora Ortega's house was and when he arrived he was shown into a splendidly decorated drawing room where the Señora was seated at a table, the remains of her breakfast before her. They were left alone and she indicated a seat to him.

"Señor, you have the advantage of me, but any friend of my astronomer friend is a friend of mine."

"Thank you, Señora. I am Captain Roberts, I am on the Earl of Wellington's staff."

She raised one eyebrow. "And how can I help you, Captain?"

Briefly, Michael told her of his meeting with Father Curtis and the task he had been set by Wellington.

"And you think that I may be able to help you?"

"I hope so, Señora, any information you have could be useful."

"You realise, I hope, that it is the French themselves who were my greatest source? It is surprising what you can pick up at dinners and soirees when the wine flows. But they have all left."

"I wonder, did you ever meet a Monsieur Renard?"

"Not a soldier?"

"No."

"Not that I can recall."

She sat quietly for a minute, sipping her coffee. "There is one thing, it might be nothing."

"Please, Señora?"

"I do remember being rather surprised on two or three occasions, in the palace, when I caught a glimpse of a priest who seemed to be on very good terms with Marshal Jourdan. I never learnt his name, but he never appeared at any social events, and each time I glimpsed him he seemed to be at pains to avoid people." She smiled at Michael, "That is all, but you must come to one of my soirees, I hold one every week. If I remember anything, or hear anything in the meantime, I will tell you then."

Michael returned to the Palacio where an orderly approached him.

"Captain Roberts, sir!"

"Yes, what is it?"

"Beg your pardon, sir, it's a bit odd, but this note was delivered for you, sir, came from the Spanish officer in charge of all the prisoners taken at the Retiro, sir."

Michael took the note and read it with increasing surprise. It was from Lieutenant Lapointe, the dragoon officer he had sent to Madrid with a message for Renard. Lapointe sent his apologies and stated that he had not been able to deliver the message to Renard as he had been placed under arrest on his arrival in Madrid.

Michael looked up at the orderly, "Do you know where the French officers from the Retiro are being held?"

Michael found Lapointe looking very sorry for himself, locked in a crowded warehouse on the edge of the city. He had to use his full authority as a member of the Earl of Wellington's staff to get Lapointe out for him to talk to. Michael was allowed to stand in a dirty courtyard with him, watched closely by three Spanish infantrymen and an officer.

Lapointe spoke before Michael could say anything. "Captain, did my men get to the British safely?"

Michael decided he rather liked this young Frenchman for his concern for his men. "Yes, Lieutenant, they did, quite safely."

Lapointe smiled with relief. "Thank you. As for myself," he shrugged, "my story was not met with sympathy and I was arrested and locked up. I was unable to see your Monsieur Renard or to send your message. My apologies, Captain."

"You didn't see him at all, or anyone from his department?"

Lapointe shook his head and looked puzzled, "No, Monsieur, no one at all."

"Did you describe me to anyone, perhaps you mentioned this?" Michael touched his scar.

"No, Monsieur, no one!"

"Thank you. I am sorry to see you like this, particularly after you gave me your parole. Is there anything I can do to help you?"

"No, Monsieur, but thank you for asking."

Michael walked slowly back to the Palacio, deep in thought, he was puzzled, troubled even. He wasn't sure why, but he believed it was important that he should discover who told Renard about his scar. He couldn't think of a single French agent who could have done it, those that he had met were all dead. There was no reason he could see for any of them to have sent a description of him to Renard, he had been in Paris until recently and a description would not have helped him at all.

Then it came to him. There was only one person who had seen him recently and who could have described him to Renard in Madrid. Montero! He had hoped the man would contact him, he had been prepared to wait a few days for him, but now he believed he knew why he hadn't seen him. He was an afrancesado and had fooled him completely. He felt foolish and angry in equal measures.

By the time he arrived back at his quarters he had calmed down enough to share the news with his party. The news was met with silence.

"And now," he began, "this is what we are going to do. Bradley, Marcello, you will stay here and look after the horses." They nodded. "Lloyd, Hall, you will be with me until we find Montero and any bloody spies in this city." He took a deep breath. "First, I want to find Antonio, I don't think we'll get anywhere without his help. So, out of stable kit and we leave in ten minutes to find him."

The three men caused a stir when they walked into the small taverna. Michael led the way to a booth and waved Lloyd and Hall to sit down.

"This is no time to stand on ceremony." A worried looking waiter approached. "Three coffees, Señor."

He waited until the waiter returned and was placing the coffees on their table. Then, very quietly, he said, "Señor, I wish to speak to Antonio from Lisbon." The waiter gave the slightest of nods and went through a door at the back.

They were only half way through the coffees when Antonio strolled in through the front door and slid into the booth, calling for coffee as he did so. He looked at the three very serious faces.

"What has happened?"

Michael told him. Told him about his error in trusting Montero. Told him as much as he knew about him. Told him he urgently wanted to find him and have a discussion with him. His tone left Antonio in no doubt about the nature of the discussion.

When Michael finished his tale, Antonio sat silent for moment, then he said, "I will do what I can." He paused. "It will require some expense, Michael, can you manage that?"

"How much"

"Fifty dollars should be enough."

"I can let you have that now if you come back to the Palacio with me."

"Good, let's go."

Back in Michael's quarters he dug out from his baggage the money he had received from the paymaster nearly four months ago. "Here's fifty, I can find more if I have to."

"That should be enough, I hope, and if this man is in Madrid."

"Even if we only find where he lives, that would be something."

Antonio nodded. "I shall be in the taverna at dusk tomorrow." He looked at Michael, Lloyd and Hall in the uniforms and tarleton with sabres hanging by their sides. "It might be helpful if you were to wear something less obvious?"

"We can do that, can you take us somewhere, now?"

Antonio nodded.

Night was just falling the following day when a Spanish gentleman and two servants walked into the taverna. It was empty save for a bored looking waiter. The gentleman waved his men to one booth, and sat in solitary splendour in another towards the back.

Even as he was ordering wine for himself and his servants he was joined by a fourth man.

"Miguel."

"Antonio. Any luck?"

"Not yet, I'm sorry, these things can take time." Antonio's head came up and he looked at the door. "A moment, Miguel."

Antonio slipped away to join another man who had just come in. They sat close together and spoke for a few minutes. Then Antonio shook the man's hand and slipped back into Michael's booth.

"That is a friend of mine. He says that someone is following you."

"What? Dressed like this?"

"Miguel, you left the Palacio in daylight, everyone knows it is where Wellington is, and this," he touched his own cheek, "is quite obvious."

Michael thought for a moment. "Why did your friend notice this?"

"Ah, probably because I asked him to keep an eye out for you, he was not expensive."

Michael shook his head. "Alright, Antonio, what do we do?"

"That depends on why he is following you. If he wants to see where you go, who you meet, it's too late to worry about it. But, Miguel, remember what happened in Lisbon when you were followed."

"Could your friend see if there's more than one man?"

At that moment two men, scarves around their faces, a pistol in each hand, came in quickly through the open doorway. Lloyd shouted out, "Sir!"

Four pistol shots rang out in quick succession, they were followed by another three, one each from Lloyd, Hall and Antonio's friend. One pistol ball had scored a line across Michael's arm as he had tried to drop. He levered himself upright.

"Antonio!"

His friend lay face down on the table, blood still oozing from two wounds in his back. Michael shook him, but Antonio's unseeing eyes told him it was hopeless.

"No!" Michael bellowed.

Then Lloyd was beside him and looked at Antonio. "I'm sorry, sir."

Hall and the other man were both reloading and standing over two figures lying half in and half out of the doorway.

"This one's alive, sir, it's Montero." Michael turned his gaze from his friend to the man on the floor, who groaned and clutched at his arm. The look on his face was one of ice cold hatred. Hall shuddered at the sight.

There were shouts from outside, the sound of running feet. Antonio's friend walked quickly towards the back of the taverna, touching his friend lightly as he passed, and then he was gone through the door at the back.

Michael strode to the door and looked down at Montero. He was conscious, his arm broken and bleeding from a pistol ball in the upper arm, his pistols lying on the floor. The other man was clearly dead. A Spanish NCO with half a dozen men appeared, muskets cocked and ready. Michael was not going to be trifled with.

"What the hell do you think you are doing, uncock those muskets now! I am Captain Roberts of the Earl of Wellington's staff. Corporal, stand your men down now or I'll have you all flogged. Now!"

Michael's tone, his whole demeanour brooked no dissension. The Corporal gave his orders, the muskets came down, and one man was dispatched for an officer.

"Thank you, Corporal." Michael's voice was hard, cold. "I'll thank you to keep out of here while I question this man." His eyes bored into those of the Corporal who just nodded and waved his men back.

Lloyd and Hall had reloaded and were standing on either side of Michael. "Drag Montero clear of the door." As he spoke, Michael took out his knife with its razor sharp blade, opened and locked the blade. "Lloyd, Hall, close the door. No one comes in."

"Aye, sir."

Michael knelt down beside Montero, whose eyes were bulging with pain and fear.

"Hurts, does it?" Michael asked. Montero managed a nod. "Believe me, you haven't felt any pain yet." He prodded the wound with the point of his knife and Montero screamed.

"Who are you working for?" Montero shook head and then screamed again.

Michael lifted the knife from the wound. "Who are you working for?"

Montero whispered, "The priest."

"What's his name?"

"I don't know, no really I don't, I swear!"

Michael paused, the knife half an inch from the wound. "You have sworn to me before, Montero, why should I believe you now?"

"I don't know his name, he worked for Renard."

"Did you tell Renard what I look like, about this?" He touched his scar with the knife and Montero nodded.

"Did Renard tell you to try this?"

"Yes, no, the priest did, but he said it was Renard's idea." Montero gritted his teeth against the pain.

"Sir! There's a Spanish officer with a lot more men, sir!" Lloyd called anxiously from the door.

"Can you give me one reason why I shouldn't kill you now?"

Montero whispered, "I can tell you where the priest's clerk is."

Michael rose to his feet. "Lloyd, come and watch this bastard."

He walked to the door and opened it, coming face to face with a Spanish officer. "Yes, who are you?"

The question threw the officer who found himself face to face with a man dressed as a Spanish gentleman, a look like thunder on his face and blood, apparently unnoticed, soaking the sleeve of his coat. "Lieutenant Risco, officer of the guard."

"Well, I am Captain Roberts of the Earl of Wellington's staff and I am questioning a prisoner. I would be grateful if you would let me get on with it. When I have finished you can help me get this man to the Palacio."

Michael had to admire the man's tenacity. "No, Señor, I do not know who you are, you are not in uniform. I must ask you to stop. I shall send a man to the Palacio for a British officer."

Michael realised that he was beaten, for the moment.

"Very well, Lieutenant. Lloyd, Hall, put up your pistols. Let the lieutenant in."

The Earl of Wellington was angry. "Roberts, what in God's name do you think you were doing, running around Madrid out of uniform, shooting people and then torturing them? Well?"

"I was following your orders, my Lord!"

Wellington looked as if he were about to explode, then he took a deep breath and looked around the room at the staff gathered about.

"Out! Everybody out, now!" He waited until there was only Michael left in the room. "Now, Captain, tell me exactly what you have been doing and why I shouldn't have you arrested and court martialled?"

When Michael had finished the long story, omitting nothing, Wellington stood, fingers drumming on a table. He stopped. "Roberts, I am sorry about your friend."

"Thank you, my Lord."

"How is your arm?" He pointed to the bandage around the top of Michael's arm.

"The surgeon said it's nothing serious, my Lord."

Wellington grunted and asked, "What about this clerk Montero mentioned?"

"I don't know, sir. I should like to question him further."

"Hmm." Wellington was silent for a few thoughtful moments. "In uniform, this time?"

"Yes, my Lord."

"And you are not to lay so much as a finger on him, I won't have my officers torturing people, d'ye hear?"

"Yes, my Lord."

Wellington stood silent again. "De Lancey can observe, take notes." It wasn't a question.

"Yes, my Lord."

"Then go and get properly dressed before I change my mind."

De Lancey was waiting for Michael outside the room where Montero was under guard.

"Roberts, not sure I like this, but The Peer says, so here I am and he says you're not to, ah, harm him."

"Yes, sir. I give you my word, sir, that I shall not lay a finger on him."

"There's a but, isn't there, damn it?"

"Yes, sir. Montero doesn't know that."

"Ah."

"Shall we, sir?" De Lancey nodded, and Michael led the way in.

Inside were two NCOs with sidearms and Montero lying on a straw palliasse on the floor, his wounded arm now bandaged. De Lancey ordered the two NCOs out and as they went Michael heard one say "Surgeon says he won't lose his arm, sir."

The door closed and Michael walked over to Montero. Standing over him, he pulled out his knife and opened and locked the blood stained blade. "Montero, you have killed a very good friend of mine. If you want to live you will answer my questions. You might keep your eyes as well."

An hour later Michael had all the information that he felt Montero knew. De Lancey's face was white, but he had to accept that Michael had not laid a finger on Montero. They called the guards back in and went to see Wellington.

Michael, with De Lancey nodding his confirmation, informed him that he got the name of a clerk, a Spaniard, who worked for the mysterious priest, handling all payments made for information. He added that Montero had repeated that it was the priest who had encouraged him to attack Michael, but that he had intimated that it was Renard's suggestion.

Wellington listened carefully and then asked, "Do you know where this clerk can be found?"

"Yes, sir."

"Then you had better go and get him. In uniform, take your men and, De Lancey, you go as well with half a dozen men."

It was midnight when they crashed into the clerk's rooms. Ramos was not a brave man, he went along with De Lancey and his men very quietly while Michael searched his rooms. It took a while, but under a loose floorboard Hall found a small note book. It was full of names, dates, and sums of money. All that was missing were the addresses. Michael flicked through it by the light of a candle. He found what he was looking for. There was only one priest, who got far more money than anyone else. Father Diego Lopez.

Back at the Palacio, Michael was shown into Wellington's office and was surprised to find, in addition to De Lancey, General de Espana, the Governor of Madrid, and another man who, it transpired, was the Chief of Police in Madrid. Michael handed over the notebook and a discussion took place on the best course of action.

Antonio's funeral was held the next day at a small church on the outskirts of Madrid. Apart from the priest, only Michael, Lloyd and Hall were in attendance. At the graveside, after the committal, Lloyd took Hall by the arm and, without a word, led him away, leaving Michael watching the grave diggers fill in the grave. Michael was angry, angrier than he could remember ever being. He wanted to roar his anger at the heavens, but his icy self control kept him in check. There was a huge weight of guilt as well. He could not help but think that if Sanchez had hanged Montero his friend would still be alive.

He had thought he was being so damned clever. He lifted his eyes to the skies as the earth covered his friend and swore that he would be avenged.

Michael paid the costs of the funeral and wrote to Furtado asking him to break the news to Bernardo and to find out if Antonio had any family or dependents, but he was sure Antonio had left only his friends. Then he set about cleansing Madrid.

It was soon discovered that Lopez was not in Madrid. A discreet watch was set on his house and the police went quietly about identifying as many of those named in the book as they could. One name interested Michael in particular. It was Diaz, after his name was a single word, "painter". With that clue he was quickly identified as a fairly successful artist. The police were puzzled, he had no known sympathies for the French, and the sums of money were only two, but very big ones, unlike any others. Michael took note and said nothing. No arrests were made, it was felt that any such action would scare off Lopez entirely and he was the one they wanted most of all. Then the clerk let something slip. He was being questioned further and asked about where Lopez might be, he denied any knowledge. Then he was asked how long he thought he might be away?

"As long as that officer is in Madrid." Asked which officer, he replied, "The one with the scar, of course."

Michael went to see Wellington. "My Lord, it seems to me that this priest, Lopez, is unlikely to return to Madrid while I am here. Might I suggest, my Lord, that you send me to Lisbon? In some way that will make it common knowledge. Then I can wait somewhere nearby and we will see if he does return."

Wellington agreed.

Michael went to one of Señora Ortega's famous soirees. There he spent the evening telling all and sundry that he was being packed off to Lisbon on confidential business for the Earl of Wellington. Wellington himself, at a dinner with local dignitaries, some of whom were known to be in the clerk's book, made a point of mentioning Michael's departure.

Michael and his party made a great show leaving Madrid. Three leagues out of the city they turned off to a small village. There they took up residence in the only inn. Four long, idle days later an orderly came galloping in with the news they had been waiting for. Lopez had returned and been taken. Before the day was out Michael was back in Madrid.

To his chagrin he was allowed no part in questioning the priest, and was only allowed to observe the arrests of afrancesados that had immediately begun. The Spanish wanted the credit. He did get agreement that he could visit Diaz the painter, mostly because no one could work out why on earth he appeared in the clerk's little book.

Michael left Lloyd and Hall outside the artists workshop. Inside, Diaz was painting a nymph, who lay sprawled naked on a bed. Diaz didn't hesitate to acknowledge the payments and said they were for a painting, of a Monsieur Renard. He pointed to an unfinished portrait in the corner, "I am, was, painting that for him." Michael stared at the portrait. It was a life sized portrait, a head and shoulders, of an ordinary looking man. A man who looked about fifty, greying hair, grey eyes, clean shaven, unremarkable. The image seared itself into Michael's memory. Just seeing the portrait caused all the hate and anger he felt to rise up and he almost smashed the painting against the wall. Even as the thought occurred, he felt the icy calm of his anger come over him. He hated this man with a passion that almost overwhelmed him, he knew that he would kill him without hesitation, but he would not lose control. And now he knew what he looked like.

Michael stood looking at it for a moment or two. He breathed deeply, calming himself. "I am afraid that I am going to take this."

"That's alright, Señor, I have been paid. Here," he added, "there are some sketches I did, studies, you might as well have those as well."

Suddenly the nymph rose from her bed and pulled on a banyan. "The bastard ran off without me."

"What?" Michael asked in surprise.

She looked coy, or tried to. "I was his mistress. Met him here, I was posing when he came for a sitting. He had money, I am sure you can imagine the rest. At least he sent me some money, sent that sad little clerk to see me, brought me a bag of dollars."

Michael asked, "What little clerk?"

Diaz broke in. "I know who she means, he made all Renard's payments for him. Came to see me, I always thought he was using official funds."

"Yes, that's right," the nymph added, "even made me sign a receipt, cheeky sod."

Michael shook his head at the thought of Renard using French money to keep his mistress and pay for his portrait. He wondered what Bonaparte would make of that. "Señorita, you need to be more careful of the company you keep." Then he took the portrait and sketches and left the artist to his work.

Over the next few days Michael watched the Madrid Police at work. Slowly, but surely, everyone on the list who could be identified was arrested. A message from King Joseph was discovered, hidden in Lopez's clothing. He refused to say much at all, except at his trial when he declared his loyalty to King Joseph. He was publicly garrotted in the Plaza Mayor, just after Montero.

Towards the end of July Michael was able to tell Wellington that Madrid was to all intents and purposes free of French agents. Wellington was delighted and told Michael so. Michael was pleased, not so much with the praise from Wellington, but because he now knew what Renard looked like.

Then Wellington said, "By the way, the Paymaster has been asking after you, you had better go and see him." He wondered how he was going to account for the money that had been advanced to him. But, first, he had a request for Wellington.

"My Lord, I have a request to make."

"And what might that be, Captain?"

Lieutenant Lapointe emerged from the warehouse, blinking at the light. He looked around, this time there was just Captain Roberts and his two men in the courtyard.

"Captain Roberts."

"Lieutenant." Michael held out a folded document towards him.

"What is this?"

"It's your parole, signed by the Earl of Wellington this time. I hope it carries more weight with your superiors."

Lapointe stepped forward and took the offered document. "Thank you, Captain, but why?"

"You still have a message to deliver."

Historical Note

The ciphered messages used by the French are not my invention. The story of those, their interception, frequently by Don Julian Sanchez, and their deciphering by Scovell, is well told in Mark Urban, The Man Who Broke Napoleon's Codes (London, 2001).

With regard to Don Julian Sanchez, he appears in many contemporary journals and Wellington's dispatches. Unfortunately, there is no significant study of him and what little that is known has to be gleaned from many sources, which does allow me a lot of leeway. He gets quite a few mentions in Wellington's dispatches, with who he appears to have been on excellent terms. A lot, but not all, of his actions are my invention and I hope I have done him justice.

The battle of Villagarcia was the finest cavalry against cavalry engagement of the war. Sir Stapleton Cotton's planning and handling of his brigades was exemplary. It deserves to be far better known, but is somewhat overshadowed by events at Badajoz. Tomkinson of the 16th records his memories of it in his Diary, which continues to be invaluable. Major Cocks, unfortunately, has little to say despite his leading role. R H Thoumine, Scientific soldier, A Life of General Le Marchant (London 1968) contains a good description and an extract from a description of the action by Le Marchant, which includes a map drawn by him. The charge of Le Marchant's brigade at Salamanca was devastatingly effective and made certain Wellington's victory. The brigade of less than a thousand heavy dragoons broke and destroyed three divisions of French infantry totalling nearly fifteen thousand men.

Fortunately for Michael, the cavalry were not involved directly in the Siege of Badajoz. For that I recommend the aptly titled, Ian Fletcher, In Hell Before Daylight (Tunbridge Wells 1984).

The battle of Salamanca is dealt with by Sir Charles Oman in Volume V of his monumental work and my constant companion, A History Of The Peninsular War. For an excellent modern account I recommend Rory Muir, Salamanca, 1812 (London 2001).

The arrest, trial and execution of Father Lopez are described in William Grattan, Adventures with the Connaught Rangers: 1809-1814 (London 1989).

BRINDLE BOOKS

Brindle Books Ltd

We hope that you have enjoyed this book. To find out more about Brindle Books Ltd, including news of new releases, please visit our website:

http://www.brindlebooks.co.uk

Should you have any queries, you can email us at:

contact@brindlebooks.co.uk

and you can let us know if you would like email updates of news and new releases. We promise that we won't spam you with lots of sales emails, and we will never sell or give your contact details to any third party.

If you purchased this book online, please consider leaving an honest review on the site from which you purchased it. Your feedback is important to us, and may influence future releases from our company.

Also by

David J Blackmore

Published by Brindle Books Ltd.

To The Douro

Wellington's Dragoon; Book One

A young man's decision to fight leads to a war within
a war…

To love…

To loss…

…and a quest for vengeance, as he plays a vital role
for the future Duke of Wellington.

Secret Lines

Wellington's Dragoon; Book Two

From the battlefield of Talavera,
by way of the guerrilla's merciless war,
to the back streets of Lisbon,
our hero fights to keep Wellington's great secret.
Can Michael gain the revenge he seeks and protect
the Secret Lines?

Behind The Lines

Wellington's Dragoon Book Three

From Buçaco to the fortified lines where the French
are finally stopped,
Behind the lines in Lisbon where the secret war
continues,
Through the devastated Portuguese countryside,
Michael Roberts continues his war, has a chance for
love, kills, and becomes a changed man.

A Different Kind of War

Wellington's Dragoon Book Four

An unhappy and angry Michael Roberts returns to
England expecting to be wasting his time at the
Regimental depot instead of fighting the French. He
soon discovers that the war is also being waged in
England, although it is a different kind of war.

Printed in Great Britain
by Amazon

49202065R00198